THE IMPOSSIBLE GIRL

ASHLEY WHITE

To my Heavenly and earthly fathers in Heaven, as well as anyone who picks up this book — this is for you. May your love for the impossible, adventure, and all things magical inspire you to do great things.

Ashley

Anabelle shoved the bassinet into Julian's oversized but awkward hands. She parted the vertical blinds of the apartment window, her hands shaky and slick with sweat. Only the dark streets of Xarcadia peered back at her.

No signs of The Registry—yet. They had time.

Time.

Something Anabelle wished she could have more of with her daughter but knew in her heart was impossible. A few hours with her newborn were all she would get. It wasn't enough, could never be enough, but had to be.

"They can't tag her, Julian," Anabelle said, her voice as shaky as her hands. "If they find out about her magic…"

Julian lowered the bassinet to the carpeted floor, then rested his meaty fingers on Anabelle's shoulders. "They won't," he said, the calm and resolve in his tone doing little to pacify her.

Anabelle regarded Julian through moist eyes. Her lifelong friend had risked his own life to help hide her pregnancy, had taken care of her, and had aided in the birth of her daughter. Now, he would do what must be done to ensure The Registry never learned about the baby's existence. Anabelle would never be able to thank him enough or repay him for his heroic deeds.

Julian grabbed an orb from his pocket and made the call. "Josie, the baby is here. You have to take Ava."

Anabelle fell to the floor and wrapped her arms around the swaddled Ava. The baby cooed, her bright blue eyes and pink, dimpled cheeks branding Anabelle's heart with a lifetime of memories from these few stolen moments. Julian dropped to his knees, flanking Ava from the other side. He pressed his head against Anabelle's, forming a protective dome over the wide-eyed Ava.

The tension in Anabelle's back released in a wave of relief. But the moment was short-lived.

Three pounding knocks at Julian's door jarred Anabelle and Julian from their troubled thoughts. They exchanged a look of panic.

Either Josie had arrived in record time to save Ava, or Anabelle's worst fear was about to come true—The Registry had found them.

Ava Marie Jones hiked up the flounces of her cotton-candy pink dress as she peeked through the velvety stage curtains. She tried to pout but the caked-on makeup kept her face frozen in a smile, and the three cans of hairspray did the same to the mounds of curls on her head.

From center stage, the pageant officiator turned toward Ava and extended a gloved hand as the spotlight reflected off his glossy, bald head. Ava fingered her amethyst necklace, trying to calm her racing heart. She edged backward in her too-big satin heels, bumping into her adoptive mother, Ulga, who nudged her forward with a tense smile of her own.

But Ava couldn't do it—endure this humiliation *again*—not on her thirteenth birthday, of all days!

She turned on her heels, sprinted past a gaping Ulga, through the back door that led into the main hallway of the auditorium, and as far away from the stage as her long legs would carry her.

"Ava, come back here at once!" Ulga bellowed in her squeaky tone as she ran after the girl. "They are about to call your name!"

"I am done!" Ava shouted over her shoulder.

Done with pageants. Done with sticky aerosol sprays. Done with pantyhose and arch-ripping heels. And foo-foo dresses, fake eyelashes, and fire-engine-red lipstick.

Ava picked up speed, refusing to dwell on the wrath that would await her when she returned home later.

"Oh, you wretched girl, you better hope I don't catch you!" Ulga almost mowed over another contestant, who stepped out of the women's restroom and reared back with shock and irritation. To Ava, the girl's expression almost matched the ridiculousness of the gowns they both wore.

Ava burst through the heavy oak front doors of the run-down community center and breathed in a mouthful of the chilly morning air.

Rain pounded down, pooling into silver puddles on the asphalt parking lot. As Ava ran, the mud plastered her legs, her makeup streaking and her curls falling loose. It was the most exhilarating, liberating feeling of Ava's life.

To be free, to not have every moment of her life planned out by self-serving strangers, was all Ava had ever wanted.

When Ulga and her pudgy, boil-covered husband, Fred, took her in six months ago, Ava had been the latest addition to their collection of four adopted and two biological children. Ava became child number seven. Her long, auburn curls, bright blue eyes, and porcelain skin gained Ulga's full attention, and the woman set to work to mold Ava into a pageant girl. Ulga claimed she herself had been quite the beauty in her youth. She had won "Ms. Astoria, Oregon," four years in a row, as a matter of fact. To this day, she seemed to treasure the memories of her pageant days.

Some people cannot let go of the past.

Ava snickered to herself as she ran.

No matter how hard she'd tried, Ava couldn't fit in. Not in Ulga's circus of a family. Not at school. And certainly not in the small, riverfront town of Astoria. It was like everyone else was on a different wavelength, and Ava couldn't tune herself right.

But today felt different. Today, Ava mustered the courage to put her foot down. A foot that was still swimming in the clunky heels. The wet winds whipped through her loose curls as she dashed into the grassy fields surrounding the edge of the parking lot. The landscape burst with vibrant green hues, full of life and filled with rows and rows of irises, Ava's favorite flower.

Her legs soon grew heavy, and she slowed her pace as she reached the incline of a familiar hillside. She stared up at where she'd been running to—the Cathedral tree, a three-hundred-year-old Sitka spruce that sprouted from a nurse log and rose two hundred feet into the air. The gaps in the trunk were large enough that she could climb in and stand inside, which she often did. The tree offered Ava shelter from the cold downpour. And comfort when she needed it.

Like Ava, the tree was alone. Most of its neighbors had been wiped out by a hurricane-force windstorm. Ava shared a kinship with this tree. It was alone, like her. The closest thing it had to family, wiped out without reason or warning.

No one asked to be an orphan. And there was probably a good reason Ava's parents had left her on the stoop of the Foundling's for Girls orphanage one cold, rainy night. But she liked to think her life—like that of the Cathedral tree—was at the mercy of unforeseen and uncontrollable forces of nature that had left her parents with no other choice.

It was easier to live with the pain that way.

The tension flowed out of Ava's body, replaced by a sense of calm and peace. It was like she'd been unable to catch her breath, like being away from the tree for too long had drained her and, by coming back, she was rejuvenated. This pull to replenish had been intensifying in Ava's gut with each passing day. Her heart rate resumed a more normal rhythm as she paused to listen to the faint notes of a song she had heard so many times before on this hillside.

She *always* ended up in front of this tree, and the *music* always played on its path.

The light melody in her head drew her closer and closer—to what, she'd never understood. But like she had done many times before, Ava allowed the music to pull her in—and she stepped into the Cathedral tree.

Instead of the anticipated ring of bark cushioning her, Ava's foot dropped, pulling the rest of her body with it. The tree's roots twisted around her as she plunged into darkness. She reached out for something to grab onto—but found nothing. Terror gripped her as she spiraled downward. A lump formed in her throat; a sense of weightlessness filled her body. As she fell, warmth seeped through her drenched clothes and hair, drying the droplets of water on her face.

Ava had been drawn to the Cathedral tree countless times, with nothing like this ever happening before. As she continued to tumble into the darkness, random thoughts flooded her head.

Maybe the rain had loosened the soil, causing the ground underneath it to become unstable?

Today, of all days. Of course, this would happen to her.

Even if Ava survived the fall, no one would be able to track her location. She'd never told anyone about this tree. It was her secret place, her oasis—and she hadn't wanted it sullied by her adoptive parents or their twin daughters, Beatrice and Elorise. They would have found some way to ruin it for her. Ava could see it: Ulga, with her suitcases of makeup and hair products, trying to beautify something already breathtakingly beautiful. Or—and much worse—Beatrice and Elorise storming the tree with an ax carried by Fred, the "yes" dad. The thought made Ava shudder, even in the midst of her free fall.

A bright light glowed below her as she *continued* her fall. She extended her limbs again, only to regret her decision.

Her right arm collided with a hard, cold surface. A loud crack like a pencil snapping in half echoed in her ears. Thick blood gushed from a deep gash in her arm, which throbbed with the blistering pain of hot embers poured over her bones. Tears welled in her eyes.

Okay, this is it.

The end.

But she didn't hit the bottom.

Strange.

Not *yet*.

In her head, Ava started to apologize for every bad thing she'd ever done.

Sure, there was the time she'd wished for Elorise and Beatrice to lose their voices for a month—and they had—after they'd said some horrible things about Ava's parents abandoning her. But, surely, that had been a coincidence.

Or the time she'd wished Ulga would stop applying hairspray, and the cans had all exploded in the woman's face. Her eyes were bloodshot for days afterward.

As Ms. Kerpopple, the persnickety headmistress at the orphanage, had always said whenever strange things happened around Ava, "The extraordinary can always be explained away. Everything that has or will ever happen already has, in some shape or form. So, don't give yourself too much credit, dear."

Ava braced herself for the inevitable impact, but something peculiar happened. Long after she should have hit the ground, she instead propelled outward and upward as if bouncing on a trampoline.

Still, she had no time to warn the pale, brown-haired boy who seemed to appear out of nowhere into her line of fire, and Ava realized too late she was about to make the worst introduction of her life.

The boy looked up, his obsidian eyes locking with hers. With swift, inhuman speed, he jutted out his muscular arms and caught her. He peered down at Ava with a perplexed expression.

"I see you like to make an entrance," he said, breaking into a grin.

Ava was in shock. Her lips moved, but no words came out. Her body was covered in a cold sweat from the fear and pain that had gripped her seconds before.

"My name's Duncan. Duncan Stavros. Are you okay?"

His deep voice reverberated with a soothing thrum of an engine.

"Put me down," Ava whispered. "Put me down *now*."

Panic overwhelmed her.

No, no, no.

This couldn't be happening.

First, she thought she was about to die. Then she thought she would maim or injure this boy from the impact of her fall. But now, all she could think about was finding a quiet corner where the boy couldn't witness an even worse embarrassment.

Duncan placed Ava back on her feet with graceful, quick movements and a bemused smile.

Ava teetered on shaky legs, her eyes darting about for a bucket—or at least some privacy. No such luck.

Her cheeks reddened and ballooned as she threw up all over what appeared to be an ornate flowerpot filled with a glossy, red flower with brown spikes for petals. Ava wiped her mouth with her sleeve and tried to steady herself.

The flower grumbled with irritation, oozing a sticky green substance to clean Ava's vomit off its petals with a most irritated huff.

Ava stared in disbelief at what she had just witnessed. She rubbed her eyes. When she opened them again, the flower was still. She shook her head, then inhaled deeply, before she turned around — *hoping, praying even* — Duncan had returned to wherever he had come from.

But no…

Those piercing eyes remained fixed on Ava. "I think we need to get you to Healer Gwyn. You're … not looking so great, Ava." Duncan gestured toward Ava's dangling arm, that annoying smile still on his face.

A "healer" sounded like a good idea. The intensifying pain of her injury had caused Ava to empty the contents of her stomach moments before. Not something she wanted to repeat.

Although, considering how far she must have fallen, things could have been a lot worse.

"Yeah, that might be wise. Let's—"

That's when it clicked.

Ava took in her surroundings for the first time. She was in a massive underground city, hundreds of levels deep, with a dome-like structure and tall, stone buildings as far as her eyes could see. There was even a sky above her with what appeared to be the sun beating down. The Cathedral tree's roots, buried deep within the earth, formed the city walls, a purple-gray bark with curved ridges, flaky plates, and green ivy growing upward.

People strolled down the streets, entering strange storefronts with signs that read Potions for Emotions, Enchant Me Nots, Wings of Fire, and Secret Leaf Tearoom—going about their lives as if a girl had not just fallen out of the sky.

But these weren't *people*—at least, not all of them.

A blue woman with sharp, pointy spikes protruding from her skin passed by with three blue-skinned, pointy-spiked children in tow. "Come along or we'll be late," the blue woman said.

Ava forgot her manners. "What *are* they?" she whispered to Duncan.

The blue woman must have overheard Ava's question, for

she flashed an indignant glare before hurrying her children along.

To Ava's left, an enormous man at least ten feet tall passed her, accompanied by a woman who appeared to be glowing with *bow-shaped* eyebrows.

Ava gaped.

People didn't grow this tall, and they certainly didn't glow or have bow-shaped eyebrows.

Then Ava heard the music. The same beautiful melody that had drawn her to the Cathedral tree for so long. Stunning, perfect people with opalescent wings played to a large crowd. The spectators danced as if they couldn't help themselves. They pirouetted with their arms waving above their heads, their movements in sync with the music.

"This … this isn't possible," Ava said, her head spinning from the pain from her arm *and* from seeing the impossible right before her eyes. "Where am I?"

"You're in Xarcadia, Ava."

Wait, he knew her name. She never told him her name.

And that's when Ava Marie Jones passed out, and Duncan caught her for the second time.

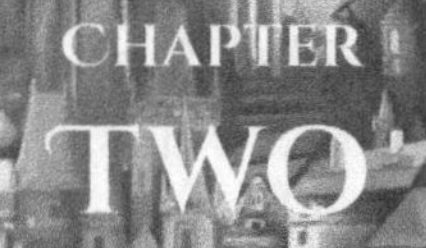

CHAPTER
TWO

"She's starting to stir," a male voice said. "That's good, right?"

"Indeed," a woman answered. "That's right, Ava. Take a deep breath. Come on, dear, open your eyes." The velvety voice lulled Ava to obey.

The city and creatures were all a dream. A terrible, frightening dream. Ava would open her eyes and find herself in a hospital.

Maybe she'd gone on stage at the pageant and fell off during her performance. She may have hit her head and broken her arm. Gone into some sort of pain-filled, psychedelic state and imagined the whole thing.

How embarrassing.

Video evidence of her pageant fall going viral played out in her mind. How Beatrice and Elorise would take such joy from Ava's two left feet. Why, oh why, had Ulga talked her into another pageant? She'd never be able to live this down. All her classmates had been there, and she had probably already become a laughingstock.

But, yes, that at least made sense.

With a huge sigh of relief, Ava opened her eyes to find

herself—*not* in a hospital—but in what appeared to be a poorly ventilated room with smoke billowing out of a large cast-iron pot over a flame. A pleasant, sweet smell wafted from its smoke with a hint of coconut.

Walls made of jade, embedded with hundreds of clear, sparkling crystals, surrounded Ava on three sides. The fourth wall, to her right, was lined with shelves of strange-looking vials full of various liquids and jars of dried—sometimes moving—contents. Throughout the dimly lit room glowed hundreds of white candles. A light flickered above Ava's head.

Rows of partitions blocked her view of the rest of the room. The ones across from her were filled with single beds and silver trays holding unfamiliar instruments.

Not like any hospital Ava was used to, but it had the components of one.

Various instructions and warning signs in bold letters covered the walls.

Witches: Remember to Cast Responsibly, Never Doing Any Harm

Vampires: Drink Your Hemoglobin Juice Three Times a Day

Fairies, Werewolves, and Vampires: Avoid Silver, Steel, and Iron at All Costs

Merpeople on Land: Stay Hydrated

Xarcadians: Please Adhere to All Decrees From the High Court of Magical Affairs

Ava clutched the amethyst amulet around her neck and twiddled the silver chain—something she did often during times of stress—and moved her injured arm unencumbered.

She stared down at her arm. The gash was gone. The pain was gone.

"Ava, dear, my name is Healer Gwyn." The woman with the velvety voice spoke again. "Do you remember coming through the gateway? I'm so sorry about that, by the way. That specific gateway has been broken for, well, it must be thirteen years!"

Ava pulled her attention back to the tall, slender woman

who now fussed over her, checking her pulse with long, bony fingers.

"The High Court of Magical Affairs hasn't gotten around to fixing it, despite many attempts by our town's Cleric of Magical Safety," Healer Gwyn continued without pause as if the explanation would make sense to Ava. "So much red tape these days. But, then again, most of you who do still get sent out are sent to places like Europe. So, you see, we haven't had anyone come through that specific gateway since it broke. It's lucky for you I was here today! I was about to pack up and head to Linhollow for the semester when Duncan brought you in. I'm one of the school's healers during the year, you see."

Healer Gwyn flashed a penlight shaped like a serpent as she peered into Ava's eyes. The woman's dark, wavy hair tickled Ava's cheeks.

"Gateway?" Ava said, her voice distorted by Healer Gwyn continuing to press against her cheekbones. "No, I was inside the Cathedral tree when the ground gave out, and I ended up … here."

Healer Gwyn appeared satisfied and stepped back, releasing Ava's face from her inspection.

Ava looked around the room again, moving her arm in disbelief.

The memories of the impossible things she'd seen flooded back and caused her head to spin.

Ava's eyes found Duncan, sitting on a stool in a dark corner. He appeared to be frozen in time, the stool tilted on two legs, his long limbs outstretched mid-air with his back leaning against the wall behind him. The swoop of his dark bangs cast a shadow over his already black eyes, and Ava couldn't tell if the boy was awake or asleep.

"Tell her!" Ava called out. "Tell her how I almost took off your head and how my arm hung broken with the skin torn open."

Duncan snapped to attention, the stool planting itself back on all four legs. "I wouldn't go that far," he said. "You barely grazed me."

The mirth on Duncan's face betrayed how much he seemed to enjoy this.

"Ava, you're where you're supposed to be," Healer Gwyn said matter-of-factly. "In our wonderful, surreptitious Xarcadia! Let me guess. Today is your thirteenth birthday?"

The woman didn't wait for an answer. "Oh, and your arm is fine. I took care of that: a little amaranth mixed with some comfrey, and you were good as new."

Ava's skin tingled. She hadn't told Duncan her name, and she certainly hadn't told him it was her birthday.

"How do you know so much about me?" Ava asked, puzzled. "How did I get here?"

Healer Gwyn bubbled with excitement. "My dear, you're what we call a Lost One—but now you're found! Returned home, where you belong, through a portal."

"Yay," Duncan added, his hands shooting up in a touchdown victory sign.

"You think I was lost?" The ridiculous thought made Ava's head hurt.

But no sooner had the question left her lips, the words lingered in her own ears. In a way, she had always been lost. Never fitting in. Always the odd one out.

"Oh, you two are terrible at this," a soprano voice said from the other side of a partition closest to Ava. "What, are you out of practice?"

"Ava," Healer Gwyn said, ignoring the girl and raising her own voice. "Our kind, magites—*your* kind—are sometimes sent out into the mortal realm at birth. It's a gift, some think."

Healer Gwyn's disapproving tone made it clear what her opinion was on this practice. "Before your powers come in, on your thirteenth birthday, it's a chance for you to experience what it's like out there. But from this point on, you can never return."

Healer Gwyn seemed much more satisfied with her final words.

Mortal realm. Our kind. Powers. Never return?

This woman must be mad.

At the same time, Ava couldn't deny what she'd seen. "If I'm never to return and must stay then, what, you think I'm like those *people* or *creatures*?" Ava asked, her incredulity seeping into her words. "What is it you think me to be?"

"Well, merwoman's out of the question with that pale complexion and skin," Healer Gwyn said with a chuckle. "So is vampire. Duncan would have been able to smell it on you. He also said you had a certain lack of, uh, grace to your movements, so that rules out fairy."

Duncan shrugged with a smirk, revealing two sharp, pointy fangs Ava hadn't noticed before.

She'd like to see *him* try to be graceful after that kind of a fall.

"But instead of trying to guess through hundreds of different species, why don't we scan your wrist and find out?" Healer Gwyn suggested.

She moved over to a metal table and turned on what appeared to be a computer. Digital, clear, and operated with the movement of Healer Gwyn's eyes.

"Registry Search" flashed on the screen in bold letters as Healer Gwyn picked up a scanner of sorts and approached Ava like a grocery item.

Healer Gwyn reached out and grabbed Ava's arm. Her pleasant face, with her oversized marble eyes and soft freckles, didn't make her *look* crazy.

"Well, that's odd," she said. "I think I'm having trouble with my system. Nothing's pulling up."

Ava looked down and noticed the woman had been trying to scan the crescent-shaped scar on her right wrist.

Of course, nothing pulled up. Ava didn't have a barcode on her arm. What she had—at least, according to Ms. Kerpopple—was a birthmark. A birthmark that happened to be shaped like a moon. Ava had fantasized about her mom having a sun-shaped scar. So, one day, they would find each other and know by their complementing birthmarks that they belonged together.

"I know my being here is no more than a terrible twist of fate," Ava said, half hoping she was wrong. That this mark did mean something—even if it wasn't what she had hoped it meant all her life. She almost hoped that Healer Gwyn would smack the scanner on the tray like Ava had done with television remotes, and then—ta-da—it would work again. The mystery of who she was, where she was from, and *what* she was finally revealed.

Ava's initial shock was already giving way to a feeling of peace, an unexplainable sense of belonging in this strange, underground place.

"Nothing pulled up?" the girl in the next partition piped up again. "Healer Gwyn, has this ever happened in The Registry's three-hundred-year history? Is it possible that this isn't a system malfunction, but a flaw in the system we've all grown to rely on to protect our way of life? *¡Qué titular!*"

The girl sounded like she was typing on a keyboard, then paused, as if waiting for a response.

"Calm down and stop typing!" Healer Gwyn snapped. She redirected her attention back to Ava. "There are no mistakes here. Let me reboot my system, and we'll see who you are, where you come from, and, most importantly, what you are."

Ava narrowed her eyes. She turned toward the mysterious girl behind the partition.

"What are you in for?" Ava asked. "Did you fall out of the sky too?"

"Too much candy from Polianne's Parlor of Tricks or

Treats," the girl answered. "I got nothing but tricks this time! My little brother, Jake, got all the treats, the little rodent!"

"You should've stuck with her one-hundred-and-one-flavored ice cream," Duncan said with a laugh.

Ava shot Duncan a confused look.

"It's great," he added. "Every flavor imaginable in a pint-sized container—and ninety-seven of them are amazing. The other four, not so much."

Ava's brain exploded at the possibility of such a wondrous thing. "I would love to try that!" she exclaimed.

Her curiosity was now piqued. She *had* to leave. To go and see this place—this world—for herself. To confirm this place wasn't an illusion. That she wouldn't walk out the doors and, magically, everything would revert to normal.

"Can we go?" Ava asked Duncan, who turned toward Healer Gwyn for approval.

When Healer Gwyn didn't provide it, Ava was quick to add, "I think, if I do belong here, I should go and explore the city—try this Polianne's Parlor of Tricks or Treats maybe."

"I'll go with you," the girl from the partition said with sounds of her jumping off the bed. "My stomach's feeling *much* better, Healer Gwyn. Thanks for the elixir."

The girl popped her head around the partition and flashed a big smile, her pristine teeth gleaming unusually bright. "Name's Tara Delarosa, by the way."

Tara looked to be about Ava's age. As she spoke, the girl's voluminous black curls engulfed her small, freckled face and fell over her dark green eyes.

"I'm in," Duncan added. He again turned toward Healer Gwyn as they all waited for her response. Ava was thankful he'd said yes, what with him having already saved her twice from falling.

"I don't see why not," Healer Gwyn said, seeming relieved to have them out of her hair. "You have one hour until my system reboots. Then we need to get you scanned in, Ava.

Lord knows they track every ounce of medicine dispensed. Plus, you'll want to know *what* you are before arriving at Linhollow Academy for the Supernaturally Gifted tonight. Off with you, time has already begun to tick away, and once this hourglass runs out, you better be back!"

Tara grabbed Ava's hand, and Duncan leapt to his feet.

Ava hoped this wasn't a concussion. She hoped she wouldn't wake up because she wanted more than anything for the outside to *not* be normal when she walked out that door.

CHAPTER

THREE

Duncan held the glass door open as Ava and Tara stepped out of Healer Gwyn's apothecary. Ava glanced back and stopped in her tracks. Her jaw dropped.

They had just exited a stone building shaped like a mushroom.

From the grout lines of the multicolored limestone bricks sprouted vines, plants, and flowers of all shapes and colors, making the structure look like a domed garden.

Tara strode down a wide, gray-cinder-block walkway that led away from the building and connected to a circular path like a bicycle spoke. Duncan followed behind her, not waiting for Ava.

"Come on, then," Tara called over her shoulder. "We only have an hour."

Ava trotted after them, looking about her with wide eyes. The walkway appeared to be floating high up in the air. Ava had never seen anything like it. Below their floating landing were layers and layers of other walkways that circled more levels of the floating city as far down as Ava's eyes could see. Weaving and spiraling around the layers was a moving conveyor belt that transported all manner of people and creatures from one tier of buildings to another.

Ava couldn't believe a place like this existed just under the human world she had just left. A place so magical, where maybe all the knowledge of the universe was *downloaded* into their brains.

"Oh, no," Duncan said with a smile. "No way we download. We take our academia very seriously. In fact, this year, I'm taking a class on glamours."

Ava tried to hide her shock at Duncan reading her thoughts *as* she thought them.

"Healer Gwyn wasn't kidding about school?" Ava asked, trying hard to keep pace with Tara and Duncan.

Ava hated school. Back in Astoria, she always sat in class watching the clock, counting down the seconds until she could escape. She would be out of her seat the moment the bell rang, dashing off to the woods, to the ocean—anywhere surrounded by nature, where her worries, fears, and problems dissipated.

"I don't know what your school was like, but it's not bad at Linhollow Academy," Tara said with a dance in her step. "This year, I get my airborne permit! No more walking around for me."

That's when Ava noticed the people above her. There must have been at least thirty of them.

Flying.

Some rode on what resembled brooms—a bundle of birch twigs bound with flexible willow wands to long staffs. They were much larger than the brooms Ava was accustomed to using to sweep the floors in the human world, with handles for steering, pedals for the feet, and a horn that appeared to be honked often to warn pedestrians to move out of the way. Most seemed to be made of ash or oak, while others were made of some sort of metal that shimmered in the daylight.

The people who weren't riding brooms rode on strange, large creatures with harnesses attached to their backs. The creatures had equine bodies with massive, white wings flapping furiously as they powered through the sky.

"Is that a … unicorn?" Ava asked, then immediately cringed at how stupid her question made her feel.

"Oh, that?" Tara said. "No, that's an alicorn. Unicorns can't fly."

"Of course, they can't," Ava said with a sheepish grin.

Ava gulped. An uneasy feeling blossomed in her stomach. She *didn't* belong here. She was sure this fact would be confirmed when they returned to Healer Gwyn's apothecary.

Healer Gwyn—*and Duncan*—had said Ava didn't resemble a merwoman, wasn't a vampire like Duncan, and lacked the grace of a fairy. She didn't have blue, spiky skin. She wasn't ten feet tall. What did that leave? She was at a loss. But she also didn't know her remaining options—what other creatures existed in this world that she couldn't imagine?

"What about me?" Ava asked. "What do you think I am?"

If she could figure it out, maybe it wouldn't matter if she didn't pull up in this *Registry*. Perhaps she'd be able to stay, regardless. The more she thought about it, the more Ava was certain she never wanted to go back to Astoria—to the world out there.

"Maybe a banshee," Duncan teased, opening his mouth wide and pretending to let out a scream.

"A banshee, really?" Ava flashed a genuine smile for the first time in, well, she didn't know how long. She didn't even care that Duncan didn't seem to be able to carry on a serious conversation.

Maybe it was her appearance that made it difficult for Duncan to take her seriously. Ava ran her fingers through her auburn curls, still matted from the rain, then picked at the patches of dried mud and blood on her pink frilly dress. But she couldn't look any more ludicrous than anything else around her at that moment.

As Ava gazed down at her dress, she veered dangerously

close to the open edge of the walkway. She imagined herself plunging over the side and falling hundreds of levels downward. Then Healer Gwyn would discover how prone Ava was to accidents. She'd broken countless bones in her thirteen years. Not to mention all the scrapes, cuts, and bruises.

"How much farther?" Ava asked.

"We're almost there," Tara said. "It's two stories down and a quick ride on the conveyor past Shirley Surley's Fairy Tavern. It's across from the city's best ring cast maker, Cast It With Us or Cast It Wrong. Oh, you'd love it. We *have* to go!"

Incredible.

Something else caught Ava's attention. "Why is this path getting narrower the farther we go?"

Tara gestured above her head at what appeared to be twenty more levels of the city. "They're still building downward—ran out of room up there," she said. "They're supposed to have another one hundred levels done by the end of the year. They haven't been able to keep up with the city's growth. I'm writing a paper on it—under my pseudonym, Arat Asoraled. The High Court of Magical Affairs does *not* take kindly to grumblings. It's titled, 'What Will Our Next Three Hundred Years Look Like at This Rate?'"

Duncan shot Tara a warning glare. "You know my parents are members of the High Court. You can't say things like that in front of me."

Tara rolled her eyes. Ava stepped between the two. "Hey, is that the conveyor belt you guys talked about?"

"Yeah, get ready to jump on," Tara said. "It never stops."

They approached an outer ring that hovered about a foot beyond the walkway. The rolling transporter looked like a band of grass on which people and creatures stood as it whizzed by at a high speed. The conveyor traveled horizontally but also spiraled up and down to reach the other levels of the city—and all the while, the passengers did not fall off. When Ava jumped onto it, following Tara and Duncan, she realized how that was possible. As soon as her soles made contact, the blades of the grass closed around her feet, holding her in place.

Ava barely had time to marvel at this wondrous grassy conveyor before she realized strangers surrounded her. She lost sight of Tara and Duncan.

Ava's heart skipped a beat as she tried to peer through the crowd. A tall, green-haired woman next to her ran a comb through her blue scales while looking into a mirror.

"Okay, it's coming up," Duncan called from somewhere in the crowd. "Get ready to jump off."

It never stops.

Tara's words echoed in Ava's head. Maybe she should have considered that *before* she'd jumped on.

"Okay, now!" Tara yelled.

Ava held her breath and jumped. The grass blades seemed to sense her movements and released its hold. She landed back on a stone walkway, with Tara and Duncan only a few paces behind.

A five-story, blue storefront loomed ahead from an intersecting walkway with a shimmering sign that said Polianne's Parlor of Tricks or Treats in red letters. White fireworks exploded every few seconds in the sign's background and danced in the irises of Ava's eyes.

"What in the worl—," Ava said as she tried to take it all in.

"Are you ready for a trick or a treat, ladies?" Duncan asked.

"Definitely a treat this time," Tara said as Duncan opened the shop's glass door, which stood at least forty feet tall with embedded images of young children—moving. Some laughed and smiled, while others clutched their stomachs and ran around with looks of alarm.

Tricks or treats?

A smile crept across Ava's lips at the anticipation as she followed Tara in, her satin heels click-clacking on the ivory floor. Just inside the door, Ava paused and looked down at her feet.

She'd have to do something about her footwear soon.

Ava glanced up, her mouth falling open wider as her head tilted farther and farther back. Sun streamed down from the glass roof covering the five-story center atrium, reflecting off all the colors of the rainbow, organized by color, from the side walls of every floor. Prominent signs labeled the fifth floor as the "Recovery Floor," the fourth floor as "Mix of Tricks," the third floor as "Treats Yourself Spa," and the second floor as "Sports and Activities," with additional signs offering "Shrink and Run" and "Gumdrops Trampolines."

Young vampires and werewolves hopped from floor to floor, while fairies flew and witches rode their brooms to scale the different levels.

On the main floor, three corners offered a "Dessert Bar," a "Drink Bar," and an open restaurant with several tables on which sat baby dragons breathing fire onto the dishes before they were served. The rest of the space offered shelves of toys, games, and candies—all organized by color and some floating through the air as customers reached out to grab them.

An eager warlock attendant wearing a crisp, white-collared shirt and a rainbow blazer dashed up to Ava with a look of eager anticipation.

"Tricks or Treats, little girl?" he said.

Ava stared back at the attendant, her mouth still gaping open. "Uhhh…"

A hand grabbed Ava's arm and yanked. "She's with us," Duncan said. "It's her first time here, so we're going to start with a drink."

The warlock shrugged. "Suit yourself," he said, turning his attention to a mother and child stepping through the doors.

Duncan pulled Ava toward the Drink Bar, where Tara waited under a sign that said, "Have a Seat or Lose Your Feet." Small, iridescent gummy bears weaved through the legs of the other teenagers packing the bar, trying to catch the feet of any violators.

Above everyone's heads, pink and yellow strands of taffy stretched by themselves, lightening in color and becoming firmer in texture before breaking to pieces into containers in front of the awaiting patrons. More taffy strands—this time, neon green and lavender—flew into the air, stretching and forming another batch for the next round of customers.

Ava and Duncan joined Tara at the red countertop. Gummy worms slithered across the surface, trying not to get snatched and eaten by the outstretched hands of eager children.

A luminescent woman greeted them from behind the counter. She wore a rainbow-colored tube dress, with sheer layers of fabric extending out from her waist as if floating on water. The strands of her short, fiery red hair also levitated outward as if they were alive, the tips glowing like lit embers.

"That's Polianne," Duncan whispered to Ava.

The lithe woman shot Ava an electrifying smile, and her bare arms—which seemed to twinkle with the light of a thousand stars from beneath her creamy skin—extended toward her, releasing a pile of rainbow-colored dust, which floated to Ava, entered her parted lips, and settled and dissolved on her tongue. An explosion of sweet, sour, and savory flavors filled Ava's mouth.

She involuntarily swallowed.

"On the house for all first-time customers," Polianne said, her voice somehow exuding the sweetness of honey. "What can I get for you two?"

"I'll take a witch's brew and a bowl of your one-hundred-and-one-flavored ice cream, Polianne," Tara said as she placed a gold coin on the counter, which was instantly absorbed by the surface.

As soon as Tara placed her order, Polianne reached below the counter and produced a steaming mug with swirling rainbow smoke. She handed it to Tara, who, after blowing on it, took a big gulp. With a loud whistle from Polianne, a bowl of ice cream levitated through a small hole in a closed door and plopped down in front of Tara.

"I'll take a hemoglobin juice," Duncan said as he set down his own gold coins, which also didn't remain on the counter for long. "Iced, please."

Polianne handed Duncan a tall, clear glass half-filled with ice and what resembled the coagulated blood Ava had seen on her arm earlier that day.

Ava shifted uncomfortably. Duncan noticed her reaction as he chugged his beverage.

"Well, it's not *real*," he said, holding up the glass in front of him. "Our alchemist makes it. What would you rather have me do, starve?"

Polianne regarded Ava with curiosity.

"She's a Lost One, with no Aurum shekels," Tara said by way of an explanation.

"Oh, I see," Polianne said with a radiant smile. "Well, whatever you want, it's on the house. Today and today only."

Ava considered her options and addressed Polianne with the utmost certainty. "I'll take what she's having," she said, pointing to Tara.

Polianne lost no time in handing Ava a smoking mug, while the ice cream levitated over and plopped down in front of her. When the ice cream hit Ava's tongue, the flavors changed faster than she could comprehend, causing her to go from delighted to displeased in seconds.

"You should get the chocolate bunnies," Duncan said with mischief in his eyes.

Tara elbowed Duncan in the ribs, which appeared to hurt her elbow more than it hurt him. "Don't listen to him," she said. "They bite you back and take off running. Get the taffy. It'll make you giddy for hours."

Tara and Duncan bickered as they advised Ava on which

free goodies to fill Ava's two large bags. Afterward, they slid into a secluded booth in the back of the shop. Ava took a sip of her witch's brew—a warm apple cider with a hint of cardamom—as she marveled at a merwoman ascending a nearby wall to reach the second floor with what looked like suctions on her multicolored, scaly fish skin.

Ava pulled her gaze back to the table just as Duncan slurped the last of his hemoglobin juice.

"So, tell me about this Registry," Ava said. "Why is it so important for it to pull something up?"

"That's an easy one," Duncan said, "Because it *has* to. For starters, our world wasn't always hidden away like this." He gestured around the shop and sounded serious for the first time since Ava had known him.

"There was a time when our world was above ground and mixed in with the mortal race," he continued. "But as their numbers grew, so did their attacks. Once they discovered vampires, witches, fairies, and various creatures existed, they began to hunt us down. Ever heard of the Salem witch trials? Our numbers dwindled so much during that time. And as the mortals developed and grew, so did their use of certain elements our kinds don't take well to—silver, steel, iron, *et cetera*."

Duncan appeared upset now and fidgeted.

"Oh, you sound like the High Court!" Tara said. "If you want my point of view, a warlock named Ambrose—the strongest warlock ever to exist—convinced everyone that if we wanted to survive, we had to go underground and live separately from the mortals. Especially after our powers came in, for fear of endangering everyone. He created The Registry, a department of the High Court of Magical Affairs, with a magical book that populates with the name and origin of every person in existence. Shortly after your birth, officials from The Registry knock on your door. False congratulations, oversized stuffed animals, and cheer aside, they move in to tag your child and go on their way."

"Why do they tag us?" Ava asked. "Why would 'Lost Ones' like me even exist if it was such a danger?"

"By tagging us, The Registry can track our *every* movement," Duncan said, "which also means they're able to stop anyone before they can try to leave and go up to the mortal world."

"Yes, yes, yes," Tara said, rolling her eyes. "As for the Lost Ones, let's say not everyone agreed with Ol' Ambrose's plan. The Resistance, as they're called, believed we could coexist with the mortals with the proper precautions in place. But when the attacks against us increased—and our people lost their friends and family members almost daily—the majority conceded.

"But The Resistance still insisted that their children, with no knowledge or magical abilities until they came of age, should be allowed to be sent out. They didn't want future generations to forget what they fought for. My *tatarabuela* was a member. Oh, the stories she's told me! Every generation in my family was sent out—until me, that is."

Tara's green eyes dimmed. She lowered them to the table, then took another small sip of her witch's brew.

"The first hundred, hundred and fifty years or so, thousands were sent out each year," Duncan said. "But most have come to realize the practice is cruel—one that denies their children the knowledge of their birth rights and sends them off into a world where they don't belong."

Duncan seemed to be at his wit's end with Tara, throwing her an exasperated look.

Maybe things would have been easier for Ava if her parents, if they were members of this Resistance, hadn't cast her out at birth. Even if they'd had the best intentions, her thirteen years among the mortals were filled with grief, heartache, and a feeling of untethered loneliness that she couldn't understand. But it all made sense now.

"I'm with Duncan on this, Tara," Ava decided. "If I'd had a choice, I would've much rather known anything about myself, about where I came from. My parents left me on an orphanage's stoop with a name card and a necklace, all alone."

Ava tried to hold back the tears that threatened to fall.

"Ava, I'm sorry," Tara said, smiling and squeezing Ava's hand. "But you *will* meet them, silly. When you return, The Registry gets alerted and lets your parents know. They'll be at the Lost Ones Ball."

Ava gasped. Meet them? Her parents?

Now more than ever, Ava hoped the grocery-store-like scanner would pull something up.

Ava gathered her bags of candy from the table. She'd barely said a word since Tara's comment about the Lost Ones Ball. She followed Tara and Duncan out of Polianne's Parlor of Tricks or Treats, her feet dragging with each step. The children embedded in the front door stopped laughing and playing. They waved goodbye in unison before their hands reached through the glass to sprinkle rainbow particles like pixie dust all over Ava.

"See you next time," they said, grinning.

Tara and Duncan led the way along the walkway back toward the conveyor, with Ava a few paces behind, lost in her own thoughts.

Meeting her parents.

Ava had imagined this countless times. Sometimes she'd imagined them having been forced to give her up only until they could reunite with her at last. Other times, Ava had imagined tracking them down. Like a private investigator who would then demand to know why they chose to be absent from her life. But these were fanciful thoughts. She'd never believed either would happen.

What would she say to them? Would she be so overjoyed

to see them, her anger would melt away—like the last thirteen years had never happened? Or would she be cross? All the hurt rising until it exploded, and she screamed in their faces?

"Ava, you've hardly said a word since we left." Tara stopped to wait for Ava to catch up to her and placed her hand on Ava's shoulder. "Are you okay?"

Ava didn't respond.

Duncan also stopped and backtracked. "Come on, Ava," he added. "You were so excited to try Polianne's popping kettle corn later. Remember—it pops in your mouth as you eat it. Albeit with some burnt pieces mixed in."

Duncan glanced at the bags in Ava's hands and grimaced, as if remembering his own distaste for the kettle corn.

Tara and Duncan were trying in their own ways to help Ava snap out of her funk, but their words only infused her with more worry.

"I never *really* imagined meeting them," Ava said. "I don't know what I'd even say. I mean, what if I don't like them—or what if they don't like *me*? It's not like I've had the opportunity to get to know them for years. Maybe they've liked being childless."

Ava pretended to fish for an eyelash in her eye as she wiped away a tear. She hoped Tara and Duncan didn't notice.

"They'll love you," Tara said. "Look at us. Duncan and I, despite our many differences, have been putting up with each other all day to get to know you."

A genuine smile spread across Ava's face. "Thanks, guys," she said.

It wasn't the first time Ava had hung out with kids her own age, but it was the first time she'd enjoyed herself. She didn't want it to end—and that was new for her.

"If we hurry, we could still go to Cast It With Us or Cast It Wrong," Tara said, pointing at a small brick-and-mortar storefront across the street. "We could be in and out in five minutes!"

Duncan shook his head and laughed. "If we're late, you're explaining it to Healer Gwyn."

"I'll take the heat," Ava said. She didn't want Tara to change her mind. "I've dealt with a lot worse than her." After all, she'd put up with Ulga, Fred, and the spiteful twins for six months.

The second time on the conveyor, Ava jumped on and off with more assurance. A shopkeeper's bell jingled as Ava shoved Tara and Duncan playfully through the narrow shop door—and stopped—crashing into a towering woman in a black cloak. The stacks of ebony-wood boxes she carried toppled to the floor, spilling hundreds of rings made of various metals and precious stones. The woman's face turned crimson.

"Watch where you're going!" she grumbled in a shrill voice.

"I'm so sorry," Ava stammered. "Here, let me help you." Ava crouched down, and Duncan and Tara joined her, all reaching for the mounds of metal rings.

The woman stepped forward and blocked their access to the rings. "No. You'll mess it up more. You three better hope you're not in my casting class this year!"

She then pointed her right index finger and uttered, "Pano Diorganose." The rings and boxes lifted off the floor and followed her out the door.

"I really hope I'm *not* in her class," Tara said, standing upright and brushing herself off. "I mean, did you see the color her face turned? She looked like she was about to blow a gasket."

"Not something I have to worry about," Duncan said, staring after the woman with a look of relief as the rings sorted themselves into the boxes trailing after her.

A man with short, blond hair bounded up. He wore dark black trousers and an intricate gold floral vest with a collared, long-sleeved black shirt underneath. "Welcome, welcome," he said. "Is this your first time here at Cast It With Us or Cast It Wrong?"

"It's my first time," Ava said as she looked around the spacious interior with black and white checkered floors. The walls around her were lined with ebony-wood shelves of alternating heights. Thousands of rings sat on the shelves, and some of the shelves floated throughout the room to stop in front of customers, who shook their heads yes or no.

A massive chandelier hung above the middle of the room, with striking crystals that cascaded around a bulb center made of a silver pearl finish.

"Mine as well," Duncan added. He looked out of place.

"Gideon, it's me, Tara! I've been coming here once a week since I was five! How can you not recognize me?"

"My apologies, dear. I see so many people," Gideon said. "I can't possibly remember them all. You understand, don't you?"

From her face, it was clear Tara didn't.

"But, for those of you not familiar," he said, directing his attention toward Duncan and Ava, "we here at Cast It With Us or Cast It Wrong make the finest, strongest casting rings imaginable. Our quality is unmatchable. Our uniqueness is unrivaled. All your casting needs in one convenient place made by the most talented gnomes in existence."

At a small workstation behind him, two gnomes—with small heads shaped like potatoes and stubby bodies— hammered away at chunks of gold and poured molten metal into a mold.

The shopkeeper's bell jingled again, and Gideon gave a curt nod and turned his attention to the two older women who entered. "Agnes, Opal!" he exclaimed. "How have you been? Agnes, how is your little one, Alaric, doing? Getting into trouble yet?"

Gideon laughed at his own joke as he led the two women into the store.

"Doesn't remember every customer, huh?" Duncan said. He seemed to be trying not to laugh at the bewildered look on Tara's face.

"Maybe he was kidding," Ava said. She knew full well he hadn't been but wanted to make Tara feel better.

"If he was or he wasn't, it doesn't matter." Tara seemed to be trying hard to appear unaffected by Gideon's slight. "I come here because I've always dreamt of owning a ring from the most illustrious shop in Xarcadia."

Ava made her way to the closest shelf of rings. "So, what do these casting rings do?"

"They help to harness a witch's power, to amplify it, even," Tara said with excitement. "It makes for safer casting. Each metal—gold, silver, iron, steel, and copper—has its own vibration. Its own unique attributes. It says a lot about the witch or warlock who wears it."

Ava's body felt electrified as she peered at all the different rings. She picked up one made of iron with three amethysts set in the center of the ring.

"It wouldn't be what *I* would pick, but I guess it's not the least attractive thing in here," Duncan said as he glanced over Ava's shoulder.

"That iron comes from the earth's crust!" Tara said with awe. "The gnomes trek for weeks to get it! Go ahead, try it on!"

Ava placed the iron ring on her left index finger. Its shape molded to her skin and created a perfect fit. A pulse deep within her veins thrummed as her hand began to glow. A bolt of energy coursed through her.

Duncan's face registered shock, and Tara's mouth dropped open.

Gideon reappeared next to Ava. "The loose stone was definitely the fault of the user, not the manufacturer," he muttered, before forcing a bright smile. "I see you found a ring you identify with. How many did you try on to find it? A hundred?"

"The very first one she put on," Tara said with shock.

"Rare, indeed," Gideon replied with a chuckle. "But, then again, you must have studied and already knew which metals and precious stones you thought you'd identify with. So nothing too out of the ordinary."

"She's a Lost One that arrived today," Tara said. "She knew nothing about any of them."

"Well, that is luck, then!" Gideon exclaimed with a look of shock and delight. "Well, unless you're planning to purchase that, my dear, you can place it back on the shelf before you leave."

Ava tried—and failed—to remove the ring.

She assumed Gideon did not share Polianne's "Today and Today Only" Lost Ones policy, and images of him trying to remove it from her finger danced in her head.

"I—it won't come off," Ava said. "Am I doing something wrong here?"

"Ava…" Tara said. "A witch who's come of age finds a ring she identifies with after trying *hundreds* on. It takes at least a hundred years of perfecting her craft for her to find her perfect fit. This never happens."

Gideon tossed his hands up in the air. "Well, it would seem that ring was made for you," he said. "Even rarer—and more problematic seeing as you have no way to pay for it, I'm assuming?"

From the nervous looks on their faces, Gideon had his answer. "Out!" he yelled. "Out of my shop before either of you"—he gestured toward Tara and Duncan—"make the same mistake she did. Send your parents to my shop after the Lost Ones Ball. Someone will make this right, or I'll curse you and the generations that come after you!"

Gideon shoved them out the door and slammed it behind them.

"Tough crowd," Ava said, trying to lighten the mood.

"Look, Tara, I know you love that place. I'm sorry if I ruined it for you."

Duncan sauntered in the direction of the conveyor. "But on the bright side, Tara," he said over his shoulder, "he'll definitely remember you next time. Maybe even plaster our faces on the wall—for security purposes."

Tara's cheeks flushed. She shot exaggerated faces at Duncan's back before addressing Ava.

"It's not your fault, Ava," she said. "On the *actual* bright side, we now know you're a witch."

A surge of relief washed over Ava. She tapped her foot and twirled her hair. She belonged in this world. It wasn't a mistake. She couldn't jeopardize her place here, but the thought that she was fifteen minutes late returning to Healer Gwyn nagged at her. She regretted having told Duncan and Tara that she would take the heat.

"Maybe she won't even notice," Ava said, her hands trembling.

"Not likely," Duncan said, running his fingers through his hair.

"She'll be at least a little understanding once we tell her what happened," Tara interjected. "As a witch herself, she'll want to hear all about it."

Ava's stomach unclenched a little at Tara's words as they entered Healer Gwyn's apothecary. "Okay, I'm ready," Ava said. "Let's do this."

Healer Gwyn rushed forward with a look of relief at the sight of Ava. She gestured toward the hourglass, then crossed her arms. "You are fifteen minutes late!"

As all three opened their mouths to provide an explanation, Healer Gwyn shut them down. "Don't even! Ava, take a seat, and let's get you sorted out at once." She led Ava back to the organized table where the computer sat.

"Healer Gwyn, did something happen?" Tara asked.

"Yes, something happened," she replied. "When I called The Registry on my orb to see how to reboot my system, the woman on the other line almost took my head off! Expected me to keep Ava here like some sort of prison ward while it rebooted. As if they don't already know of everyone who has passed through today. If their gateway hadn't been broken, there would have been no need for me to scan you. A watchman would have been there to greet you. Hardly *my* fault."

Healer Gwyn turned back toward her computer as she continued to mumble under her breath. "Wrist, now," she demanded. "I was to call her back fifteen minutes ago, and each minute we waste makes me look worse. Any chance I'd had at moving on from the school to the Department of Health and Magical Safety is gone!"

Unlike the first time Ava had handed Healer Gwyn her wrist, a rush of serenity filled her as "Registry Search" again flashed on the screen.

Ava's mind was calm, her pulse was steady, and a feeling of belonging coursed through her.

She watched as … nothing flashed on the screen again.

"Oh, this is impossible," Healer Gwyn exclaimed. "Absolutely impossible!" She stared in disbelief and almost looked like she would smack the screen.

A knot formed in Ava's stomach. "Er, is there still a problem with the system?" she asked.

"No, no." Healer Gwyn replied. "The problem, young lady, seems to be with you! Wait here while I go in the other room and call the curator from The Registry back. No reason your young ears should hear what's about to be said."

With that, the woman picked up a spherical crystal ball and left the room in a hurry.

Tara reached into her bag. "Smile," she screamed at Ava.

A flat piece of metal the size of a business card flew through the air and stopped inches away from Ava's face. A holographic comb extended out on accordion arms, brushed an errant strand of Ava's hair, then flashed a bright light. A picture printed out of thin air, and both the card and picture shot back into Tara's hands.

"This is quite the exclusive," she said. "Arat Asoraled is about to get a lot more famous! In three hundred years—since The Registry's inception—this has never happened. It's not even supposed to be possible!"

Tara looked as if she would burst from the excitement. "I've got to go and write this up. I should be able to get it ready and picked up for the three-o-clock *Daily Believe It or Not* column. I'm thinking front page! I'll see both of you at five. We'll read it as we head over to Linhollow on the kelpies."

Tara placed the picture and camera back in her bag before shooting Duncan a warning look. "And remember, you've never heard of Arat Asoraled."

Before Ava or Duncan could say a word, Tara was gone.

Healer Gwyn returned to the room, distress plastered all over her face.

"Ava, there are some people from The Registry coming to help us," she said, although she didn't look like she believed it herself. "They'll know what to do."

A tense silence settled in the room as they waited. Healer Gwyn bustled about, straightening containers of dried plants that were already straight and reorganizing a shelf of books that sneezed as she dusted them off.

Duncan had resumed his perch on the corner stool and appeared to be deep in thought.

"This isn't going to be a problem, you think?" Ava asked in a whisper.

Duncan's obsidian eyes met Ava's. "I'm not sure," he whispered back. "As Tara said, this has never happened. I don't know how this—*how you*—are even possible. It goes against everything I've been raised to believe."

Could they make Ava leave if she wasn't in the system? She'd accepted the idea of meeting her parents. She now wanted more than anything to attend the Lost Ones Ball. She could picture it, her parents waiting for her. If she wasn't there, would they be upset or relieved?

Ava glanced down at the ring on her finger. What would her life look like from that point on? If she was cast out, back into the mortal realm, would the longing return? Would she still feel the pull to the Cathedral tree, the gateway back to this world?

It wasn't as though she'd be able to tell anyone what she'd seen, what she'd experienced. Oh, Elorise and Beatrice would love it if she did. Their mother, Ulga, wouldn't hesitate to take Ava straight to the psych ward.

Ava realized she already considered Duncan and Tara her friends. She felt like she'd known them forever. After what she'd already experienced, she couldn't imagine going back. How could she return to the mortal realm when she now knew an entire civilization—filled with *her* kind—existed?

The doors to Healer Gwyn's apothecary flung open, and three men with garnet-red hooded cloaks draped over black trousers and black collared shirts stormed in, the stomping of their heavy boots on the marble floor resembling the sound of rolling thunder.

Healer Gwyn ignored the short, jumpy man on the left and the bulbous man with the beady green eyes on the right and addressed the man in the middle—the tall, fair-haired one with the cold eyes.

"Julian … I thought associates from The Registry would be coming," she said, her surprise evident in her voice. "What brings advisors of the High Court here?"

"That was the case until a story broke ten minutes ago about young Ava's unexpected arrival," the man in the middle, whose name must have been Julian, answered. "Your lack of discretion has forced our presence."

Healer Gwyn scanned the room. With no Tara in sight, she seemed to put the puzzle pieces together. She said nothing about who had leaked the story.

Julian turned his hard gaze toward Ava. "So she's the reason our whole world is in chaos?" He seemed unimpressed as he approached Ava—as if this was all some big misunderstanding. As if this girl couldn't be the one creating such a stir.

"Let me see her wrist," he said as he continued to address Healer Gwyn.

"I've already tried twice," she answered. "It's not my system."

Ava could tell Healer Gwyn wanted her words to hold true. The last thing she probably wanted was to have made an enormous mistake in front of these men.

"I'll need to see that for myself, thank you," Julian said, a harshness to his voice.

Tired of no one in the room addressing *her*, Ava bit her lip and decided to speak up. This wouldn't be like the times at home when she'd let Ulga walk all over her. Ava would put an end to that today. She wouldn't start her new life the same way she had her last.

"Well, what are we waiting for?" Ava asked as she tried to sound braver than she felt.

Julian ignored her question and turned to the jumpy, short man, who handed him a black velvet bag. From it, Julian pulled out a greenish-gray labradorite stone with iridescent specks of blue and yellow. Attached to it was a thick, metal chain, far heavier looking than any chain Ava had ever seen.

With steady hands, Julian grabbed Ava's right wrist, causing her heartbeat to accelerate. He closed his eyes and stretched one arm over hers. The stone began to move. As it did, Ava could sense Julian scanning her wrist with his mind.

From the look on his face, she could tell what was *supposed* to be there was not there. The stone's momentum began to fade, a pulse coursed through it, and all its color vanished. With the iridescent flashes gone, it resembled the black depths of Duncan's eyes.

Julian tossed the stone aside with frustration. The jumpy man dropped to the floor to pick it up and placed it back into its bag.

Julian reached into a sheath inside his cloak and pulled out a black-handled, double-edged steel dagger with a clear crystal base.

He began to spin the dagger in his hands with his eyes fixated on the blade. His grip tightened around the dagger's hilt, which displayed ornate carvings, his knuckles turning white. He spun the blade and pointed it at Ava's head with a menacing glint in his eye. The bulbous man laughed, but the jumpy man turned his head.

Ava's heart squeezed in her chest. Was this man going to kill her? Right here, right now? In front of a room full of people?

Julian stepped toward Ava, his dagger's point leading the way.

The door burst open for a second time, and a towering man sauntered in. The light reflected off his slicked-back bronze hair like a halo, the scowl on his face causing the stubbles on his chin to quiver. He wore the same garb as Julian and his men, but the others lowered their heads and inched backward as he approached.

Everyone froze as if awaiting instruction. Healer Gwyn stood straighter and seemed to hold her breath.

Ava couldn't take her eyes off the mysterious man. He seemed to have a magnetic pull that Ava could have sworn she sensed *before* he'd entered.

"Lower that at once," the man said, his booming baritone lending gravity to his order, "and stop frightening our newest arrival!" With that, the man broke into a wide smile, his icy blue eyes sparkling with mirth.

Julian bowed his head and backed away from Ava, the dagger still in his hand. "Your will be done, Ambrose."

Julian snapped into action, jumping about the apothecary, gathering items from the jars and vials before returning to a silver tray next to a single bed, chopping the items with his blade and brushing them into a small, silver bowl. He placed the bowl over a flame and melted the ingredients into a bubbling liquid. From his pocket, he produced a box containing a syringe with a long needle. He placed the syringe into the liquid and pulled back the plunger.

Julian tapped at the murky green liquid inside the syringe, then turned toward Ava.

When he stepped within inches of her, a shockwave blasted the room, the sharp change in the room's pressure hurling Julian and everyone else backward—all except Ava and Ambrose, who remained right where they were.

Ava sat on her bed, frozen, her eyes locked with Ambrose's. The others moaned as they pulled themselves back up to their feet. Out of the corner of her eye, Ava saw Duncan rub his head and Healer Gwyn stanch a cut on her hand.

"Very interesting," Ambrose said. "It would seem our young Ava is unable to be scanned *or* tagged."

Ava's eyes ballooned even larger.

Had she done that?

She hadn't wanted Julian to shoot something into her arm. When he had approached, an electricity pulsed through her. Her free hand had moved to her amulet, and a voice—not her own—in her mind had said, *"No,"* before the shockwave had blown everyone back.

"Mr. Ambrose … I know that looked bad, but I don't know what that was or how I did it…" Ava's voice sounded smaller than she would have liked, so she straightened her posture and held Ambrose's gaze. She needed him to understand she meant what she said, even if her shaky voice betrayed her. "I *do* think I can be an asset around here if you let me stay—tagged or not."

Ava didn't know how she'd be an asset and hoped he wouldn't ask her to elaborate. She reckoned she could figure that part out later.

Ambrose flashed a warm smile. "Sending you back is not an option, Ava," he said. "You are a part of this world, for better or worse. You must be frightened. What must you think of me? Of us? What with my cohorts"—he gestured toward Julian and the other two men—"coming across so harshly after the news broke."

Ambrose darted a disapproving glare about the room, and the other men lowered their own gazes to the floor. "You must understand, their wish is to preserve our way of life," he continued. "A way of life that has stopped our kind from being hunted and slaughtered. Kept us in a peaceful state for three hundred years. Outside this apothecary, there are many scared for their lives—for their children's lives. You see, there's no way you can exist, but here you are."

The man turned back and regarded Ava with the briefest confused expression before his face lit up with a smile again.

"Regardless, I'd like to be the first to welcome you to Xarcadia," he said, extending welcoming arms toward Ava. "I'd also like it if you held a press conference with me in a moment to help reassure everyone of your intent here. You see, you're all they're talking about! They even have a name for you: The Impossible Girl."

"After she changes, of course," Julian added, disdain in his voice after giving Ava a quick once over.

Ambrose nodded. "That would be best."

CHAPTER

SIX

For the first time since her arrival in Xarcadia, Ava was left alone in Healer Gwyn's "powder room," as she'd called it. Ava didn't want Ambrose to change his mind about allowing her to stay, so she ripped off her pageant dress and let it fall to the floor without another thought, standing with satisfaction in her white cotton tank top and bloomers.

A wave of relief washed over her—that with this simple action, she would close the door to her old life.

For the first time, she thought about what this would mean. It wasn't that Ulga, Fred, the twins, or her foster brothers and sisters were hard to leave. But what would they think had become of her? Would they report her missing? Now a Lost One to that world?

Ava imagined Ulga holding a press conference of her own. Forced tears would spill from her eyes, her perfect makeup smudged just enough to make them appear genuine. The mean twins would hover in the background. They'd have their mother back and get their moment in the spotlight. The kids at school would comfort them during their period of "grief."

Ava glanced at the clothes Healer Gwyn had left out for

her. A plain T-shirt, dark denim pants, and an azure hooded cloak. Ulga had only allowed Ava to wear dresses and skirts.

More ladylike, her adoptive mom had insisted.

For the first time, people weren't trying to make Ava into something she wasn't.

At least outward-appearance-wise, they weren't.

Ava stood in front of the opal-resin vanity that held the stack of clothes, a small bowl, and a large, graphite hairbrush, extending her arms out to the side as Healer Gwyn had instructed. A damp washcloth from inside a bowl shot up and wiped away the remnants of makeup from Ava's face. It sounded like it sputtered and spat as it returned to the bowl. The hairbrush flew up next and wrangled with the tangles in Ava's hair.

A standing mirror floated out from a corner of the room and hovered in front of her. A very different girl than the one who had gotten up that morning stared back at her. This was Ava's true self—who the people of Xarcadia would meet in a few moments.

Moments later, Ambrose guided Ava out of Healer Gwyn's apothecary, followed by Julian and the other two advisors, but they couldn't take more than a few steps out the door. Hundreds of people—frantic looks on their faces—greeted them, filling the walkways and spilling out into the streets. Some jostled the people ahead of them as they tried to get a better view of Ava, causing someone to yell out, "Giants and Ogres to the back! I mean, come on!"

Dozens of metallic cameras flew toward Ava from every direction, flashing bright lights in her face. Ava shielded her eyes. The resulting photos and the cameras flew back to their owners, members of the press forming a semi-circle in front of them.

"Ava, over here," a voice called out.

"Give us a smile," another person said.

"Is it true you found your perfect fit at Cast It With Us or Cast It Wrong?" a third voice asked.

All three scribbled away on their notepads even though Ava hadn't uttered a single word.

Ava sucked in a lung full of air and kept her head down. Being riddled with questions wasn't foreign to her. Pageant judges lobbed questions to contestants all the time—but nothing like this. She felt dazed, lightheaded even.

To his credit, Duncan didn't leave Ava's side and appeared to shield her from the onslaught of attention. He met her eyes and nodded as if to say, *You're fine. You're going to be fine.*

She wasn't sure if she needed to speak and turned to Ambrose for a cue.

Ambrose stepped forward, his red velvet cloak billowing behind him, and the audience grew quiet with anticipation. A stage materialized with shimmers of light, elevating Ambrose a couple of feet into the air. He turned back toward Ava as a podium and a microphone appeared in front of him.

"Come, Ava," Ambrose said, his voice booming through the crowd. "Don't be shy. They've all been waiting to meet you."

A railing appeared in front of Ava. She grabbed hold and climbed three small steps to take her place beside Ambrose at the podium.

Ambrose flashed a smile at Ava before directing his attention back to the frenzied crowd. He pointed a willowy finger. "Yes, you down in front."

A woman with a slicked-back, blond ponytail, red lipstick, and a too-tight, red leather jacket spoke. "Ambrose, are there others like her? What can you tell us?"

"Ambrosia, you look beautiful today," Ambrose said with a wink, causing the woman's face to match her lipstick shade.

"I assure you, our young Ava is an anomaly," he continued. "By whatever means, she *was* able to be born without The

Registry's knowledge. It was, and always will, remain an isolated incident."

"What about now?" a short man with glowing skin asked. "Is she tagged now?"

"Ah, Warren, I think you know the answer to that," Ambrose said with a hard glare. "Word travels fast, doesn't it? It's true. Ava was not tagged at birth *and* wasn't able to be tagged now. She shows exceptional promise in her craft—and yes, Donella," he addressed a dark-haired elfin girl, "she did find her perfect fit today!"

Ambrose paused for a moment before continuing.

"Ms. Ava Marie Jones—the name she was given in the mortal realm—shows more promise and power than any young witch her age that I've come across in the last five hundred years."

Five hundred years.

Ava gulped.

How old was this guy? She'd guessed him to be in his forties, at most.

"As for what it means, it means nothing to our society's impregnable security," Ambrose declared. "Ms. Jones is excited to become an upstanding member of our society. Moreover, I've assigned two of my top advisors—Julian and Geoffrey—to oversee her until a more permanent solution can be reached. Xarcadia and its citizens are as safe as when they woke up this morning."

"Do we know who her parents are?" Ambrosia asked. "Do we know how and why they allowed this to happen? Have they stepped forward?"

Ambrose's smile of reassurance appeared to turn a little more tense. "While they have not yet stepped forward, we have every reason to believe they will. *No one is in trouble here.* Every system, even an almost perfect one, is bound to have growing pains. One in three hundred years isn't bad in my book. I'm eager to have a one-on-one with them, so we can make sure this never happens again. I assume they'll be at the Lost Ones Ball to embrace young Ava, as we all should."

Ambrose's smile faded as gasps erupted throughout the crowd. He followed their gaze to the sky. Three witches flew in circles high above their heads, at a much greater speed than the witches Ava saw earlier in the day.

The hoods of their long brown cloaks shielded their faces, and lustrous silver glitter trailed out the ends of their brooms, further shrouding their identity.

Silver letters in perfect penmanship formed in the sky: "The Resistance Lives."

Louder gasps burst from the crowd. All around, people hugged each other with looks of shock and fear. Cameras flew up and snapped pictures.

In another instant, the three witches disappeared behind a cloud of silver.

Ambrose whispered into the ears of Julian and Geoffrey, and the two men dashed away. He then spoke again into the microphone.

"Now, if you'll excuse us," Ambrose said, "Ava here is expected at Linhollow by five-o-clock, and—well, you know how the kelpies hate to be kept waiting."

CHAPTER

SEVEN

Ava sat on the same bed inside the apothecary. Duncan tilted back on his corner stool as Healer Gwyn rushed about, throwing "last-minute essentials" into a tiny, rubbery suitcase that inexplicably expanded to accommodate every item it swallowed. A glass jar fell off a shelf, and a mossy mound escaped when the lid popped off.

Ava yanked a foot off the floor as the mossy mound scuttled past. She almost fell off the bed before she caught herself.

Her body slumped, losing its stiff posture. Her lips parted and she let out a loud sigh of relief. She unclenched her hands, the marks from where she'd dug in with her nails still aching. The press conference was done. Behind her. But it could have gone better.

It would have been nice if Ambrose had asked her to address the crowd. She wanted to reassure them of her intent, and it would've been better coming from her. Instead, she had been paraded out for the people to gape at like a contestant at a pageant.

She had promised herself this was behind her. With the excitement of everything, she'd fallen back into the bad habit of going along with whatever she was told to do.

Then there was the writing in the sky, which had nothing to do with her, but she could tell the people of Xarcadia associated it with her arrival. Their eyes had darted back and forth from the writing to her.

"Ava, Duncan," Healer Gwyn said. "Hurry, so we're not late."

Ava shook the memories from her head and jumped off the bed. "How far is this place?" she asked, noticing the time.

Duncan also hopped to his feet. "It's about two hundred stories down." Then to Healer Gwyn, "Please don't tell me we're going the way I think we are."

Healer Gwyn zipped the suitcase shut. It now reached her shoulders.

"Oh, Duncan, you know it's the quickest way—and they will leave with or without us if we don't make it in time to listen to that long safety speech they insist on doing every year," she said. "As if we all don't know: Don't touch the kelpies!"

Healer Gwyn snapped her fingers, as if remembering something. "I'll be right back. I need to grab my dragon's blood oil. Lord knows the school's always running out halfway through the year."

"Perfect, just perfect," Duncan said solemnly.

Not once had Duncan looked fearful in the hours Ava had known him. Worried, yes, but never fearful. But at that moment, he looked as if someone had gut-punched him.

"It can't be that bad, right?" Ava asked. "What do we have to do?"

"We're flying," he answered back. "I *hate* flying. It's not natural for my kind, but even I wouldn't be able to get there in time."

"I guess you have me to thank for that," Ava said with a nervous laugh.

"You'll make it up to me," Duncan said. "Since you're

familiar with humans, you can help me with my Mortals 101 homework all month."

"Two months," she promised. She was an expert after all, especially since she considered herself to be one up until a few hours ago.

Healer Gwyn parted the ruby red window curtains and peered out at the crowds lingering outside. "For heaven's sake, still there," she mumbled. "Out the back. It'll be faster and more discrete."

She motioned to Ava and Duncan and dashed toward the back of the room. The black suitcase jiggled and burped as it floated after her. Duncan groaned, looking like he dreaded what was coming next.

Ava followed Duncan out the back door of Healer Gwyn's shop into a magnificent botanical garden. Some of the plants were twenty feet tall. Shrubberies shaped like unicorns with gold hooves and horns with thick manes made of moss lined the sides of a running stream. The unicorn heads tilted downward as if eating the flora off the ground.

To their left, was a large herb garden with a sign above it that read, "Garden of the Apothecaries, Take What You Need, Nothing More." Rows and rows of colorful plants, with tall ferns mixed in, grew haphazardly.

"I hate doing this, but I don't see any other way," Healer Gwyn said.

The woman's voice startled Ava, pulling her back from her inner thoughts. She realized she had been veering toward the unicorn shrubberies with her hands outstretched to touch them.

Healer Gwyn reached into her pocket and pulled out a gold coin and a heart-shaped locket. She raised them above her head as her free hand went to her mouth and blew a loud whistle.

A massive creature with the head of an eagle and the body

of a lion flew in their direction from high above. It had metallic feathered wings, a curved beak, and golden talons.

It landed in front of Healer Gwyn and nudged her with its expectant beak.

She placed the gold coin and locket in its mouth.

"It's payment," she explained to Ava. "Griffins are a last-resort transportation for us. Their price is high, but you can always count on them to appear if you have something worth giving. As neither of you can fly, this qualifies as a last resort."

"I'm not riding in front," Duncan said.

Healer Gwyn put her foot into the stirrup of the golden saddle and hopped on. She grabbed onto the reins.

"You can sit behind me, dear," she said to Ava.

Ava almost fell when she tried to mount the griffin but managed to grab onto Healer Gwyn's waist and pull herself up. Duncan jumped on effortlessly behind her.

"What? If you've got a power, use it," he said with a shrug.

Was everything that easy for Duncan? Would it, over time, get easier for Ava as well?

"We need to be at the Kelpie Port in five minutes," Healer Gwyn said to the griffin. "We cannot be late."

She leaned forward in her seat, and the griffin lifted up.

Odd. Didn't Duncan say they were traveling two hundred levels below?

The griffin picked up speed before it changed trajectory and dive-bombed over the railing. Witches and warlocks on brooms narrowly dodged the creature's descent.

The wind slapped Ava's face and whipped her hair in every direction. Her heart raced as her hands tightened around Healer Gwyn's waist. This was much faster than when she'd fallen into Xarcadia, but she loved every moment of it. It was the most natural thing in the world. As effortless as breathing in air. She wished the ride would last longer than five minutes. She wished the thrill, the excitement, would never end. She wished the griffin could carry them all over Xarcadia, showing her its every level.

People, from every direction, stared at them. It was clear griffins were only used as a last resort. A rideshare for the sky —and of all people, Ava was on it. No one back home would ever experience this. It was hers and hers alone.

"How much did that cost you, Healer Gwyn?" a man's voice called out as they plummeted past.

"Too much!" she said with a girlish chuckle.

Healer Gwyn glanced back at Ava and seemed to misinterpret the mystified look on Ava's face for fear. "The first time's always a little jarring, dear," she shouted over the heavy winds that almost drowned out her voice. "It'll get easier once you start flying by yourself."

"Are you kidding?" Ava exclaimed. "This is amazing!"

Duncan, on the other hand, wore the same unsure and terrified look that Ava had when she fell *into* Xarcadia from the Cathedral tree.

This provided Ava a small sense of enjoyment. Here he was, perfectly safe, and he looked as if he was about to be sick. It was a kink in his impenetrable armor, and she was over-joyed that this boy who had saved her and stood by her could now benefit from her strength.

"You okay back there?" she asked, trying to egg him on the same way he'd done with her and Tara all day.

"Not now," he replied, his teeth clenched and his face whiter than usual.

Ava turned back around and loosened her grip on Healer Gwyn's waist. She stretched out her arms, realizing she didn't need to hold on to remain seated. The golden saddle held them in place. She was like a bird that'd been let out of a cage and trusted wherever this creature took her. She would stay on its back forever if she could. She'd have to find some things she could offer to beckon it down from its resting place high in the sky. This wouldn't be her first and last time on its back.

If riding a broom, all by herself, would be half as exhilarating as this, she'd be content.

The griffin slowed its speed and landed with a loud thud. Its impact with the ground caused dirt to mushroom into the air, temporarily blinding them. Ava wanted to remain seated on the griffin's back and follow it back to its home in the clouds, but Healer Gwyn pulled her off. She then helped Duncan off.

Ava walked around to face the griffin and gaze into its fiery eyes. "Until we meet again," she said, reaching out her hand to touch its cold, hard beak.

The griffin nuzzled her arm, and Ava was certain it smiled back at her.

The griffin's departure was as quick as its arrival. After dropping off its passengers in front of a ten-foot stone wall, the creature launched up and disappeared into the sky. Ava, Duncan, and Healer Gwyn were dusted with dirt from the griffin's powerful wings.

Healer Gwyn waved away the dust particles in front of her before leading Ava and Duncan toward a large, iron gate in the middle of the fortress-like stone walls. The iron bars within the gate swirled in the image of the Cathedral tree, its metal roots branching outward to meet the moving vines that slithered up and down the domed stone entrance.

"You okay?" Ava whispered to Duncan.

"I've been better," he said. "Healer Gwyn gave me some benzoin oil; seems to be working."

The gate swung open on its own as they approached. A sign above the stone archway that read "Kelpie Port" morphed to "Welcome" in letters formed by dark green seaweed.

When they stepped inside, Ava's breath caught in her throat. Hundreds of students packed the earthen courtyard just beyond the gate. But Ava's eyes traveled past them to the turquoise lake beyond. For within the lake were large, bronze boats attached to the backs of horse-like creatures. The creatures had the appearance of Clydesdales—if Clydesdales were fifty feet tall and had silver, scale-like skin that shimmered like diamonds in the sunlight.

The creatures wore silver and black bridles adorned with green calcite stones. The animals' manes—the only things about them that *didn't* shimmer—were intermixed with lake-weeds. Every time a creature shifted in the still waters, it unleashed a thunderous boom.

A chill licked Ava's face and crept under her skin. Her teeth chattered and she had to pull her cloak tighter around her body.

Tara broke through the throng of students and dashed up to Ava.

"Ava! Duncan!" Tara called. "I've been waiting for you. I was beginning to think you wouldn't make it!"

Tara greeted Ava with the familiarity of a long-lost friend. She even shot Duncan a warm smile.

"We ran into some … complications," Ava said. She didn't know how else to phrase the last hour of her life.

"I know!" Tara moved closer and whispered, "I should have come back! Quite the missed opportunity for Arat Asoraled."

"Maybe it's best *not* to poke the hornet's nest—anymore than you already have," Duncan whispered back. "Your article put the world in chaos!"

Ava agreed with Duncan but didn't have the heart to say so. Tara beamed as she clutched her newspaper article to her chest. She looked so proud to have been the first to break the story. It was a shame she couldn't openly enjoy the credit, since only Ava and Duncan knew the true identity of Arat Asoraled.

Tara grabbed Ava's hand and squeezed it. "Oh, and did you see Gideon released a press statement?" she asked. "He said he gave you the ring as a gift after discovering it was your perfect fit. Said we're all welcome in his shop any time, the snake!"

"Unbelievable," Ava responded, tracing the cool ridges of the ring on her finger.

Healer Gwyn, who had overheard their conversation, appeared at a loss for words. Her cheeks burned red, and she shot Tara an exasperated look before trotting away.

Tara pulled Ava closer to the crowd of students.

A tall, tan boy with copper hair who stood alone a few feet away from the group caught Ava's eye. He looked jittery, like, if he could, he would sneak out the main entrance.

"What's his deal?" Ava asked Tara and Duncan.

"Probably another Lost One," Duncan replied. "You guys always stick out like a sore thumb."

Another Lost One.

"Well, come on then!" Ava exclaimed, pulling Duncan and Tara toward the boy.

The boy seemed to pretend not to notice them as they approached.

Ava continued forward anyway, overcome with a sudden desire to make the boy feel less alone—like Duncan and Tara had done for Ava.

"Hi!" Ava said, trying, but failing, to make eye contact. "I'm Ava, and this is Duncan and Tara. What's your name?"

The boy appeared startled. Like he hadn't watched their every step toward him under his eyelids. He kept his eyes downcast. "Colin Arion," he told his feet in a British accent.

"Are you a Lost One?" Ava asked. "Because I am—and well, you'd be the first person I've met who is too."

"Yeah, I'm a bloody Lost One," he answered back. "They tell me I'm a bloody *Summer fairy*. A fairy! It's embarrassing, is what it is."

"Could be worse, man," Duncan said. "You could be a werewolf."

Colin's cheeks flushed bright pink. He probably would prefer to be a werewolf.

A woman wearing a long, brown coat, suede boots, and a riding cap pulled over her bobbed silver hair swooped down from the sky. Her opalescent petal-like wings fluttered, holding her in place above the students' heads as she blew a high-pitched whistle.

"All right, all right, settle down," the woman said in a melodic voice. "My name is Eve Sable, and I'm the keeper of the kelpies. Freshmen, this will be new for you, so listen closely. For those of you who've heard this before—even a *couple* times—entertain me here and *appear* to give me your full attention."

As the woman continued to speak, Ava drifted from the crowd, her attention drawn by a kelpie a short distance from where they all gathered. It was the most beautiful thing Ava had ever laid eyes on. She edged farther away from everyone, unnoticed even by her new friends.

Ava stepped closer to the edge of the water—and the kelpie moved its massive head toward her in response, its white eyes meeting hers.

It had called to her. Spoken into her. A voice in her head that summoned her to the water. Pulled her closer.

Ava reached out her hand. The kelpie shook its head up and down and seemed to encourage her. She touched the animal. Its skin was rough and sharp, but also sticky and smooth in some places.

Ava sensed the creature wanted her to keep her hand there —for what, she didn't know. It shifted its massive hooves as it held her gaze.

A shrill voice behind Ava made her break eye contact with the beautiful creature. The girl, tall and blond with an athletic build, screamed and pointed in Ava's direction as silence fell over the crowd. "Keeper Sable, that freak girl from the papers —she touched one!"

For the second time that day, all eyes were on Ava. Fear and shock plastered everyone's face.

"*Why* would she touch one?" a deeper voice asked.

Low murmurs spread through the crowd.

"Ms. Jones, keep yourself perfectly still," Keeper Sable instructed as her delicate wings carried her closer to Ava. "Do not move *one iota*."

Ava kept her hand in place and didn't move even one iota, as instructed.

Keeper Sable peered closer and confirmed Ava had touched the kelpie's skin.

"I'm sorry, young lady," she said, sounding almost breathless, "but it looks like we're going to have to take off that hand —a couple weeks though, and Healer Gwyn can have a new one regenerated. It won't have the same mobility, but you should've thought of that before you did this."

The woman reached into a brown satchel on her hip for something Ava assumed would be used to remove her hand. Ava stepped back at once. Her hand free.

Gasps erupted from the crowd.

"How did she do that?" the athletic girl asked. "Only Ambrose himself is said to be able to touch them!"

A stout boy reached out his hand toward the kelpie. Keeper Sable screamed.

"Triston, unless you want to lose three fingers like your brother last year and miss even trying out for the Assembly Games, you'll move your hand away!"

An embarrassed Triston retreated to the crowd as Keeper Sable returned her attention to Ava. "Ms. Jones, step away from the kelpie and rejoin your class," she ordered with a confused look. "Regardless of what you saw—touching a kelpie is forbidden. Many before you have lost limbs—or worse, *their lives*—by making that same mistake."

She again eyed Ava with curiosity, then cleared her throat. "Let us finish going over the rules of engagement prior to departing to Linhollow," she said. "First and foremost, never touch a kelpie's skin. Second, once we depart, keep your hands and feet in the boat. Third, do not, under any circumstance, look a kelpie directly in the eyes. Last, Lost Ones, check your pockets for a letter delivered from Linhollow's Department of Housing that requires your attention. Until the Lost Ones Ball, your food and housing will be comped until your parents can assume their financial responsibilities."

Ava checked her pockets. Sure enough, a small envelope appeared in her left pocket. She stepped back toward Duncan, Tara, and Colin, all three stared at her with bewildered looks.

"*Why* would you touch one?" Tara asked. "You know, Xarcadia isn't called the Graveyard of the Pacific for nothing."

"You're like a magnet," Duncan added. "You can't help yourself, can you?"

Colin only stared at Ava with raised eyebrows, his head tilted to the side.

Ava's cheeks reddened as she tried to find the words to explain herself. All she could come up with was, "It called me."

"Kelpies do not talk, Ava," Duncan said.

"It wasn't out loud," Ava said. "It was in my head, I swear."

"In the past, yes, sure, kelpies could get in your head," Tara said. "But that green calcite on their bridles blocks that. The High Court charmed the gems to break their old mental patterns, make them more docile and accepting of their new roles ... there's no way it could've talked to you, Ava."

Tara spoke a mile a minute and didn't wait for Ava to respond. "On a more positive note, I can't wait to write this up tonight! Layla" — Tara gestured to the tall, athletic girl — "was right—once the kelpies were taken by force out of the mortal realm, only Ambrose, the one who subjugated them, could touch them. If you think everyone here was shocked, wait until the rest of Xarcadia and Linhollow finds out!"

"Tara…" Duncan said.

"Okay, okay. I won't," Tara said, but it was clear she didn't mean it and she would.

Ava *had* heard a voice. It didn't matter if anyone believed her. At the same time, she hated that she had, unknowingly, broken two out of three rules from Keeper Sable's speech. Maybe she was a magnet for disaster. If she was ever going to fly under the radar, she'd need to be more careful and not follow her every whim.

"Okay, everyone, separate by class into groups of twenty and line up—orderly—in front of a kelpie," Keeper Sable said as she flew above them once again. "Freshmen to the left, seniors to the right. The rest of you, you get the idea. Get ready for departure."

Feet shuffled in every direction, everyone eager to ride with their friends.

The kelpie called to Ava again. She bit her lip, ignoring the echoes of its voice in her head, and stepped away from it toward the next kelpie. She didn't want to cause another scene. She didn't understand why she'd been spared—while that boy, Triston's brother, had lost fingers and still others had lost their lives.

Ava's new friends rushed to group themselves with her.

The kelpies knelt at the edge of the water. An adult sat at the stern of each boat on the kelpies' backs. Some of them looked like giants, fairies, and vampires, while others were harder to identify. Ava reminded herself not to ask anyone what they were. It seemed an impolite question here, as it would be in the mortal world.

The one thing they all had in common was they wore the same aquamarine cloaks, tall black boots, and tan trousers with white shirts.

Out of the corner of her eye, Ava saw Julian and Geoffrey pushing their way toward Ava with stern expressions.

Great.

"You two," Julian barked to two students in Ava's line, "find another kelpie." It was clear from all the shocked stares they garnered, advisors of the High Court didn't typically journey with the students, let alone talk to them.

The men took their place behind Ava.

She shuddered. She didn't like Julian or Geoffrey, or their fixed scowls, and wished Ambrose would have sent anyone else in their place. She decided to ignore her new shadows and turned her attention forward again.

One by one, the students in her group were helped onto the boat by a stout, dark-haired warlock. Ava's senses seemed to heighten, and she recognized some of the students around her were also witches, *her* kind. Others, she guessed to be vampires by their pale skin or werewolves by their oversized, athletic physique. Because of Colin, she guessed a couple to be fairies—their wings seeming to retract when not in use—and a couple more to be merpeople who resembled the woman she'd seen on the conveyor. But they weren't anything like the merpeople she'd seen in movies and books. While their bodies were covered in scales, they had two legs and feet—the expected tail missing. They had fishtail eyebrows and noticeable gills in their necks.

The warlock helped Ava onto the boat, and she took a seat at the bow. Tara sat next to her, and Duncan and Colin slid in behind them. Julian and Geoffrey embarked last and took the starboard seats near the middle, a little ways away from Ava, which comforted her. She gazed at the seemingly endless body of water around her and leaned into Tara. "So how far is this place? It looks like it goes on forever. Will it take us long to get there?"

"You're asking the wrong questions," Duncan said from behind her.

"It's not how far out it is," Tara replied. "It's how far under."

"Under!" Ava and Colin said, gasping at the same time.

Ava wasn't sure how long she could hold her breath. Colin seemed to share her thoughts and fidgeted in his seat.

"I don't know about vampires and fairies and everyone else, but I have never heard of a witch being able to breathe underwater in any stories I've read," Ava whispered, her tone taking on an urgency.

"Seeing as how you're the Impossible Girl, I'm sure you'll find a way," Duncan said.

This was payback. Ava could tell. Because she'd teased him about the griffin, Duncan appeared to enjoy the roles being reversed a little too much.

"Don't worry," Tara said, gesturing to the warlock at the stern of the boat. "He'll pass out potions that allow us to breathe underwater until we get to Linhollow. It's a mixture of feverfew, agrimony, chicory, and burdock root. Does *not* go down smoothly."

Ava turned back to Colin. "That make you feel any better?"

"It might," Colin said, "if I was being called the Impossible Boy … so no, not really."

As if on cue, the warlock passed out small glass vials to everyone but the merwoman and merman, who were seated to Ava's right.

Before the warlock could hand vials to Ava and her friends, Julian jumped back up to his feet, sending a ripple through the air that bumped the warlock. His satchel fell to the floor, spilling the remaining vials. Julian rushed over to help pick them up.

"My apologies," Julian said.

The warlock seemed unphased and amiable. "It was no problem at all. These types of things happen." He accepted the vials Julian handed him and returned to his feet.

"Does everyone treat them like they can do no wrong?" Ava whispered to Tara.

"Pretty much," Tara whispered back.

The warlock approached Ava and handed her the clear, crystal vial with a cork topper. "Make sure to drink the entire thing," he instructed, handing the rest of the vials to Tara, Duncan, and Colin.

Ava removed the cork, raised the vial to her nose, and sniffed its contents. A foul odor greeted her nostrils. She hoped it tasted better than it smelled.

"Bottoms up," Duncan said, as he raised his vial to his lips.

"Cheers," Colin said unenthusiastically.

Ava took a big gulp. She did not get her wish. The contents were bitter and sour at the same time, with a misplaced sweetness on the backend.

Ava glanced around. Everyone seemed to share her revulsion to the taste. The merwoman and merman laughed as they took in everyone's expressions.

Keeper Sable floated offshore in front of the boats. She rang a small, ornate bell three times.

With that, the kelpies rose to attention.

The potion turned Ava's stomach. That was the only thing it seemed to do. She felt no different than she had before—which worried her. She inhaled, she exhaled—as she always did. She touched her neck, arms, and hands. She was positive no gills had sprouted on her skin. And after trying to hold her breath for a few moments, she also was positive she still needed to breathe.

Everyone around Ava appeared calm—as well as confused—when she held her breath, her face turning red. She tried to calm her nerves, to reassure herself that she had nothing to worry about. She'd already seen so many things she couldn't have fathomed the day before and hoped this to just be another. She was now surrounded by magical beings, feared and loved in the mortal realm, so this was probably the safest place to be. Bones were mended, and limbs could be regenerated. She hoped she wouldn't need either, but she was eager to learn what else this world had to offer.

The first kelpie began to gallop. It charged about twenty feet before it jumped high into the sky, then dove into the water, a large splash in its wake. She glanced over the boat, which garnered her a disapproving look from the warlock.

Still, Ava could find no trails of the kelpie *or* the students who had been on it.

A knot formed in Ava's stomach.

A few seconds later, a second kelpie took off, and a third. Then Ava's kelpie took off in a gallop. The creature's massive legs pushed off and rose thirty feet into the air before it dove, headfirst, into the water.

The water, to Ava's great delight, was like the warm rays of the sun kissing her skin on a midsummer's day. Her arms immediately floated to her side, free from gravity, and the particles around her seemed to hug her like the softest of blankets.

Ava's body had the same sensation of riding on the griffin. It frightened and exhilarated her at the same time—and she loved it. The speed at which they traveled through the depths of the water seemed *faster* than the griffin, if that was possible. They streaked by large underwater sand dunes with protruding reefs, a colorful school of fish, and a gaggle of mermen and merwomen carrying sharp wooden spears.

As they swam by, Ava could see why people in her old world thought they had a tail. They swam fast, with their legs close together. If Ava hadn't seen them outside the water, she'd have thought the same thing everyone else did in the mortal realm.

Each time Ava exhaled, air bubbles floated up toward the surface. They seemed to be the only thing in a hurry to leave this place. Even though she was surrounded by a boat full of people, the silence was infinite and calming.

The other students followed Keeper Sable's instructions—with some creative liberties. Many turned around and peered out the side of the boat. They pointed at a long spindly looking dragon, wingless and blue, while the warlock gestured for them to remain seated.

Julian and Geoffrey, who did not share in the excitement of the students, maintained a stoic demeanor.

Julian's eyes were fixed on Ava, and he appeared to be deep in thought. Ava shifted in her seat. Something in her gut told her he was not to be trusted.

Geoffrey, on the other hand, stared down at his massive, gorilla-sized hands. Compared to Julian, he didn't seem like a threat. He appeared to be all brawn and no brains, and she imagined a lot of empty space between his oversized ears.

The kelpie slowed down and changed from a vertical to a horizontal course. Ahead of them, a few kelpies—with no students or instructors on their massive backs—swam away and disappeared. Ava sensed the creatures probably preferred it that way, some semblance of their previous freedom.

Ava craned her neck but couldn't pinpoint an apparent destination. But as the kelpie swam closer, she saw it: a massive waterfall with white water cascading down in a whimsical way. How such a thing was possible at such depths, she had no idea, but Ava marveled at its beauty.

She elbowed Colin in the ribs before gesturing at Duncan and Tara, trying to mouth, "Is this it?" Only one kelpie remained in front of them.

A weird sensation took hold of Ava before she could gauge their response. Her head pounded. Every cell in her body screamed for oxygen. Her lungs felt as though they were on fire, every breath she'd taken moments before burning from the inside out.

Duncan and Tara noticed Ava's agitated state and shot out of their seats. Colin ran to the warlock, who was busy scolding the merwoman and merman for getting out of their seats.

The kelpie edged forward and stopped.

Duncan and Tara didn't wait for the warlock to give instructions. They each took Ava's arms, placed them over their shoulders, and tried to move her. Ava's feet dragged up a couple stairs, then on a hard surface, as her friends carried her.

Ava couldn't focus her eyes; black spots clouded her

vision. Sharp sheets of water pounded her head and shoulders as she was dragged through the waterfall. She collapsed to a hard, cold surface and coughed up water.

Duncan and Tara said something to Ava, but she couldn't make out the words. She greedily inhaled oxygen from where she lay on the ground. Her body remained on high alert, but her pulse began to slow. She heard others pass through the waterfall.

"Ms. Jones!" the warlock's voice boomed. "You didn't drink the entire contents of the potion. You're lucky we weren't one kelpie back in line or we would not be having this conversation!"

One kelpie back in line.

Ava's head throbbed. If she had ridden the kelpie that had called out to her, she would not have survived this trip.

"I … I did drink the whole thing," Ava said as she tried to formulate more words, her throat burning.

"Ms. Jones, I will not have you lie to my face. If—"

"Can we talk about this later, perhaps?" an annoyed Tara interjected. "She's been through enough without you yelling at her!"

"Young lady, you will watch your tone, lest you've forgotten who's in charge here!" the warlock said to Tara before redirecting his attention to Ava. "I assure you, a full report will be written up on your escapades today, and you will answer to Headmistress Astrae."

Ava hoped this headmistress would be more understanding than the warlock.

More students crossed through the waterfall, and Ava became uncomfortable with the way everyone watched her. She was tired of being the center of attention. She'd had enough of it for one day—for one lifetime.

Ava struggled to stand and reached for Colin's outstretched hand. Duncan and Tara stood in front of her and formed a protective barrier of sorts between her and everyone else.

Julian and Geoffrey ambled over.

"He's right," Julian said, a threatening edge in his tone. "It's best if you do exactly as you're told."

The warlock appeared pleased about Julian taking his side. "If you're well enough to move, Ms. Jones, we must be on our way," he said, gesturing for Ava to move along. "Sixteen more groups of students are behind us."

"I'm fine," Ava lied. While her mind did feel fine, her body threatened to collapse. She refused to give everyone the satisfaction. She'd deal with her emotions and pain later.

Ava gathered her bearings, following the warlock and the rest of her group down an elongated hallway. Her feet stumbled over the multicolored-blue stone ground, which was embedded with white pebbles that sparkled, each one its own unique size and shape. No two pebbles were alike, and they reminded Ava of snowflakes. Her arms reached out to the deep aquamarine slate walls for balance as they reached an elevator at the end of the hallway. The elevator doors opened on their own, revealing what Ava thought was a man—but he had the front legs, hindquarters, and ears of a horse. His tail swayed behind him.

"He's an ipotane—half man, half horse," Duncan said, always ready with answers to questions Ava didn't ask.

She would have to find out how he did that. While useful in this instance, she could already tell how annoying it would be under other circumstances.

"Alastair," the warlock said to the half human-half horse, "my apologies for the delay."

The ipotane ignored the warlock and turned to address the students instead with a jovial smile.

"Students, welcome! On behalf of Linhollow's residents and instructors, I'd like to be the first to welcome you to our esteemed city. Please file in, quickly. Once we get to the academy, remain with the other students until everyone has retrieved their luggage. Afterward, make your way to Cromwell Hall, where you will hear Headmistress Astrae's welcoming speech and receive your room assignments."

The warlock stepped in the elevator first and seemed annoyed by Alastair's dismissal. But Alastair continued to ignore the warlock as Ava and the others crowded in.

Alastair closed the elevator door and pulled a large, golden lever.

Ava's stomach lurched as she once again descended to an unknown place.

CHAPTER TEN

The descent lasted seconds and for that, Ava was grateful. She wished Linhollow Academy for the Supernaturally Gifted was located back in Xarcadia —on solid ground and with the assurance of oxygen. She had no idea what to expect on the other side of the elevator door. And while part of her wanted to jump up and down and turn cartwheels, a bigger part fought the urge to vomit.

The elevator door opened, and the other students jostled Ava forward onto a shiny white marble walkway laced with blue veins.

Ava's group joined a large crowd of students who had already arrived, crowding the walkway ahead of them. A few fairies flew about, while some of the vampires and werewolves, Layla and Triston included, lunged and tried unsuccessfully to catch them. Never were they fast enough, although the vampires had come much closer than the werewolves. Would a witch on a broom be able to catch them? Ava wanted to find out and hoped she could do it in front of Layla, the athletic vampire who had called her a freak.

The students who'd already arrived carried backpacks or

luggage. Luggage that hadn't been with them when they'd departed.

Ava gazed around her, her mouth gaping open. The elevator had opened into one side of a domed underwater city that shimmered like sunlight bouncing off the ocean's surface. That was probably because the outer layer of the dome that protected the city looked like nothing more than running water. Ava reached out her hand to see if her imagination was playing tricks on her. Her fingers struck a see-through barrier, but to her delight, water trickled cooly over her fingertips. She turned around and splashed some of the residual droplets at a distracted Tara, whose hair bounced as she laughed.

Ahead of Ava, the marble walkway stretched as far as her eyes could see, winding around storefronts and houses and away from a forest of tall, colorful trees to the west and a white, sandy beach abutting aquamarine water to the east.

An enormous golden statue, rising thousands of feet into the air, marked the center of the city. The statue of a bearded, muscular man seemed to reach all the way to the top of the dome, seeming to bear its weight.

The walkway wrapped around the statue and continued to a hilltop, where a stately castle with majestic towers over-looked the city.

"Where we come from," Ava said, gesturing to herself and Colin, "there's stories of a lost, ancient city called Atlantis. Is this … it?"

Had Ava traveled to a city the mortal realm had been searching for? Her mind raced at the exciting prospect. She'd often dreamt of such a place.

"That's a legend we find funny around here," Tara said with a chuckle. "Before we moved underground, a witch, in her travels, got drunk one night in a tavern in Greece and told everyone there all about the city of Linhollow. She went on and on while they listened. They were enthralled by her. She was so sloshed that when they asked her the name of this magical place, she'd thought they asked for *her* name, so she replied, 'Atlantis' before passing out."

"They went and told some people, who told some people, who told Plato, and that's how the legends started," Duncan added.

Duncan and Tara shared a laugh, for once not bickering.

More students and instructors arrived, and they had to shift forward from their spot near the dome's edge.

A few feet ahead of Ava, a merman stood in the center of a rectangular area, cordoned off with yellow tape. Fairies flew above him, and he jumped into the air, trying to catch one. From what Ava had read about merpeople in her old world, he didn't have a good chance. An instructor yelled for the boy to move out of the landing dock, and he sprang outside the yellow tape just in time to avoid the piles of luggage that dropped down.

Students rushed over and scanned the newly arrived mound of luggage. They didn't touch any until they found the right bags.

Ava and Colin watched the scene and exchanged confused looks.

"Why are they being so cautious?" Ava asked Duncan and Tara.

"Come find out," Duncan said, mischief returning to his eyes. "There. That one right there is mine. Can you grab it for me, Colin?"

Colin reached out his hand to pick up Duncan's bag. Its handle turned into a snake that tried to nip at his fingers. Colin reared back and screamed, tripped over his own feet, and landed with a hard thud on the marble ground.

Duncan burst into a fit of laughter.

"Everything gets sent via teleportation by Xarcadia's postmaster," Duncan said after regaining his composure. "You can pay extra for added security, and you never know whose parents shelled out the extra Aurum shekels until it's too late —thus why everyone is so cautious."

A gangly boy to their right shrieked as he reached out his hand to retrieve his bag. The handle was overrun by large spiders. "But it's *my* bag," he screamed at anyone who would listen.

The spiders shook their heads at him and hissed in response.

The boy removed an orb from his pocket and spoke into it, causing it to light up with images. "Mom, please say you used the orange brush beside my dresser when you sent my things."

"No, the blue one, Theodore. What's wrong?"

"What's wrong is you used the *cat's* brush—I can't grab my bag."

"Oh, well, that's your fault, isn't it, Theodore," the woman snapped. "You're the one who insisted on the extra security! Ask an instructor to levitate it in for you. I purchased a twenty-four-hour charm, so it'll be fine by tomorrow."

The boy flushed as he said goodbye. He stuffed the orb back into his pocket and rushed over to an instructor.

"What's that smaller pile, to the left?" Ava asked, trying not to further embarrass the boy by redirecting her attention elsewhere. An older woman with gray hair and a black cloak bent over the small boxes and read the name cards aloud.

"Those are for Lost Ones," Tara replied. "Sometimes parents like to send notes and other items before the Lost Ones Ball."

Hope blossomed in Ava's chest. Only three parcels remained. She prayed one of them would be for her. Geoffrey stood near the woman, almost as if he planned to inspect any package meant for Ava.

In the woman's hand was a large tan parcel—the last one —wrapped with coarse string and a note attached. Geoffrey shook his head at a disinterested Julian and walked away.

"Aedan Ariti … The Registry also has you listed as Colin Arion," the woman said, when no one stepped forward.

Ava's heart skipped a beat but she forced a smile. "Colin, that's great," she said. "Are you excited?"

Colin didn't move or respond. Ava nudged him forward, but he still appeared hesitant to grab the package. Ava assumed the package wasn't magically secured since no spiders had attacked the woman, so she grabbed it instead.

"Err … do you want us to open it for you?" she asked.

"Sure," Colin said, his face a mixture of distrust and sadness.

Ava opened the box, which was no bigger than the width of her palm. But out of it came a gold jacket with puffy shoulders, gold-embroidered pants, and a pair of ostentatious dress shoes.

"They can't be serious!" Colin's cheeks burned red. "Who would wear such a thing?"

"The note's nice…" Ava stammered. "They ask you to wear it to the Lost Ones Ball. They say it's been in the family for generations…"

"It *looks* to be generations old," Tara said, eyeing the outfit with distaste.

"Yeah, fairies tend to go … garish for these types of events," Duncan added. "Maybe you could tell them it got lost…"

"Give it here," Colin said, grabbing the clothes from Ava and trying to stuff them back into the parcel before anyone else could see it.

After all the students claimed their luggage, Keeper Sable flew high into the air. "All right, all right, students, instructors. Now that everyone has finished trying to see who the fastest magical being is and retrieved their belongings, let's make our way inside."

Colin kept his eyes downcast. He chose to walk a couple of

paces behind in silence as the students made their way toward the castle.

The pathway was composed of a white sand with electric blue specks. Under the walkway, the raging waters in a wide moat rippled down the hill into the center of the city below in several canals.

The castle's exterior appeared to be made of crystals and adorned with pearls and diamonds that blinded Ava with a reflective light as she approached. Several tall towers, linked by criss-crossing walking bridges, rose high into the sky. Large, ornate windows appeared to have been asymmetrically placed throughout the many floors. The glass main entrance, which opened as if to welcome the students as they approached, was flanked by an earthen trellis, out of which bloomed white flowers with bright blue pistils and leaves. The same melody that had greeted Ava when she arrived in Xarcadia drifted toward them in visible waves from somewhere inside.

The main entrance was so large, it allowed all the students to file through together. The inside of the castle was more majestic than the exterior. The snow-colored marble floors click-clacked under the students' feet, the sound echoing throughout the castle. A large, double-sided staircase—with ivory railings and marble steps—appeared to twist and turn upward for hundreds of flights.

Just beyond the staircase was a large entrance to another room. The music grew louder as they neared it. A line of creatures stood on either side of the double doors.

"Goblins," someone whispered behind Ava.

Two short-tempered goblins swung open the doors, muttering and complaining under their breaths, as the students began to file through. The closest goblin grabbed the luggage from each student and haphazardly tossed it down an assembly line of goblins stretching down the hall. The luggage frequently missed its intended recipient, crashing to the marble floor before another goblin grabbed it and tossed it down. Where the line ended, Ava had no idea.

Ava stepped through the doors into a grand room with a vaulted ceiling. On a stage to her left, adult fairies with earthen harps, sweet-toned silver bells, and walnut guitars played beautiful music. The rest of the room was furnished with large, round tables that surrounded one long rectangular table, which sat directly in front of the stage.

Cylinders of light shined down from the ceiling over the round tables, casting translucent shapes of stars, suns, crescents, and other symbols Ava did not recognize.

Ava followed the other students to claim a chair at one of the round tables while the instructors sat at the rectangular table.

An elaborate menu several pages long appeared in front of Ava and the other students with green buttons next to each item listed.

"Do we press the button, and someone brings us what we want?" Ava asked.

"Even better," Tara replied as she pressed several buttons in the desserts section—and a chocolate chip cookie, hot fudge sundae, and chocolate pudding materialized in front of her.

"You are going to be so sick," Duncan said with a look of disapproval.

"And it'll be worth it," Tara replied as she dove into her sundae, then bit into the cookie.

Ava pored over the menu. *Ladies shouldn't eat red meat!* Ulga's mantra rang in Ava's ears. She smirked and made her choice: steak and potatoes.

The dish appeared in front of Ava the instant she pushed the green button. She scarfed it down. She'd forgotten how hungry she was after all the excitement from the day. Duncan ordered another iced hemoglobin juice and a leafy sandwich. Colin, to their horror, ordered a mushy dish that smelled of fish with brown bread and a lemon wedge.

"What?" Colin asked when he noticed eyes on him. "It's kippers; you should try it."

Tara snorted. "Not likely," she said, moving on to her chocolate pudding.

Julian and Geoffrey stood near the end of the instructors' table, watching Ava closely.

"Do they not eat?" Ava asked.

"Not while on duty," Duncan said. "It's an honor to be Ambrose's advisors; I doubt they'll lighten up."

Duncan's inflection changed, as if sensing the last part of his comments wasn't what Ava wanted to hear. She didn't know if her face or her thoughts gave her away.

Ava pretended the advisors were there for someone else, that she wasn't the Impossible Girl, and returned to her meal. An uneasiness settled over her anyway. She wasn't sure how long Ambrose planned to have them watch over her, but she hoped it would only be until the Lost Ones Ball.

An instructor with long, chestnut-colored hair and a kind face stood from the head table and clapped her hands. The noise in the room immediately died down, as if sucked into a vacuum. All the food vanished, and the students looked up with anticipation. She wore a beautiful white gown with a skirt that flowed out around her. Even with Ava's distaste for dresses, the woman's gown—and the woman herself— mesmerized her.

"Welcome," the woman's voice boomed. "Sophomores, Juniors, and Seniors, we welcome you back. We are excited for you to continue your education with us. To those of you who are new," she directed her gaze toward a group of wide-eyed younger students, "my name is Headmistress Astrae, and we are so excited for you to begin your journey with us. This school was founded three hundred years ago to bring us all together, united and stronger than ever. Our differences, set aside. For, it is in these differences, we find our strength. The following four years of your life will be some of the hardest years you'll face. You will be tested physically and emotionally. Your expertise in your individual crafts and your knowledge of the workings of our world will grow exponentially. I know some of you are tired."

She stopped for a moment and met Ava's eyes. "Rest tonight, for tomorrow begins a new year filled with challenges and opportunities. Classes begin at nine, and this year's Lost Ones Ball will be held in three days, on Wednesday."

Headmistress Astrae gave a nod and sat back down. The warlock who'd escorted Ava's group hovered behind her chair, then leaned in and whispered to the headmistress and Keeper Sable. All three glanced in Ava's direction.

Ava wanted to march over and explain herself before this warlock gave her a bad rep, but her attention was drawn by two students approaching.

"My name is Evander, and this is Priam," the boy said, gesturing to the girl. "Classes start tomorrow so it's time to clear out. We'll be your freshmen resident advisors. Get ready to catch your room assignments."

Evander winked as he and Priam turned and walked away.

"Catch?" Ava asked. She shifted her gaze just as hundreds of spherical, translucent balls materialized above their heads. Each one shined like the sun as it descended and landed in front of its intended student. Ava stared at hers, transfixed.

Duncan, Colin, and the rest of their male counterparts followed Evander and their spheres out of Cromwell Hall and climbed the staircase to their left. Priam led Ava, Tara, and the girls to the right.

After that meal—the biggest Ava had had in months—she regretted not taking into consideration all the steps she'd have to take with a full stomach. Her legs dragged and her eyes struggled to stay open. They rounded the top of the staircase to find a long hall to their right and several more flights of stairs. One went to the left, one to the right, and the third shot straight up. Ava's sphere led her up the third staircase.

"This is a lot of walking," Priam said, wiping sweat from her brow. "Once some of you lucky ones are cleared to fly, you can navigate the halls at a faster speed. Until then, consider it your exercise, and do your best not to complain."

Tara walked beside Ava, unaffected by all the sweets she'd eaten. She hadn't even opted for one green thing on her plate. "You're going to have to tell me how you do that," Ava whispered.

Tara smiled.

Ava's legs were about to give out when they reached the end of the staircase.

This better be the dormitories.

The group started to splinter off. Individual spheres led their respective students in various directions. Priam continued to lead Ava and Tara's group down a long hall. Elaborate, silver-framed paintings lined both sides. Some were landscapes while others were portraits of people and creatures.

"On the walls, you'll find illustrations of famous places, things, and the magical beings that were lost during our persecution." Priam gestured with only her back visible. "The losses prior to The Registry's formation by Ambrose could fill this entire castle, which is why these frames rotate themselves out."

Tara bit her lip and rolled her eyes in Ava's direction.

A picture flew off the wall in front of them, let out a loud shriek, and disappeared. A new picture appeared, and the man pictured in it smiled and took his place on the wall. Other frames did the same with screams or laughter along the wall. Ava ducked to avoid being struck by a flying picture.

The spheres stopped in front of a large door made of frosted glass and crystal. To its right was a small, rectangular device. Priam placed her right wrist to it, and the doors opened.

"You'll need to do the same," Priam said as she walked through.

"How's that going to work for me?" Ava whispered to Tara. Additional attention was the last thing she needed.

"Make sure I'm with you, I guess," Tara said with a shrug.

The hairs on the back of her neck stood on ends, and Ava was reminded of her shadows: Julian and Geoffrey. She spun around. "So, do you plan on watching me sleep also?" Ava asked. "Or is this where we say our goodbyes?"

A smile tugged at Julian's lips, recognition or something in his eyes. "No, this is where we say goodbye. But we will be back in the morning to escort you to your classes."

Ava chose not to say goodnight as she turned back around and walked into the enormous living quarters. To her left was a game room filled with a grand pool table, arcade games, a dartboard, and several sitting areas for chess. To her right were lavatories, and in the center was a large sitting area filled with several tables with lit candles atop each one. She had a suspicion this was a designated study area. Up and to the left and right were two small sets of stairs.

"Curfew is at ten," Priam said as she plopped down at one of the tables. "Your butts better be in bed by then. I can be fun, but I'm not lenient when it comes to breaking the rules, and I will not be made a fool of.

"To show off how fun I can be," Priam added with a large smile, "rather than assigning you to rooms—which I know you'd all hate—I'm going to let you work it out. Once you find a room and have your luggage delivered there by speaking into your orbs, you'll get dibs on that room. Four people to a room! Go!"

Tara grabbed Ava's hand and pulled her along.

When was the last time she had walked this much?

Tara opted for the right staircase, followed by a pack of girls who tried to push and shove their way closer to the front.

Thirteen closed doors were visible down the long, candlelit hallway. There were six on each side with one final door at the end of the hall.

Tara and Ava chose the second door on the right.

The room was unlike any Ava had ever been in—and not at all what she'd expected. Back home, she'd shared a single room with four small twin beds—one in each corner—with her foster brothers and sisters. The twins insisted they needed to sleep alone, in separate rooms. It'd been so cramped in Ava's room that when she got out of bed each morning, she would hit her shin on the footboards.

It seemed a distant, bad memory compared to Ava's living quarters now. Four beds were spread throughout the spacious room with enough floor space for her to do cartwheels in between.

Each bed was unlike the others, seeming to represent a different element in nature. Ava somehow sensed this distinction was important in Xarcadia and Linhollow.

One bed seemed to be a cross between water and solid furniture. Its headboard, footboard, and side rails appeared to be composed of flowing water. But none of the moisture spilled onto the floor. It stayed in its place—rooted but not. The mattress rippled with soft waves and looked like it would mold to Ava's body.

The second bed looked like Ava would fall right through. Its cloud-like appearance didn't inspire security, and she eyed it with distrust.

The third bed looked like a blazing ball of fire. Flames engulfed it, and Ava reared back.

The final bed, the one she ran to and jumped on, was earthen. Its mattress was the most plain, but its exterior the most beautiful. Beautiful green vines covered the bedframe with blue flowers sprouting out.

Tara chose the cloudlike bed and plopped down much harder than Ava would have. To her surprise, Tara didn't fall. She spoke into her orb, and her luggage appeared on the bed. She rolled over and looked at Ava to see what she'd picked.

The merwoman from their boat ride entered and chose the water bed, which swayed as she jumped on it.

"I'm Kailani, by the way," she said in a beautiful sing-song voice before requesting her luggage and tossing the orb aside. "Now, I know who *you* are, we *all* do"—she gestured to Ava— "but what's your name?"

"Tara Delarosa. Nice to meet you."

Layla and a group of girls walked in. When they saw that three of the four beds were taken, and that Ava was one of the takers, Layla looked Ava dead in the eyes and said, "Let's go back to the other staircase, and get as far away from that one as possible." Her entourage laughed before leaving the room.

"Is it me, or is she insufferable?" Ava asked, frustrated by her second slight of the day.

"Definitely not you," Kailani said with a laugh. "Layla's an entitled nincompoop, her hate even sharper than her fangs." Kailani jutted her teeth over her bottom lip in a way that made them all laugh.

A fourth girl, pale and tall with long black hair, walked in, and seemed uncomfortable with Kailani's current impression. "You, um, mind if a *vampire* takes the fourth bed?" she asked and gestured to the fire bed.

"No, of course not," Kailani said with another laugh that made her long blond hair sway and cover her face. "Layla's the only vampire I dislike this week."

The girl seemed to relax. She didn't look like she wanted to do much more walking. "I'm Mira," she said with a bright smile.

The other girls also introduced themselves.

"Ava, catch!" Tara yelled, tossing a pair of pajamas at Ava. "Until you get some. They may be a little short, what with the height difference, and they are old…" She rambled on and seemed embarrassed by a tiny hole in a pajama leg.

"No, they're perfect," Ava said and meant it. "Thank you."

She jumped up and made her way to the dresser beside her bed. She opened the drawer to stash her candy from Polianne's—the only thing that had come when she spoke into her orb. The drawers were full of what looked to be sets of matching uniforms. As she examined one, she also found it to be her size.

"How'd they know what room we'd pick?" Ava asked.

"They didn't, but once we did, the school's seamstress, a very talented nymph, whipped it all up and had a witch teleport them—kind of like with the luggage," Tara said, changing into her own pajamas.

Ava closed the drawers, changed, and laid back down. The day that never felt like it would end was finally over. She had no idea what tomorrow would bring. She had no idea if she'd like her classes or the rest of her classmates. And she had no idea how she'd be received, being the Impossible Girl with two impossible-to-lose shadows. But as she drifted to sleep, she didn't care. Whatever came, she'd face it, as she had today. The place already felt more like a home than she'd ever had, and she'd do whatever it took to stay.

Ava fiddled with her casting ring the next morning as she studied her appearance in the crystal, floor-length mirror by her bed.

She wore an aquamarine sweater vest over a long-sleeved, white button-down shirt with a white pleated skirt and an aquamarine cloak. She wore her amethyst amulet, as always, around her neck. It was the one thing Ms. Kerpopple said had come with Ava when she was left as a baby on the orphanage's doorstep. Ava only removed the necklace to shower. While the amulet usually gave her strength, even it wasn't enough to make her feel better.

"I don't know about this, Tara," Ava said for the millionth time that morning. "Are you certain there's no pants that go with this uniform?"

Ava again tossed everything out of her drawers. Once more—to her dismay—she found nine more knee-length pleated skirts. The same nine she'd already tossed out and then placed back. She willed for a pair of pants to appear from the mess that lay on the floor. When that didn't work, she closed her eyes and pointed her left index finger at the drawer's contents—to no avail.

"If you're finished with that..." Tara said with a laugh, pointing toward Ava's clothes pile on the floor.

Although Tara, Kailani, and Mira had already all said no, Ava had still hoped for a different response.

"We can always stop in and see the school's seamstress later," Tara said. "I'm sure she'll be able to whip something up ... but you'll be fine for now, and we're going to be *late* for our first class if you don't hurry up." She gestured around the already empty room as if to make her words sink in. Mira and Kailani had already left ten minutes earlier.

"Okay, alright, fine. But you're taking me to this seamstress after our first class. Deal?"

"Deal."

"Where do we even go to get our schedules?" Ava asked. She had no idea what her classes were or where they were.

"They'll be downstairs," Tara said, appearing eager to have Ava move away from the dresser.

Ava grabbed two cotton candy burritos filled with fruity pebbles and some unmelting vanilla ice cream out of her bag of goodies from Polianne's before she ran out the door with Tara. She handed a burrito to Tara, who had missed breakfast because of her and would be missing lunch as well.

Downstairs, two small, ornate placards awaited them on a long, crystal table with cabriole legs made of ivory. The table had not been there the night before, and its purpose seemed to be to display their schedules.

The rest of the room was empty. They weren't the last ones to leave their room—but the last ones to leave their *entire* dorm. Ava again apologized to Tara as her cheeks reddened.

Tara shook her head and brushed it off. She read over her schedule with one hand, taking a bite out of the cotton candy burrito with the other, a fruity pebble stuck to her chin.

Ava laughed and pointed it out to Tara before she grabbed and read over her own schedule.

Monday:

Casting 101: 9:00 A.M. — 12:00 P.M.
History of Magic: 1:00 P.M. — 4:00 P.M.
Tuesday:
Book of Mystiká: *9:00 A.M. — 12:00 P.M.*
Botany for Beginners: 1:00 P.M. — 4:00 P.M.
Wednesday:
Flying: A Beginner's Introduction: 9:00 A.M. — 12:00 P.M.
Potions and Charms: 1:00 P.M. — 4:00 P.M.
Thursday:
Magical Etiquette: 9:00 A.M. — 12:00 P.M.
Mortals 101: 1:00 P.M. — 4:00 P.M.
Friday:
Casting 101 9:00 A.M. — 12:00 P.M.
Crystal Balls and How to Use Them 1:00 P.M. — 4:00 P.M.

After Ava and Tara read through their schedules, they switched placards.

"Almost all our classes are together!" Tara exclaimed happily.

"Yes! But … it's eight fifty-five," Ava said, as she glanced at the oversized clock above the marble fireplace. "We have five minutes to get *here*." She traced her finger on the "you are here" star and dragged it to their intended destination. The diagram on the lower portion of the card looked more like an impossible maze than a usable map, especially for someone who'd always hated geography.

"This looks far, Tara…"

"Then we better move," Tara said, shoving the last bite of her cotton candy burrito into her mouth.

Ava dashed out the door and hoped Julian and Geoffrey would've thought they'd lost her, possibly mixed in with the crowd of girls who had left earlier. She hoped they would have divided and tried to find her, but, no. There, they stood.

Ava frowned.

"Cutting it close, aren't you?" Julian said in a dry tone.

"Try to keep up with us, old man," Tara said as she nudged Ava to run. "We can't be late."

They had five minutes to climb ten flights of stairs. Ava and Tara ran like they were being chased—which they were. Ava stole a glance over her shoulder at Julian and Geoffrey, who followed but at a more labored pace.

Ava was relieved to see a conveyor like the one they'd used in Xarcadia midway down a large hallway after they'd climbed six flights of stairs. She envied each fairy and witch who flew by. Sweat dripped from Ava's brows as she hopped on the conveyor, and she was able to catch her breath as it ascended the remaining four floors. Julian and Geoffrey stepped onto the conveyor behind them.

Ava checked her map again and turned left onto a bridge that led outside to another tower, where her class was located. Ava had never been so high up with such an amazing view of the entire city down below.

Ava and Tara peered through the door to see a roomful of witches and warlocks in their seats. They conversed back and forth and ignored the books in front of them. It was seven minutes past nine if the clock above the instructor's desk was to be trusted. It didn't appear the instructor had arrived yet. Ava's wardrobe hesitations this morning wouldn't be getting them into trouble, after all.

Ava's heartbeat recovered a little as she slipped inside the classroom, with Tara, Julian, and Geoffrey close behind. Ava and Tara scurried to the front, ten rows down a tiered, auditorium-style seats, and took their places next to each other. They exchanged satisfied smiles.

A woman's voice—a familiar voice—echoed down from the top row. "Now that we are all here, we can stop wasting everyone's time and begin our lecture."

Her heels scraped against the marble as she walked down to the front of the classroom and stopped in front of a large, crystal desk. Her back still turned, she stepped behind the desk and pointed her index finger at a large chalkboard that occupied most of the wall. The chalk raised itself and wrote her name in cursive, large enough for even the people in the back to see: Sibyl Kataros. "You are to address me as Mrs. Kataros."

She turned around and locked eyes with Ava, then Tara.

The *woman* from Cast It With Us or Cast It Wrong.

"And how nice it is to see you two again—and on better terms—without running into me and knocking anything out of my hands this time," Mrs. Kataros said with a frown. "You two have demonstrated a failure to pay attention to your surroundings and tardiness in all of two days. I expect nothing but your full attention for the remainder of the semester."

Ava didn't know whether she wanted an audible response and nodded in agreement as the rest of the class looked on. Once her back was turned, Ava and Tara exchanged wide-eyed looks.

The chalk rose as Mrs. Kataros spoke again, "Casting is an art form. Much like art, you begin with finger painting and coloring outside the lines, your work sloppy. As it is with being a child, this is acceptable for a time—a short one, at that. As we progress this year, it will become unacceptable rather quickly. Your goal in this class is to color as precisely in the lines I give you. You will hone your crafts, most of you being average. Some of you will be great. But it's up to you which category you fall into. Understood?"

When all the students nodded, Mrs. Kataros seemed satisfied and proceeded.

"Before you learn how to crawl, you must first find a casting ring you identify with. A casting ring is a witch and warlock's most valuable tool. The vibrations of the ring will help to balance your powers, better control them, and allow you to cast with more precision and dexterity. Can anyone tell me the five metals most used in a casting ring?"

Tara's hand shot up first. This was a topic she had

expressed interest in at Cast It With Us or Cast It Wrong, and Ava was not surprised she knew the answer. Maybe it would even help her to make a better impression.

Mrs. Kataros glanced in her direction. "Anyone else? Come, I won't bite."

Theodore, the gangly boy who'd had trouble with his luggage, raised his hand. He looked nervous, as though he knew the answer but was afraid to say it.

"Yes, then, speak," Mrs. Kataros urged.

"Gold, silver, iron, steel, and copper," Theodore mumbled.

"That's correct. A gold band helps to harness one's power and protection. Silver, like gold, is an excellent conductor of energy. Silver helps with balancing one's emotions."

Mrs. Kataros directed a hard glare toward Theodore, and the poor boy looked like he was going to be sick from her attention.

"It also reflects negativity and increases one's psychic awareness in reality as well as in their dreams," Mrs. Kataros continued. "Iron and steel are also protective metals. More so, they help to ward off malevolent forces with their power, strength, and aggression. Copper helps conduct energies in things relating to health and one's foundations. People who identify with copper tend to end up as healers."

The instructor walked up and down the rows, checking that the students were taking notes. A scowl spread over her already serious face at the sight of one student with his face down, buried behind a book. She pointed her right index finger, and the book hurled to the floor. The boy startled awake.

A black cat Ava hadn't noticed before jumped onto the boy's desk with a loud hiss.

"You'll stay after class," was all Mrs. Kataros said to the boy, whose eyes were still locked with the hissing cat's. "And to the rest of you, that's Gregory" —gesturing to the cat— "and he'll be watching you."

Tara leaned in. "That's her familiar," she whispered to Ava. "He *will* be watching us. Familiars find you and serve the witch or warlock they choose. Some are more powerful than others."

"Moving on," Mrs. Kataros said. "Now that we've gone over metals used in casting rings, who can tell me how many stones are set in each one?"

Tara's hand shot up and was, again, ignored.

"Three,"Ava said, looking down at the perfectly fitting casting ring on her own finger.

"Correct, Ms. Jones, but you'll do well to wait to be called on in the future."

Ava gulped and nodded.

"The gemstones, much like the metals used, in a casting ring say much about the witch or warlock who wears them and what parts of our craft they identify with most," Mrs. Kataros continued. "Amber, for instance, is associated with fire and the energy of the sun. Strength and confidence exude from it as well as the witch or warlock whose finger it adorns. Alternatively, azurite is associated with tapping into one's third-eye abilities. We'll go more in-depth on the different gemstones in next week's lessons. As you grow over the next several hundred years, you will have a better understanding of what metals and gemstones you identify with and, if you're lucky, you'll grow enough to find your perfect fit and master your craft."

Mrs. Kataros absentmindedly tugged at her own snug ring.

"Until then, for those of you who did not out of sheer luck find your perfect fit on your first try, if the papers are to be believed" — Mrs. Kataros shot Ava a stern look like she didn't like exceptions to her rules — "today will be the day you find *a* fit. Go ahead and break into ten groups of ten and spend the duration of class trying to find something you identify with — and you'll know when it happens, so don't call me over for every try."

The instructor opened the top drawer of her desk, and the same ten boxes from the shop flew onto her desk.

Ava pushed her desk closer to a few students as the boxes flew across the classroom. One dropped down in front of Ava's group, and the top flung open to reveal one hundred rings. Her fellow students frantically grabbed at the rings, trying them on, one by one. Every few minutes, the boxes flew up and shifted to the next group. Ava sat back, fiddling with her own snug-fitting ring.

Tara reached into a box with her eyes closed and grabbed a ring. "This is the one, I can feel it!" She said the same thing at least sixty times, each time dismayed. Then, it happened.

Tara raised her glowing hand high up in the air, her face beaming.

For the duration of class, hands continued to shoot up as students around them also found a fit.

After class, Tara kept her promise and took Ava to the school's seamstress. The workroom, tucked away in a tower on the thirty-third floor, was no larger than their living quarters. Stacked from ceiling to floor were numerous, breathtaking textiles. Ava had never seen such beautiful fabrics and wondered what this woman could design, given creative freedom. The space was much too small for all its contents or the seamstresses's bubbly personality.

A short woman with a floral wreath in her silver-blue hair bounded toward them and introduced herself as Rhapso.

"It's nice to meet you, Rhapso," Ava said. "I was hoping you could do something about this?" Ava held the fabric of her pleated white skirt between her fingers.

The seamstress looked Ava up and down as though she'd

made a mistake with her uniform. She fiddled with the measuring tape around her neck. She must not receive many visitors, and she seemed overly excited about their visit.

"I'd much rather prefer pants," Ava said with a nervous smile.

Rhapso laughed, her cherub face beaming. "Oh my stars, yes, of course," she said. "When you return from dinner, you'll find several pairs of white pants in your drawers."

Ava wanted to jump up and down. She wanted to do a victory dance. Instead, she said, "Thank you. Really. We'll visit again soon."

"One more question," Tara said, grabbing Ava and spinning her around. "Just how hard would it be to craft clothes with spaces for small, secret recording devices?"

Rhapso fell silent. Her mouth opened, then closed. She seemed at a loss for words.

"She's joking," Ava said before Tara could utter another word. "Really. Thanks again."

Ava pushed Tara to the door.

Their lunch hour was nearly up which made Ava grateful. Anymore time in that room could have proved disastrous for Tara.

"Are you sure you don't want people to know you're Arat Asoraled?" Ava asked, making sure Geoffrey and Julian were outside earshot. "Because with questions like that, you're likely to be found out—and sooner rather than later."

Ava didn't know how the High Court dealt with grumblings and was concerned.

"Oh, you give me no credit!" Tara replied, unfazed. "If she'd even bothered to ask why I needed it, I would have told her it was for my studies. I'll have to ask her again next time."

Julian and Geoffrey's footsteps grew closer. Tara had pointed out that Rhapso's workroom had no exit and unless they wanted to hear some *very* personal things, they'd better wait outside. Ava laughed at her friend's fearlessness as the men caught up with them. She hoped it would rub off on her.

With only ten minutes left, Ava was thankful their History of Magic class also was located on the thirty-third floor. This time, they'd be early.

"What do you know about instructor Alaraic Viscardi?" Ava asked as she stared at her schedule.

Before Tara could answer, Duncan and Colin rounded the corner, laughing, and walked up to the large, glass doors to the classroom.

Ava and Tara exchanged a mischievous smile and tiptoed up to the boys. Duncan spun around.

"You're going to have to try a lot harder if you want to surprise us," he said with a large grin.

"You're going to have to tell me how you keep doing that," Ava said.

"I'm a vampire. It's in our genetic makeup to sense things and read minds. Some of us are better at it than others."

"You're kidding!" Ava exclaimed, half-intrigued and half-furious he could listen in on her private thoughts.

"Don't worry so much," Duncan whispered into her ear so no one else would hear. "I won't tell Tara you agree with me more than her most of the time."

"That is not true," Ava said, even though the warmth rising in her cheeks said otherwise.

"You'll learn how to block it; they'll teach you." Duncan raised his voice, now loud enough for everyone to hear. "The higher a wall you build, the harder it is for our kind to get in. Take him, for example."

Duncan gestured to a boy coming down the hall. "He's got secrets to hide. Day one, and he's already got his wall so high I don't even want to know what he's thinking."

Ava was eager to change the subject and to start building this wall. "So you guys are in this class?" she asked.

"Well, since we're all magical in some way or another,

we're all required to take it," Duncan said. "Don't tell me you're already thinking witches are better than everyone else? One day must be a record."

"No, of course not," Ava said, defensiveness creeping into her words.

"Glad to hear that," Colin said. "Because from what I can tell, most of the warlocks in our dormitories are complete snobs. Duncan and I had to chase one out of our room before he got comfortable."

"Yes, yes, we get it," Tara said with a roll of her eyes "Tensions with other magical beings run ever so high between you testosterone-filled men—can we get to class please? I want to get a good seat."

Mr. Viscardi's class went a lot smoother than Mrs. Kataros's. Not only had Ava not been made the center of attention, but she found the instructor—a six-foot-eight tower of a man with trim black hair, pale skin, and hazel eyes—to be much more pleasant.

Ava liked how this school differed from her old school. Besides the obvious difference in course content, instructors at Linhollow Academy didn't force students to go back and forth and awkwardly introduce themselves. Ava had never been good at that and had always stumbled with her words until the instructor had deemed her to have spoken enough. It had been hard to introduce herself when she hadn't even known who she was or where she came from.

But, as she listened to Mr. Viscardi explain the history of different magites, Ava hoped she would discover more soon.

From Mr. Viscardi's lecture, Ava learned all fae fell into three courts: seelie, unseelie, or solitary. The seelie court was ruled by summer fae, and, to a lesser extent, spring fae. The unseelie court was ruled by winter fae, with the autumn fae submissive to the winter fae. Then there were the courtless, the solitary fae, who preferred to go about their own business.

There used to be a fourth court, the shadow court, but that was said to no longer exist and sounded like something out of a nightmare. Ava shuddered at the thought that these fairies had given literal bits and pieces of themselves to control the shadow magic, a sacrifice required to access their dark powers.

Ava also learned vampires came into existence through a horrible twist of fate after a young apprentice had betrayed his then-master—a powerful witch, Aurora Cromwell—double-crossing her and stealing her Book of Mystiká for an unnamed warlock who tried to rid the world of the mortal race. Aurora Cromwell cursed the young apprentice, causing his skin to burn from silver and sunlight. She also gave him fangs and a bloodlust so strong, the young apprentice killed his entire family that night, draining their bodies of their blood. Her intent was to ensure he lost everything that mattered to him in one night, then ceased to exist at sunrise.

What she hadn't expected was for him to feel no remorse once he'd slaughtered his family. He delivered the Book of Mystiká to the warlock anyway. With the book and the centuries' worth of spells it contained, the warlock gave the apprentice super strength, immortality, and the ability to glamour, listen in on thoughts, and step out into the sunlight.

Aurora Cromwell struck down the warlock a week later, but she let the vampire live on, the magic from which he was created much too dark for her to do anything about. As the years passed, the apprentice went on to create more and more of his kind—occupying every city in the mortal realm—and his identity became lost to time.

Instead of fighting the vampires themselves, the witches and warlocks created werewolves to combat the rising vampire attacks that drew attention to magites everywhere.

Over centuries, the werewolves and vampires balanced each other out. The tumultuous relationship remained, however, even after the original vampire had been slain and the bloodlust that had connected them had been broken. Ava remembered Duncan's earlier words about werewolves and his apparent disdain for them, as though it was ingrained in him—and probably in werewolves, as well.

Ava glanced to her left, past Tara, to Duncan. She'd never have guessed such a dark history could link her to him. What did it say about witches and warlocks that they were responsible for much of the creatures of the night she'd grown up fearing?

Mr. Viscardi's classroom was shaped like a hemicycle, filled with tables instead of the individual desks in Mrs. Kataros's class. As Mr. Viscardi lectured in the center of the large classroom, with its domed ceiling and crystal windows—next to a desk with similar ornate crystals—Ava couldn't help but imagine that the only things missing from this trip down memory lane was the curtains drawn, the candles lit, and someone jumping out and yelling, "Boo!" Ava struggled to accept what she heard, that this could be actual history.

But the curtains were open, the candles weren't lit, and no one jumped out to shatter the illusion. No, all the other students scribbled away in their notebooks.

"Regardless of our continued efforts to hide our existence from the mortals, we failed, and countless lives were lost," Mr. Viscardi said. "Too many of our kind were ostentatious with their actions, uncaring of the consequences. You probably saw some of the lives lost as you walked through Remembrance Hall.

"You see, I knew some of those magites," he continued. "They were, mostly, wonderful people. Innocent people. People who were lost because we had no system, no way to govern with all magites under one unified front. It was chaos, and had Ambrose not brought all our Elders together and convinced them there was a better way, we'd still be in hiding, always fearful of our shadows."

Mr. Viscardi paused as if to let his words sink in. To let the gratitude to Ambrose sink in.

"Once all the elders signed off on his plan to relocate all magites underground, the violence stopped," the instructor said. "He went on to create the Scrolls of Parturition, a magical book that populates with the name and origin of every child born. He then created The Registry to manage it, to go in when a name popped up, to tag the child, and protect our way of life. Those already born also were tagged. This was necessary, as in the beginning, the rebellion group, known as The Resistance, tried many times to leave, to fight back. They didn't believe the attacks warranted such drastic measures. The majority believed we could find a way to coexist with the mortals, with a smaller portion believing we could rid the world of mortals. But, with the tags having been inserted into each person"—Mr. Viscardi pointed at the crescent-shaped scar they all bore—"and with the Keepers, those designated to stop any potential flight risks, we were able to contain any potential outbreak, track their whereabouts and bring them back, and place them into Desmios for eternity. Its location remains unknown except by Ambrose and those who guard it."

Several students shuddered at the mere mention of the name. It did not sound like someplace anyone would want to spend the rest of their days, let alone an eternity.

A couple of rows behind Ava, someone snickered.

"And what, might I ask, is so funny back there?" Mr. Viscardi asked with a frown. "Does Desmios amuse you? Because it shouldn't. The detainees are said to be tortured, trapped in their minds. Immobile in their cells and left to replay their darkest fears over and over."

"I apologize, Mr. Viscardi," Layla spoke up. "I agree with what you said—about being tagged. How it protects us. But I'm curious why our own Impossible Girl hasn't been shipped off to Desmios. My mother, who works as a cleric at the High

Court, says it's a matter of time. I received a letter from her this morning."

Ava's cheeks reddened and a red-hot anger flared in her stomach at Layla's words.

If Ava belonged in Desmios, wouldn't Ambrose already have put her there? Why allow her to attend these classes and have his advisors follow her around?

No, Layla was wrong. Once Ava's parents stepped forward at the Lost Ones Ball, it would be revealed to have been a horrible mistake—she did have the mark, even if she wasn't tagged. That meant her parents had tried, maybe some mistake having happened on The Registry's part and not theirs.

Duncan, who looked like he could finish off Layla with one bite, seemed like he was about to rise from his chair. Ava placed her hand on Tara's arm and gave Duncan a look.

On the offhand chance Ava could end up in Desmios, it was best to take the higher road. A road Layla and her cronies, who all sported smug grins, knew nothing about. Layla had gotten the reaction she'd wanted: everyone stole glances at Ava and whispered to one another.

Mr. Viscardi clapped his hands and cleared his throat.

"You know full well no child chooses to be tagged—you included, Ms. Lelantos," he said to Layla. "It's not a choice you made; it's not a choice *she* made. In whatever manner Ms. Jones came to us was not of her doing, and there is no magite at the High Court or Elder's Court that would wish her harm."

Ava's cheeks still burned. Mr. Viscardi's kind words didn't provide any comfort. She doubted the other students agreed with him.

Mr. Viscardi gave Ava a small smile before he turned, signaling that the matter was closed and there'd be no more questions.

"Back to the topic at hand," he said. "That same year, the High Court was created. Led by Ambrose and formed to regulate and work in conjunction with the Elder's Court—which remains to this day with one elected magite to represent each of its constituents— guaranteeing equal representation for magites everywhere. The longest-standing member is Samael Stavros, our own Duncan Stavros's father."

Duncan slumped lower in his chair.

Mr. Viscardi paused, glancing at the depleting sand in the hourglass on his desk. "By our next class, I'd like you all to write five hundred words, by hand. Explain what The Registry, High Court, and Elder's Court mean to you and your families. You're excused."

Ava released a long breath, a wave of relief washing over her.

"Mr. Stavros," Mr. Viscardi yelled over the frenzy of students shuffling out of the class. "Stay behind for a moment. I'd like to speak with you."

Duncan nodded. He turned his back on Mr. Viscardi and rolled his eyes. "I'll see you at dinner," he said to Ava and Tara. "It's probably the usual, 'Tell your father I said hello,' or 'Do you think your father will be coming to lecture anytime soon?' I get that one a lot."

"We'll save you a seat," Ava said with a smile.

"I even promise not to write about what you tell me—this once," Tara said, seeming to want to make sure Duncan understood it wasn't a blanket pass for perpetuity.

Ava walked in silence to Cromwell Hall with Tara and Colin. Maybe that was why Duncan took such a liking to her and Colin. They were Lost Ones, with no knowledge of who Duncan's father was. They had no ulterior motives to be his friend and wanted nothing in exchange for his friendship.

Maybe she wasn't the only one who had trouble making friends and finding a place where she belonged that hadn't already been decided by her parents.

After she'd pushed the unpleasant encounter with Layla out of her mind, Ava was surprised at how much she enjoyed dinner that night—and that they were allowed to order whatever they wanted with the push of a button. She had a craving for cereal. She laughed so hard as they talked about the day's events that milk spilled out her nose. It was an occurrence she'd hoped would repeat itself throughout the year, albeit without the milk coming out of her nose.

Tara plopped onto her bed the second they got back to their room. Even though it was structurally sound, the airy bed still made Ava nervous. She imagined Tara falling through its cloudlike frame with a loud thud. She hoped she wouldn't laugh if it did happen.

"I have never been so tired," Tara said with a groan. "Listening to Mr. Viscardi drone on and on about how wonderful everyone is—it's exhausting."

Ava glanced around the room, checking to make sure they were alone. "I don't know, he seemed nice," Ava replied. "And he got under Layla's skin. Did you see her face when he reprimanded her? She doesn't get that a lot, you can tell. Gives him major points with me."

"You can be nice *and* boring, Ava."

That much Ava knew to be true. Her foster brothers and sisters who, while nice, had never elicited more than the mildest of reactions from her. Their actions never even caught the attention, or wrath, of Ulga, Fred, or the twins.

"I want to keep an open mind," Ava said. She knew how Tara felt and still needed to decide how she, herself, felt. She smiled playfully, which seemed to appease Tara. "Ask me again next Monday what I think of him."

Ava sat up, remembering the pants Rhapso had promised

would be waiting in her dresser. Before she could jump up to check, a loud bang over her head preceded something falling from the ceiling with a loud clunk.

Tara shrieked and pulled her bed covers over her head.

The room returned to silence.

Ava now noticed what she hadn't the night before: a series of clear, quartz pipes lining the edges of the walls. They blended, almost perfectly, into the walls themselves before stopping in the corner near the bedroom door.

Ava walked toward it and saw a small glass door with a shelf inside. On it was a clear bottle with a brown cork holding a piece of parchment. She opened the glass door and retrieved the bottle.

"Don't worry, Tara, I've secured the perimeter, captured the culprit and, I have good news—we're going to be fine," Ava said as she held up the bottle.

"I'm fine," Tara said, peeping out from her covers with a sheepish grin. "I don't like loud noises."

When it was clear Ava didn't buy it, Tara added, "When I was younger and at my abuela's house one night, the High Court and some seekers used a battering ram to break into her house in the middle of the night. They claimed someone had reported my abuela for causing stirrings in The Resistance, which was ludicrous. While she does sympathize—and was in the past a leading member—she's been dormant for years! That didn't stop them from trashing her house and scaring us half to death, though. They treated us like common criminals! I'll never forget that feeling, the way they looked at us…"

"I'm sorry … I didn't know," Ava said.

"It's fine, you're fine," Tara said, seeming to shake the memories away. "Know I can hold my own if the situation calls for it. I'm no damsel in distress; I'm the tiger yet to be unleashed that everyone else needs protection from. Besides, what you have there is a message in a bottle. Before other magites moved underground, it's how the merpeople sent secret messages! It hasn't been used in centuries."

"I can tell," Ava replied, brushing a heavy coat of dust off her fingers.

"Well, what are you waiting for?" Tara said. "Open it up."

Ava removed the cork and turned the bottle upside down. The rolled-up, brown piece of parchment fell out.

"This must be wrong," Ava said, staring at the paper. "It's addressed to me. But who would send me anything?"

Her hands shook as she unrolled the parchment. Was it from her parents? A letter explaining that it wasn't a mistake that she wasn't tagged or that they wouldn't be coming to the Lost Ones Ball? Or maybe it was a threatening letter from Layla or others like her. Ava couldn't decide which would be worse.

In the center of the parchment were only three words, neatly written by hand: TRUST NO ONE.

"It says *trust no one*," Ava said, confused. "No one" would leave her with no confidants.

"Oh, it's probably somebody who wants to scare you," Tara said."Layla, even. A great, great, great something-or-other probably told her how to use the message tubes. Throw it away, and don't give it a second thought."

Ava followed the first part of Tara's instructions and tossed the parchment into the wastebasket next to the door, but she had a lingering feeling the message wasn't from Layla. It must be someone who wanted to warn her, to protect her even—but who? The words echoed in her mind.

Kailani and Mira burst in, interrupting Ava's thoughts. Mira plopped down on her bed and rubbed her tummy. Kailani went to the mirror to pluck an "errant" eyebrow as a sparkly brush combed through her hair. The girls didn't look like people Ava needed to worry about.

"I ate way too much," Mira said. "If anyone needs me, I'll be over here, unconscious."

Kailani returned from the mirror and plopped on Tara's bed with a wide grin. "Word on the street is Layla got scolded in front of everyone today," she said, appearing delighted. "Do tell!"

Tara and Kailani went back and forth as Tara recollected how it'd gone down. It was clear Tara knew how to tell a great story, emphasizing the right words, slowing down, and speeding up at the right points.

Ava couldn't help but stay quiet, though. She had a foreboding feeling in the pit of her stomach. Who was the message from? Why had they remained anonymous? And, if they wanted to warn her, why hadn't they said what they wanted to warn her about? Why be so cryptic?

Ava forgot to check if Rhapso kept her promise about the pants that night. Wardrobe issues were the least of her worries. She fell asleep with dreams of being sent to, and trapped forever in, Desmios and prayed that wasn't her destiny.

THIRTEEN

The next morning, Ava wore a pair of crisp, white pants that Rhapso made for her. But even that didn't improve her mood. As she and Tara made their way to their first class, Ava was hyper-aware of Julian and Geoffrey's loud footsteps behind her. She felt like a caged animal. Someone watched her, knew her movements, and had known the right time to send a letter for her to discover.

Their Book of Mystiká class was on the twenty-sixth floor. While the conveyor did most of the legwork on the upper levels, Ava's legs ached from the first four floors. Her feet dragged on the cold, snowy marble which felt much like her current mood.

Her body had never felt so sore as it had these last three days. She needed to get accustomed to this new routine soon —so she wouldn't walk like a cowboy with too much swagger.

Tara raised an eyebrow at Ava's funny movements. "You know, if you're going to try out for the Assembly Games, you're going to have to get in a lot more physical activity to even make it past the qualifiers."

"Assembly Games?" That was the second time she'd heard the phrase, but she'd never asked what they were. What came to mind was an auditorium filled with students doing one-legged races, tug of war, and wall climbing—but here, that didn't seem likely.

"Yeah, they hold them every year. Everyone tries out. Two magites from each grade and species are chosen."

Ava closed her eyes and calculated with her fingers. "So forty students out of two thousand are chosen," Ava said. "The odds are not in anyone's favor."

A reprieve from the doom and gloom that had preoccupied Ava's mind all morning was welcome. Not to mention, they had to climb two more flights of stairs before getting to the glorious conveyor.

"Okay, I'll bite," Ava said as her mood continued to lighten. "What is it? Magites compete against each other? Who usually wins?"

"If I remember correctly—and I always do—the fairies won it last year, and the year before, we took it," Tara said with pride. "The year before that, the vampires won. It goes back and forth among the three of us each year, like a yo-yo. But it's been years since the werewolves or merpeople won. And believe me, they are bitter and hungry this year!"

The thought of a win brought a smile to Ava's face. "Besides obvious bragging rights, what do you get if you win?" she asked.

"A three-hundred-year-old trophy, the respect from the adult witching community, and some extra privileges in Linhollow," Tara said.

Ava considered this as they finally reached the conveyor, her jellylike legs thankful for the respite as they ascended the rest of the way.

When they entered the classroom and took their seats, Ava wished she could sneak out and disappear again. Everyone around her pulled out large, leather-bound books that varied in size and style.

Ava glanced toward Tara's, which had her family's name embossed on the front.

"It's a copy of my family's Book of Mystiká," Tara said, noticing Ava's stare. "We'll create our own this year. We'll take what we find useful from the witches and warlocks of our past and add in our own spells, potions, herbs, and things."

"I guess I'll have a clean slate," Ava said as she tried to make light of the fact that this was another reminder that she didn't know her lineage.

A woman with tightly wound blond curls and large, doe-like eyes walked in. She apologized for having kept them waiting and introduced herself as Cassandra Rathmore. She insisted the students call her Cassie, making Ava more relaxed than Mrs. Kataros.

But like Mrs. Kataros, Cassie lifted the chalk into the air with her casting finger as it wrote on the chalkboard for her. What would these instructors think of a normal classroom? One where you couldn't magically do the simplest of things.

"This week, we'll cover the Book of Mystiká," she said. "I see you've all brought a copy of your family's sacred books." She scanned the room and looked pleased, before her eyes reached Ava's empty desk and smiled tightly. "A Book of Mystiká is a wonderful thing. A sacred place for a witch to keep the generations of magic his or her family has mastered. It allows for you to take what you need and add in your own achievements and discoveries for later generations. The most powerful witches are the ones who take this book seriously and follow their family's rede and honor the book in everything they do. If one is in danger, if one is lost or at a standstill in their craft, this is where one turns. The knowledge contained in the book in front of you is invaluable—and that is where we'll begin this week."

Cassie instructed them to break into two groups and share their family rede and at least one entry.

Ava listened to Tara and the others around her and

couldn't help but feel empty inside. She had no rede or entries to share. The students who spoke around her—Tara included —all sounded so proud. They would copy their families' entries into their own books this week. They even seemed grateful as they spoke about each entry and its author.

When class ended, Cassie pulled Ava aside and handed her a black, leather-bound book of her own. All the pages were empty.

"After the Lost Ones Ball, you'll need this," she said with a smile. "Look forward to that. It'll open your eyes to where you came from and give you more purpose than you ever could have imagined."

Ava liked Cassie, despite the fact the instructor's class filled her with emptiness and sadness. After her parting words, Ava had trouble swallowing her lunch. She wanted this to be over. More importantly, she wanted it to be tomorrow—the night she would meet her parents.

The fresh air as she made her way to her next class, Botany for Beginners, provided Ava with some relief and helped to clear her head.

While the enclosed space appeared dull and lifeless from the outside, the inside of the classroom was anything but those things. Garlands of ivy with pink sprouting flowers lined the arched entrance all the way to the stations that had been set up for them in the middle of the room. Streams of running water circled trees—moving and still—that reached toward the ceiling. Rows of different herbs and plants stretched around the room, intermingling with large shrubberies in the shape of creatures. Hundreds of different types of flowers grew in patches and vines, most of the walls and ceiling of the unorthodox classroom covered in them.

Moll Damia, their instructor, planned a treasure hunt for their first class. She allowed them to pick their own groups and passed out pictures and descriptions of what she wanted them to collect. The first team to complete the challenge would have no homework.

Ava and Tara teamed up with Theodore, who appeared awkward and stood by himself. He looked so dejected, like he'd already given up hope of being picked for a group, that Ava was drawn to him.

After forty-five minutes, Ava, Tara, and Theodore had already collected ten of the twenty items from the list. Theodore proved to have an eye for botany and was invaluable. He'd found more than half of the items himself.

"Does this look like mugwort?" Ava asked as she read the description and then stared at the angular, purple stalks that looked to be about four feet tall.

"The leaves growing out of it do appear to be the right hue," Tara said as she looked at the description over Ava's shoulder and then back at the plant. "And their undersides are cotton-like! Yes, grab it."

"Hey, guys," Theodore called from a couple of feet ahead of them, "I found the agrimony."

Ava looked down at her paper and read its description. "Make sure you're wearing gloves," Ava yelled. "It says if it's not handled properly, it can put you to sleep when exposed."

They rounded the corner and found Theodore had been a little overzealous and not heeded Ava's warning. He lay sprawled out on the floor in a deep slumber.

"You know that's going to slow us down," Tara said and left Ava to wait with Theodore while she fetched Ms. Damia for help. Theodore snored loudly.

Ms. Damia arrived in a huff, woke him with ambergris,

and ordered him to sit out with the other students who hadn't followed instructions.

One man down, Ava and Tara rushed to complete the challenge before anyone else could.

But their scramble to win proved to be their downfall. They'd mistaken bee-balm, a flower essence used to manifest intense joy, for dogwood, something used to protect one's Book of Mystiká.

"The purpose of this exercise," Ms. Damia said, "was to show you the importance of following directions as precisely as possible. When practiced improperly—or too rashly, as in many of your cases—the results can be detrimental. While no deadly items were placed on your list today, it's important to remember that this may not always be the case. To the winning team—Raz, Josefina, and Andrew—you'll be excused from the homework assignment this week. For the rest of you, have a paper on my desk by next Tuesday listing the most dangerous herbs and plants used in botany, so you'll be more aware in the future."

With the exercise proving to be a lesson more than anything else, Ava was frustrated by the fact that nothing seemed to go her way today.

She hoped that tomorrow night would be different.

"Ava, wake up!"

Ava opened her eyes with difficulty. The curtains were drawn, and bright light poured into the room. Tara stood over her with a look of impatience. She was already dressed, her book bag over her shoulder. Kailani and Mira were still sound asleep.

Ava pulled her covers over her head. "Are you crazy?" she mumbled. "What time is it?"

Memories of the last few days flooded her head and made Ava want to stay in bed.

"Does that even matter today?" Tara moaned. "Today we fly, actually *fly*—by ourselves!"

Tara ripped the covers off Ava. A cold breeze that seemed to be ever-present throughout the castle caused Ava to shiver.

"Listen here, I am not risking us being late today, so up and at 'em. Get dressed, and let's go." It was the pushiest Tara had ever been and, while Ava loved her forceful nature, she resented it when it disturbed her sleep.

"Can you two please keep it down?" an annoyed Mira yelled, revealing her pointy fangs. "I'd hate to make you." She was not a morning person either and pulled the covers back over her head as she continued to mumble threats. Kailani seemed able to sleep through anything, though. She didn't stir from the raucous or the light Tara had allowed into the room.

Ava didn't want to annoy Mira or risk how far Tara would go to make her comply. Against her body's objections, Ava sat up. "Okay, I'm up. Geez," she said with defeat.

For such a small girl, Tara could command the room when she wanted to. Even though Ava hadn't spent much time with Mira and Kailani, she liked them already. She'd grown accustomed to their nightly chats, listening as they rattled off the gossip from the day. Kailani somehow knew everything that went on in the school.

"How early is it?" Ava asked Tara a second time.

"It's six fifty-five," Tara answered. "And before you say anything, that gives you plenty of time to have whatever wardrobe meltdowns or any other drama and still leaves me time to get in a good breakfast and warmup, which we'll need. You never want to fly on an empty stomach."

Ava begrudgingly got out of bed. The knowledge that she'd lost an extra hour of sleep made her move slower.

Twenty minutes later, they were out the door. Tara practically shoved Ava to get her to move faster. At the sight of Julian and Geoffrey, Ava shrugged and directed them toward Cromwell Hall, too tired to care about their presence.

Tara scarfed down enough food to have fed at least five people. She wouldn't fly on an empty stomach, that was for sure. Despite Tara's warning, Ava didn't have much of an appetite and munched on some toast. Besides a boy buried in a stack of books, they were the only ones in Cromwell Hall at such an early hour.

"Let's go warm up," Tara said with a squeal as she grabbed Ava by the arm and led her down the hall to go outside.

"Are we going to see Duncan out there?" Ava asked as she tried to keep pace with her friend. "Do vampires have to take this class?" With Duncan's reaction to the griffin, she thought it unlikely.

"Don't be silly. Vampires don't fly. He'll be stuck in 'Controlling Your Hunger With Hemoglobin Juice' or something." Tara chuckled as they exited through the large doors.

For the first time since she'd arrived at Linhollow Academy, Ava stepped back outside the castle, breathing in the outdoor air. The fresh breeze ruffled her hair, the sunlight kissing her skin. Ava had the sensation of a weight being lifted off her shoulders.

Her feet sunk into the white sand pathway, its shimmering blue specks reflecting the sunlight with stunning majesty, as she followed Tara down discrete, transparent stairs that she hadn't noticed the night she'd arrived. The combination of the see-through glass and the height of the winding stairs made her question the sanity of the architect.

The city of Linhollow was quiet. There wasn't another soul in sight. The only thing that kept them company was the large, gold statue in the center of the city. It shone under the sun, whose warmth would hopefully soon reach them.

With no one else around, no Duncan to tease her, no Layla to overhear and mock her, Ava asked a question that had been burning a hole in her brain for days.

"How does that work?" Ava gestured toward the sun and the clouds in the sky.

"Oh that? It's a fairy thing," Tara replied matter-of-factly. "They control all the weather patterns in Linhollow and Xarcadia. Even the air."

Ava could tell Tara was a woman with a mission—to fly—and wasn't interested in small talk.

Tara slowed her pace as they entered a massive green field with hills that stretched for miles. The gentle breeze swayed the branches of some nearby century-old trees. They approached a large, marble building that looked like an oversized shed.

Tara started doing jumping jacks. Ava, Julian, and Geoffrey stared, slack-jawed.

"What are you doing?" Ava asked.

"I'm warming up," Tara answered between heavy breaths. "I want to be limber and ready. There's a new instructor this year. Since she's having our first class outside, she definitely intends to let us fly! And I want to be on point when she arrives."

"You mean to do that for another hour?"

Julian and Geoffrey inched closer, curious looks on their faces that seemed to say Ava may not be the only one who needed close supervision.

Tara didn't answer, so Ava opted to leave her to her calisthenics. Ava noticed, a short distance away, the same white flowers with bright blue pistils and leaves from the day of her arrival and decided to take a closer look.

Ava reached out her hand to grab a flower and narrowly avoided being bitten. Its pistil transformed into something that resembled a mouth with sharp teeth.

"They're nocturnal," an exasperated Geoffrey said from behind Ava. "You woke them up."

Nocturnal plants. Great, just great. Something not covered by Ms. Damia yesterday. Not only had Ava been woken up early with Tweedledum and Tweedledee following her around like some sort of magnet, but she'd also been unsuccessful in picking a single flower. This morning had started out great, again.

Tara continued her Olympic-worthy warm-ups by running laps. Her frenetic activity coupled with the early hour made Tara look like a madwoman. No one else was going to such extreme lengths to prepare for class.

Ava turned around and glared at her two shadows. Images of them trying to follow her even as she flew made her stomach turn. She already got enough attention without them, with constant whispers in the halls about her being the Impossible Girl. If they trailed her today, it would send the wrong message: that she couldn't be trusted for five minutes without supervision. Like some sort of dangerous escapee from Desmios.

Geoffrey, a werewolf, didn't concern Ava. Unless someone flew with him or there was a spare griffin around she didn't know about, he wouldn't be able to fly. The thought, though, intrigued her. Healer Gwyn had said if you offered something of value, the griffins always came. Could they be summoned this far beneath the waters if the situation called for it?

Julian was the bigger cause for concern, as he was a warlock and did know how to fly. She couldn't wait and find out once everyone else arrived, so she bit the bullet and questioned them.

"So, are you planning on flying with me today too?"

Julian smirked.

"Mrs. Avilasa won't let you get far, so I'll stay where I am," he said. "But don't think that, at a moment's notice, I can't be right behind you."

I'd like to see you try.

As if he read Ava's mind, Julian smiled in response. It was impossible, but she didn't like the way he looked at her. She preferred the doom-and-gloom Julian to the smiling Julian.

The sound of approaching voices caused Ava to break eye contact with Julian.

Tara stopped her warmups and rushed to Ava's side. She pulled her friend away from Julian and Geoffrey, who didn't bother to follow.

"Say nothing of what I've been doing," Tara whispered to Ava before she turned around as if to give Julian and Geoffrey a warning glance as well. "I want to look like a natural."

Tara had nothing to worry about. The other students were preoccupied and talked amongst themselves. Julian and Geoffrey kept to themselves on one side. Ava wished Duncan was there to overhear what the two men discussed in such secrecy.

A massive crowd of students soon gathered around them. It looked like all one hundred witches and warlocks from their freshman class were in attendance. Their hands were stuffed into their fur-lined cloak pockets as they conversed back and forth and tried to stay warm. All appeared as excited as Tara. The crowd's energy was palpable, and their excitement spread to Ava too.

She hoped it would be as exhilarating as when she'd flown on the griffin. Some distance—even briefly—from Julian and Geoffrey would do her some good. Their ever-watchful eyes would struggle to keep tabs on her for once, because of the speed she planned to fly. If that even was an option for her to choose—she wasn't sure how it worked.

The thoughts made Ava's pulse quicken. She didn't plan to do anything she shouldn't, but she did plan to make it as hard as possible for them to follow her.

An older woman with gray messy hair and large rimmed glasses dropped down from high up in the sky, coming in fast and landing hard. The woman could have been there for as long as they were, for all Ava knew ... could have seen Tara's antics. They hadn't thought to look up. She had a smile and a large brown bag in her right hand. Behind her glasses, her eyes appeared kind.

"Students, students, gather around. My name is Mrs. Avilasa, Linhollow Academy's newest flying instructor. I'm thrilled to see so many excited faces this morning!"

She dismounted her broom, and it remained upright next to her. She placed her brown bag on the ground, pointing her right index finger at it before pronouncing, "Yatsa." At once, one hundred individually wrapped packages flew down and landed in each student's surprised hands.

"Apricot jelly sandwiches," Mrs. Avilasa said. "You never want to fly on an empty stomach, and I suspect many of you opted for sleep rather than breakfast." Her smile seemed to say she didn't blame them.

"I told you so," Tara whispered. She looked ready to burst from the excitement of it all.

Mrs. Avilasa walked over and addressed Tara. "You're going to want to eat that, dear. I saw you earlier; you expended a lot of energy."

Tara blushed as Mrs. Avilasa stepped back to address everyone. Tara scarfed the whole sandwich down in seconds.

Ava did not like apricot, so she handed Tara hers. "You should have mine too."

Once Mrs. Avilasa gave them adequate time to finish eating, she instructed them to gather around in a circle.

"Flying is a witch's most sacred gift, after casting," she said. "It's a gift our kind has always been able to tap into, and it's one you will learn to master today."

"So, to be clear," a mousy girl said, "we will be flying today?"

"While past instructors have had students spend weeks poring over textbooks, learning every rule and sanction listed in the Department of Flying Vehicles handbook, I prefer a more hands-on method—and I have a feeling most of you here today will as well."

"She's amazing," Ava whispered to Tara.

Ava no longer resented being woken up. This was the most excited she'd felt since she arrived at Linhollow Academy.

"Dear, what's your name?" Mrs. Avilasa asked as she walked toward the mousy girl. She seemed to have noticed the same thing Ava had—the girl looked worse off after her question had been answered.

"It's Raz Samena," the girl replied.

"This runs in your blood," Mrs. Avilasa said with a reassuring tone. "You have nothing to worry about. I'll be with you the entire time."

Raz smiled back but still didn't look convinced as Mrs. Avilasa returned to the front of the class.

"Now, throughout this year, I'll have the same five rules for each class," she said. "One, fly safely—no funny business, no crashing into each other, *et cetera*. Two, keep your mind clear. A distracted mind can and has led to disastrous results in the past, and I don't want to be the first instructor to send a student to Healer Gwyn this semester. Three, keep a safe distance behind others. This goes back to rule number one and not crashing into anyone. Until you grow in your skill level, it's normal for you to lose control of your speed. Four, always land somewhere safe, somewhere flat. Five, do not try to showboat before you're ready. There have been plenty of students in the past who have tried to land in trees, only to fall and break their arms, legs, hands—you get the point. Now, does everyone understand?"

Every head, even the mousy girl's, nodded.

"Alright then, let's begin! And yes, it *will* be better than you ever could have imagined." Again, Mrs. Avilasa raised her right index finger and pointed at the marble shed. This time, she uttered the word "Erchomai" toward the far-right corner of the field. The shed doors flew open, and one hundred brooms flew out and landed, upright, behind her.

They were all identical. Unlike some of the flashier models Ava had seen in Xarcadia, these resembled the brooms she'd seen as a child: bundles of birch twigs attached to staffs of oak and ash with their bindings made from willow wands. The only differences being that wooden roses with handles were attached to one end of the staff and hemicycle-shaped horns were affixed to the center.

Before the students could dash to grab a broom, Mrs. Avilasa emphasized, "*Orderly*, I want you to each grab a broom and line up in rows of twenty in front of me. And before you think the first row will go first and disobey the *orderly* part of my instructions, please keep in mind that I'll randomly choose which group goes first."

The eager students tried—and failed—to follow the instructor's directions as they all rushed forward. Some shoved to get their hands on a broom. After almost being knocked down by Theodore, Ava and Tara each had their hands on a broom.

Ava's body felt electrified. The broom was more like an extension of her body than a staff with some birch twigs.

"What row do you think she'll have go first?" Tara asked in a frenzy. More and more students picked their spots, most only having gotten there seconds before them.

Ava could almost swear Mrs. Avilasa blinked three times at her.

"Third row—now," Ava whispered, and Tara and Ava scrambled to the third row without a second thought.

The instructor hadn't said one word to Ava, and it was ludicrous to think she would give Ava a secret signal that would allow them to go first. It was what every other witch and warlock there wanted.

But Ava had a feeling she was right. And Tara didn't second-guess her. Tara went along at once, and they scored the last two spots in the third row.

Several students switched lines. Each time they looked confident for a moment before they'd get a doubtful look on their faces and then switch again.

"Five, four, three—be in a line by the time I say one, or sit out the rest of this lesson completely—two, ONE." That was the most effective thing she could have said, and all the students stood frozen in the five rows by the time she had gotten to two.

"Now for those of you who are lefties with casting, bring your broom out to the left side of your body," Mrs. Avilasa said. "For those of you who are righties, bring your broom out to the right side of your body. Each time you fly, you'll want to begin like this with the broom closest to your casting finger."

With uniform movements, the students moved their brooms. At least four students bumped their horns, which blared and caused some students to cover their ears.

"It's important that once you mount your brooms, you visualize them rising off the ground," Mrs. Avilasa said. "Until this becomes second nature, this is easiest to do with your eyes closed. Those of you lucky enough to be in the *third* row, please mount your brooms."

FIFTEEN

"Oh my gosh, I freaking love you, Ava," Tara yelled over the disappointed mumbles that reverberated throughout the crowd.

Behind them someone yelled, "I told you we should have moved, Josefina! This is all your fault!"

Ava didn't know if it was a coincidence or if Mrs. Avilasa had been giving her a helpful hint. Regardless, Ava kept the thoughts to herself. "You deserve it, Tara," Ava whispered. "Those warmups were legendary."

Tara smiled in response before they followed Mrs. Avilasa's instructions and mounted their brooms.

Ava imagined herself lifting off the ground. Imagined herself taking flight. Even with her eyes closed for concentration, even without visual confirmation that she had actually lifted off the ground, a feeling of weightlessness took hold of her.

She opened her eyes to see Tara and the others still on the ground some twenty feet beneath her. Tara's face was a mixture of frustration and disappointment as she rose two feet off the ground, only to fall the minute she opened her eyes. Mixed in around her were eighteen other students who all had their eyes closed and their brows furrowed. Some even jumped off the ground and tried to bypass the initial instructions.

In a field not too far from them, a group of fairies gathered around—Colin included. Their wings were outstretched and shimmered as the sun beat down on them. The fairies would likely join her in the air shortly and crowd her airspace. Ava turned toward Mrs. Avilasa for permission to move. Even for a moment, she was excited to experience this first flight alone.

"Ms. Jones, excellent," an excited Mrs. Avilasa called from below. "Go ahead and lean forward for increased speed, backward for decreased—and use the handles to steer, of course. You have twenty minutes to fly wherever you'd like until my familiar comes to get you."

Down below, a small, black raven flew beside her and circled the hourglass Mrs. Avilasa had turned upside down on Ava's ascent.

Tara or even Colin would join her soon—before the hourglass ran out. Ava closed her eyes again and imagined herself rising higher.

She opened her eyes. It worked! The people down below were no more than fuzzy specks, like dandelion seeds in the wind.

She leaned forward, toward the city of Linhollow, and was surprised by how fast she zipped away. While not as fast as the griffin, her flight speed wasn't too far off.

Thanks to Tara's advice, her hair was in a high ponytail. This was more practical, her vision otherwise would have been impeded by flopping hair.

The wind hit Ava's skin. The fur-lined aquamarine cloak she wore provided some warmth. Her flying wasn't as smooth as the griffin's, but it wasn't terrible either. As she stopped to look over the city and its many storefronts, she came to an abrupt halt as her speed decreased much too quickly. It didn't bother her that much because every time she'd ever ridden in a car with Ulga, she'd had a similar experience. Ulga had always driven at forty miles per hour until the absolute last second before a stop sign. Ava had whipped forward and backward in her seat plenty of times. At least now, it was within Ava's own volition.

The streets below were packed with people, going about their day. While she wanted to go down and explore, she wasn't sure if that was against the rules.

Instead, Ava raised her gaze toward the gold statue that stood thousands of feet tall. Presently, she flew at the level of its calves and wondered how long it would take her to fly to its top.

She decided this would be the best way to test out her newly acquired skill. Eyes closed, she shifted upward once more by visualizing it in her mind. She leaned forward, her eyes open, and barreled upward. The outline of the golden structure was the only thing that told her she hadn't reached its top. Her eyes didn't have time to register much of anything as she moved, everything around her a complete blur.

After a few moments, the outline of a face came into view. She turned toward it, not bothering to check how much space remained between her and the water perimeter that domed the city.

Ava crashed into the top of the dome, her head bouncing off like a rubber ball. While she was able to put her hands up against the side of the dome when she first arrived in the city to feel the cool, running water over her palms, there had been an impenetrable barrier on the other side of the water that protected the city. The top of the dome was the same way, and Ava's head struck the barrier with a painful clunk. The impact threw off Ava's balance on the broom, and her legs slipped over its side. Her hands were the only things that kept their grip on the ash staff.

She fell—fast. Her once neat ponytail came loose, and her

hair covered her eyes. She struggled and tried to shake it off, too scared to lift a hand off the broom.

Her heart raced. Her ears pounded.

As she descended with her precarious grip on the broom, she tried to devise a plan.

She would pull herself up with her arms and swing her legs over. All would be fine.

As she tried to act out this plan, she discovered she lacked the upper body strength. Her continued efforts only weakened her grip. She had thousands of feet left to fall—each second bringing her closer to the reality of her loosening grip.

The broom continued its descent, forcing Ava's stomach into her throat. She had no control over the broom's trajectory. She tried again to visualize, to focus, but no matter how tightly she closed her eyes, she couldn't regain control.

It had been stupid to fly to the highest point of the city. It had been stupid to veer off from her class, from Tara. Tara, to whom she would never have a chance to say goodbye. Who would be there to look out for her and her wild ideas, if not Ava?

Nothing flashed before her eyes like she'd imagined it would from movies, which had to be a positive. But there was a lot of regret. Regret that she may not discover more about herself and her powers. Regret that she would never meet her parents at the Lost Ones Ball. Regret that she'd insisted Julian not follow her.

"I can't leave you alone for five minutes, can I?"

She snapped her head around and tried to find where the voice had come from.

To Ava's left, Julian sat on his broom as it descended and kept pace with hers.

Ava was somewhat annoyed that he had broken his promise to allow her a moment of peace, but she also had never been happier to see the warlock than at that moment.

The happiness faded as he continued to stare at her and not offer any help.

"Do you mean to scare me, or do you intend to watch me fall to my death?"Ava yelled. "I'm sure people saw you leave, so there would be rumors this was done by your hand—and that can't be what Ambrose would want. From the papers, you guys have enough to deal with as it is."

The wind muffled Ava's words and made her threatening tone less effective.

"I don't intend to let you fall," Julian said. He flew closer and placed his outstretched hand on her broom. Its descent stopped. They hovered hundreds of feet above the ground.

Ava's tired fingers began to sweat. She couldn't hold on much longer.

"I think this is the perfect time for us to set some ground rules."

"Of course, you would," Ava said. Her threatening tone returned and was more audible since they were no longer plummeting through the air.

Ava's right hand slipped, her full weight now pulling on her tired left hand.

"I do, so let's make this quick," Julian said, eyeing Ava's precarious fingers.

"You're a psychopath," Ava said. Not her smartest choice of words considering her predicament, but they tasted good as she'd said them.

Julian smiled at her outburst. "One, you'll lose the attitude," he said. "Two, you and your friends will stop insulting Geoffrey—to his face and behind his back—he's a softie underneath all that muscle, and antagonizing him will only make things harder. Three, stop thinking of us as the enemy rather than a detail that has been placed to protect our kind as well as you. Lastly, there's to be no funny business. Anything you do, you tell me about. Anything you even *think* about doing, you tell me about. Do we have a deal?"

Ava blew a raspberry. "You leave me no other choice, you realize that, right?"

"Of course, you have a choice," Julian said with all seriousness. "You have three: you can choose to accept my terms, you can choose to try to regain your composure and focus as I let go, saving yourself, or—and least appealing to you, I would imagine—you can fall."

Ava hadn't been able to regain her composure on her own, and she also didn't want to die today. She'd choose option one, which somehow felt worse than the other two.

"Deal."

With that, Julian reached out for her hand.

Ava froze and stared at it like some foreign object that she didn't know what to do with.

"This comes back to rule number three, Ava. Don't think of me as the enemy, and trust that I'll keep my word. When you remove your hand, I'll grab it."

Against her better judgment, Ava loosened her grip. Her body swayed to the left as she stretched her right hand toward Julian. His coarse hand locked onto hers. He kept his word and pulled her up and helped her to mount her broom.

Ava's heart rate slowed, her ears no longer pounded, and the adrenaline eased from her body. She felt a connection to the broom once more and was able to control it.

She took a deep breath and steadied herself. She would never again fly without paying closer attention. She would never again be placed in a situation where she needed to be rescued, least of all by Julian.

"Perfect timing," Julian said, as he gestured toward the raven that arrived to signal Ava's time was up.

"Just perfect."

Ava followed the raven back toward her classmates.

"Ava, over here!" Tara yelled.

Ava landed near Tara, glad to have her feet on the ground.

Tara eyed Julian, who had landed beside Ava. "I thought he let you fly solo?"

"That was the plan ... but I guess he doesn't need to check with me when he changes his mind." Eager to change the subject, Ava asked, "So, how'd you do?"

"It was magnificent!" Tara answered. "I got twenty or thirty feet off the ground—although I did lose height several times whenever I got distracted, so there's that ... but an admirable first try, I think. Several didn't even get more than a couple feet off the ground." She'd whispered the last part, always seeming to put other's feelings ahead of her own.

The students in the first row began their turn. Ava and Tara watched for several minutes as the students only managed to fly a couple feet off the ground. When the second, fourth, and fifth rows had their turns, a couple students crashed into each other, while a couple more crashed into the surrounding trees. Only a handful were able to go more than thirty feet off the ground.

"I forgot to ask you," Tara said as they watched. "How'd you do? You took off, and I couldn't see where you went."

Ava didn't want to make her friend feel bad or hold a lengthy discussion of how she'd been extremely successful and then extremely unsuccessful.

"It went okay," she replied.

In less than a week's time, Ava had had more near-death experiences than she cared to think about. Still, she was able to take some joy in the fact that, compared to everyone else, she had been the most successful at flying.

As the last students finished, Mrs. Avilasa called for them to gather around.

"Foundations are important," she said. "Today's lesson was meant to demonstrate that. Young witches and warlocks often want to skip the foundational studies to rush to the 'fun parts.' Today"—she eyed several students who rubbed injured appendages—"you learned this is not an option. To be successful at anything requires proper training, which is why our next class will be in the classroom. I guarantee by doing this, the next time we come out here, your individual flights will be much more successful."

No one argued with Mrs. Avilasa's logic. Most looked embarrassed that the grandiose flights they'd expected to take did not happen.

"Go refuel and read chapters one and two of your DFV handbook, and be prepared for a short quiz next week." She pointed her casting finger at the brooms assembled in front of everyone and uttered, "Fyge." All one hundred brooms flew back into the shed as the doors swung shut and locked behind them.

Everyone dispersed. No one wanted to stick around and discuss their failed attempts any more than they had to.

"How much do you want to bet that Andrew goes off and tells everyone he flew the highest of us all?" Tara joked as they picked up their bags. Andrew, who had been in row four, had talked a big game and tried to get in everyone's heads only to never leave the ground at all.

"Ms. Jones, a moment, please," Mrs. Avilasa called.

Ava turned back.

"What do you think that's about?" Tara whispered.

"Not sure, but I'll catch up," Ava said. "Save me a seat, and order me a sandwich if you can."

Mrs. Avilasa waited for Ava near a large oak tree, her raven on her shoulder. Julian and Geoffrey stood back and gave them some privacy.

"Ms. Jones, my raven here tells me you flew to the top of the city, yet you, yourself, told no one of your amazing feat. Why is that?"

Ava blushed. "I didn't want to make anyone feel bad, and let's just say, it didn't go the way I'd intended."

"Yes, yes, he also told me that."

With no one else there, Ava didn't think anyone could

know what had transpired. She also wondered how the creature on Mrs. Avilasa's shoulder spoke to her.

"You show incredible promise, Ms. Jones," the instructor said over the silence that lingered in the air between them. "Don't hide that. It's okay to make others uncomfortable from time to time. It betters them. Let it inspire your classmates and push them to what they're capable of—and most importantly, what you, yourself, are capable of. Don't let anyone count you out for being whatever it is they're calling you."

"Er … thank you, Mrs. Avilasa."

"And, if you didn't plan on trying out for the Assembly Games on Friday, make sure that you do. You have a real shot at getting the freshman girl slot and putting on a performance for our kind."

Ava thanked her instructor again and walked away, a smile curling the ends of her lips, a bounce in her step. Despite the slim odds, Ava started to believe she had a chance to get past the tryouts. At doing something that would help cement her into this world while also changing people's negative impressions of her.

Ava broke into a run to catch up to Tara when a group of students sprinted past her, their clothes shredding and falling by the wayside as they transformed into large, wolf-like creatures. *That* had to be awkward. Ava was relieved she wasn't a werewolf—and grateful she didn't have to take that class.

At lunch, a group of fairies flew into Cromwell Hall and sprinkled gold dust into the air that spelled out: CLASSES CANCELED, PREPARE FOR THE LOST ONES BALL THIS EVENING.

The students cheered. They used the extra time to eat, laugh, and go over their classes.

Colin showed off his newly grown wings. He spread them and retracted them several times with giddy delight.

Duncan announced he had worked on glamours that morning and believed he made real progress. When asked if anyone wanted to volunteer so he could display his new skill, everyone declined and changed the subject. If he had made progress, there was no telling what he would try to get them to do or believe, even if only for a moment.

Tara, who had remained silent for much of lunch, couldn't tear her eyes away from the latest issue of the *Daily Believe It or Nots*. They yanked the paper out of her hands, before she shared the story that had her so enthralled.

"They're saying The Resistance's movements in Xarcadia are rising, even getting violent," Tara said, frustrated. "There's a mention of an attempted break-in at The Registry. It makes no sense. They've never been a violent group." She looked down, deep in thought.

"Times change, and so do the people," Duncan replied.

Ava and Colin, the least familiar with the topic, listened to them go back and forth without saying a word.

Duncan scooted his chair back and stood. "Let's get ready for the festivities," he said.

The students cleared out of Cromwell Hall, chatting and laughing as they left. Whether they were more excited for the ball or for the fact there was no class after lunch, Ava couldn't tell.

She made her way back to her room with Tara, butterflies in her stomach. This was it. This was the night she'd waited for. She hoped it would be the night she *hoped* for, as opposed to the night she'd had nightmares about.

CHAPTER

SIXTEEN

"You've got to be kidding me?" Ava asked, face-planting onto her bed before sitting back up. She stared down at the official invitation to the Lost Ones Ball later that evening. Its silver calligraphy read: FORMAL ATTIRE REQUIRED. Beneath the instructions, images of people danced and moved around as they smiled, cheered, and clapped at the festivities.

"Well, it *is* a ball, Ava," Tara said with a chuckle. "More importantly, it's a tradition we've had in place for three hundred years, and it's not likely to change. It's old school, I know, and yes, it's something you're going to need to wear a dress to."

"And if I don't?" Ava jumped back up and darted to the window, as if needing a dose of nature to calm her down. "Why wasn't this told to us before?"

"If you don't, your 'detail' won't let you attend," Tara said. "It'd be disrespectful and counterintuitive to what Ambrose told everyone about you at his little press conference: that you're one of us, here to follow our traditions and laws. Plus, with the growing number of Resistance sightings around

Xarcadia and Linhollow since you arrived, it would make things even worse—like you're publicly siding with them. Which, if you wanted to, I'd understand, don't get me wrong."

The look on Ava's face said more than she could with words: Why was that her problem? She'd done nothing wrong. She hadn't chosen to be the Impossible Girl or to have sparked a surge in this Resistance she knew nothing about. So why should she be kept in a little box, unable to express herself lest everyone else lose their minds over it? It was insane, and maybe if these were the rules by which she had to play, she wouldn't play at all. She'd stay in tonight, maybe force her parents to come to her.

"You *are* going tonight, Ava," Tara said, her tone sounding like a mother speaking to a rebellious child. "If you don't, you'll regret it. Your parents are going to be there. If you're not there, the press is going to have a field day, drawing all kinds of speculations about your absence. 'The Impossible Girl turns her back on her parents at the Lost Ones Ball' or 'The Impossible Girl refuses to attend an institution that has been a part of our society since its inception—The Resistance grows.'"

"This is so unfair," Ava said, frustrated. She lowered to the ground, her head between her knees. "None of that should be my problem. I'm one person. It shouldn't matter what I do or don't do."

"Ava, put it all out of your mind for a minute." Tara's tone softened. "If you don't go, it will hurt your parents. And, if you don't go, you won't have another opportunity to see them until after the school year. We remain at school for all breaks. Our parents are not allowed on campus during those breaks. Most importantly—if you don't go, it's going to hurt *you*. You'll regret it as soon as it's too late to change your mind. You deserve an explanation from them. You deserve to know where you come from. Don't throw all that away because you have our whole world's eyes on you. It's unfair, yes, you didn't do anything, but don't let them take this away from you."

Tara was a force when she had a narrative she wanted you to grab hold of; with her many published articles at thirteen, Ava wasn't surprised in the least. But it overwhelmed Ava when it was directed at her. Tara was right. She *would* regret it if she didn't go. She'd go crazy if she had to wait a full year to get answers.

Accepting defeat, Ava raised her head and looked at Tara. "We need to see Rhapso."

"Oh, my stars, you two are back sooner than I imagined!" Rhapso exclaimed, her face glowing with pleasure. "But you, Ava, look miserable to be here."

Ava sighed. "It's not you; it's the Lost Ones Ball. The invites went out this afternoon, and it's formal attire. I only have my school uniform and some borrowed pajamas from Tara. I have nothing to wear."

"Well," Rhapso said with a delighted laugh, "that's nothing to be glum about, is it? Look where you are! What are we thinking? Oh, wait, I've got it—an A-line, scoop, floor-length, tulle dress with rhinestones on the bodice!"

Ava stood, frozen, as Rhapso showed them some of the rhinestones she had in mind.

"Rhapso, before Ava starts to hyperventilate," Tara interjected, "she wants simple. Definitely nothing pink. If it were up to her, she'd wear a white T-shirt and some denim, if that helps you stylistically."

Tara rattled off all the words that Ava had failed to formulate herself.

"Oh, I see," Rhapso said, not at all fazed as she set the rhinestones down and moved to grab less sparkly items. "Well, that's not a problem, dearie. It'll take me less time too. I promise you'll have something you'll love when you get back to your room."

"Thank you," Ava said. "Really."

The idea that she'd meet her parents in a couple of hours weighed on Ava. She did want to start out on the right foot with them. She didn't want to cause a scene by choosing not to follow the rules. And she didn't want to be turned away from even entering the ball. But her parents deserved to know the real her, and after she met them, she would make sure they did.

So many times as a child, Ava had been told she acted more like a boy than a girl. She'd never enjoyed dolls, dress-up, or pretending to be a princess that needed to be rescued. No, she'd preferred to watch and play sports rather than gossip with her classmates about the latest episode of *Princesses Sent Into Hiding—Are You One of Them?*

She'd found it ludicrous that anyone could try to define how a girl or a boy should act at all: how they should behave, how they should think, and what they should like. As if it were that simple. As if they all fit into these neat, little boxes that, if they dared to exit, they were somehow "odd," "off," or "wrong." By that definition, even Tara would be off, as she preferred to write the story than be featured in it.

"About that last conversation we had," Tara said to Rhapso. "What I thought of is a shirt with a secret compartment in its side for discrete recording purposes and maybe a camera fastened to a button—discreetly, of course. Would you be able to make something like that?"

Before Rhapso could respond, Ava jumped in. "She's planning to use it for her studies." While this could be true, Tara had other plans for it. Plans centered around Arat Asoraled.

"I see, you're rather dedicated, dearie," Rhapso said with a baffled look. "Let me work on it this week once things calm down, and I'll let you know how it turns out."

Tara beamed as they left. So much so that Julian side-eyed them.

"She's excited about my dress," Ava said, before any questions could be asked.

Geoffrey shrugged, uninterested and satisfied with the answer that placed them in the "normal" boxes. Julian shot Ava a look that said he *was* interested and was also unsatisfied with her answer. To Ava's delight, he didn't press it, following the girls down the halls as they searched for a pre-ball snack.

They entered Cromwell Hall and made their way to their usual table.

"Duncan, Colin, over here!" Ava called.

Tara tore into the enormous turkey leg she'd ordered with all the sides as the boys ambled over. Ava wondered—not for the first time—how her friend was so small.

"You guys excited for tonight?" Duncan asked, more to Ava than Tara, who was still distracted by her "snack" and hadn't yet looked up.

The boys ordered their own food, and Ava ate a spoonful of her yogurt.

"I'm optimistic," Ava said. "We saw Rhapso, and she's promised to make me something I'll be comfortable in."

"Well, that's a shame," Colin said. "I guess I'll be alone in my embarrassment. This one,"—he cast a distrustful glance at Duncan—"convinced me to wear that atrocious thing my parents sent. I still can't tell if he's messing with me or not."

"It's the thought that counts, and I guarantee most of your kind will wear similar outfits," was all Duncan said.

"Well, what are you wearing?" Ava asked Duncan.

"Oh, leave this to me," Tara said, as she came up for air, her mouth still full. "A black tux with your family's red crest engraved on your lapel. Mr. Stavros would definitely have his son represent the family tonight, am I right?"

"You are," Duncan said with a nonchalant air and a flick of his wrist.

"So how does this work, anyway?" Ava asked. "Colin, me, and all the other Lost Ones are going to parade around and have a magnifying glass on us as we meet our parents for the first time?"

"Kinda, sorta, but not really," Tara answered. "Head-mistress Astrae will give a speech, then his majesty Ambrose will give a speech, then you'll be called, one-by-one, to go down and embrace your long-lost parents, all right with the world. It's the same every year. This will be my first time in attendance instead of being forced to watch from home. So, who knows, maybe something crazy happens that they never show on-screen."

"Be thankful that you and Colin arrived when you did," Duncan said. "Two days later, and you would've had to wait to start your classes and be kept in Xarcadia until next year. Unable to attend this year's Lost Ones Ball or meet your parents until the next one."

"What type of society would make you wait a full year to meet your parents because your birthday doesn't coincide with the Lost Ones Ball?" Ava asked, confused by the logic.

"One that values its traditions and heritage," Duncan replied, obviously seeing no problems with them. "One that has an agreement with the parents who choose to send you Lost Ones out. That's how it works. The fact they still chose to send you out is their acceptance of that."

"It seems wrong," Ava mumbled, saddened for anyone who would arrive any time after today.

"It may also be a blessing," Colin said. "I would have loved more time to accept this new identity before meeting them. Maybe if I'd had a full year, I'd be more prepared. But, I don't understand why they did what they did, and I intend to tell them that tonight."

"So, to recap, Ava will be dragging her feet, Colin will potentially be telling off his parents, you—Duncan—will be toeing the line with your father, and I, Tara, will be there to take it all in and record tonight's events for future generations. I can't wait!"

SEVENTEEN

Ava parted the heavy curtains of her bedroom window and looked down at the vast forest on the outskirts of the city. How she longed to be there. To run through it. To explore. Instead, she was surrounded by excited girls putting on gowns and doing their hair and makeup for the Lost Ones Ball—which was an hour away.

The pit in Ava's stomach grew larger with every minute that passed. It was about to happen. She'd meet her parents tonight—but not only meet them, meet them in front of the whole world. Such a private, intimate moment on display for everyone to see and judge.

She'd also started to wonder at the name of this event. Lost Ones *Ball*. A ball implied dancing. If she had to dance, she would be in a lot of trouble. Her two left feet could no more follow a tune than they could stay planted on flat surfaces.

Ava closed her eyes and drew in a long breath. She forced a smile and turned around to face her roommates.

Tara bubbled with surprising excitement as she pulled on her dress—a short A-line, off-the-shoulder, pearl-pink-and-lace number—then placed a matching headband with three large pink flowers on her head.

The outfit was the last thing Ava would have guessed Tara would want to wear.

"You look stunning, Tara," Ava said, appraising the outfit and how beautiful Tara looked.

"Thank you!" Tara said, staring at herself in the mirror and tucking some of her bouncy curls behind her ears. "I never get to dress up like this."

"Do you want to try some of this glitter on your arms and legs?" Kailani asked, as she applied a generous amount to her own green arms, legs, and chest. She truly looked like a merwoman tonight. Her wavy, blond hair fell down her back, and she wore a form-fitting, sparkly, emerald green gown. Kailani's skin shimmered as brightly as her dress with the added glitter.

"No, I don't want to get anything on the dress," Tara said, embarrassed. "After the ball, I have to send it back so my abuela can sell it."

Tara's comment hung in the air for a moment, the other girls not knowing how to respond.

"What about you, Ava?" Kailani asked, trying to keep the mood light. "Mira?"

Mira wore a two-piece halter dress, her midriff exposed, with a long train. The bodice was black with eyelet lace, and a black waistband flowed into a red skirt with a slit halfway up her leg. Her black hair was pulled back into an elaborate bun, which she kept adjusting.

"Keep that stuff away from me!" Mira said, laughing through a mouthful of bobby pins.

"Same," Ava said. "But thank you for offering…"

"All right, all right, I get it," Kailani joked. "I'll shine by myself over here."

Tara's glance went from Ava to the closed garment bag by her side. "Ava, do you need help getting into your dress?"

Images of Tara pushing her out the door for their flight lessons flooded her mind. She wouldn't wait for Tara to force her into whatever frock Rhapso had concocted. Ava took a deep breath and bit the bullet, opening her garment bag.

The other girls gasped.

"That's breathtaking, Ava!" Kailani said.

"Rhapso kept her word," Tara said with a smile.

Inside was a teal, scoop neck, knee-length dress. Its bodice shimmered with sequins while its A-line skirt was soft and fluid. It was nicer than Ava had imagined. Its color even reminded her of nature, of running waters, of the things she felt close to.

Ava forgot about the pit in her stomach and started to put the dress on. "Can someone help me zip it up?" she asked.

"On the case," Tara replied, seeming all-too-happy to lock Ava into the dress for the night.

Ava's auburn curls cascaded down her shoulders. Her blue eyes somehow seemed even bluer as she stared at herself in the mirror. She reached into the small, white box that had been left next to the garment bag and pulled out a pair of iridescent, silver flats and a headband. No heels! Rhapso had come through three times for her, and Ava was grateful. Most of the adults she knew were the opposite of Rhapso and preferred to tell you how you should do things rather than ask what you wanted.

Ava stared at her reflection once more and tried to imagine her parents next to her: what they would look like, how they would look together, but her mind came up blank. It was crazy. How could you imagine people you hadn't seen since birth? But it still made her nervous. Still made her eager to go and have everything said and done.

"Are we ready, ladies?" an excited Tara asked. She gave them a look that said there was one right answer to her question.

"Ready," they all said in unison.

Ava and Tara split up with Kailani and Mira as they left their dorm and hurried down the hall to meet up with Duncan and Colin.

"Well, don't you two look fancy," Duncan teased.

Duncan was dressed in an all-black tux that looked to be more expensive than all their outfits combined.

"Watch yourself," Tara said, clearly in no mood to be teased.

"Well, at least you don't have to walk around wearing *this*," Colin said. His outfit was even gaudier on him than it had appeared when it was first delivered. The gold satin jacket, vest, and pants were embroidered with flowers. The gold-speckled white satin shirt puffed out at the sleeves, and the white lace pocket square and ascot pushed the entire ensemble over the top.

"Your parents will ... be happy you wore it," was all Ava could muster, the sheen of the gold fabric practically blinding her.

"What do you two think?" Colin asked Geoffrey and Julian, who followed a few feet behind them. "Fairies dress like this?"

Geoffrey smiled and provided no answer. He looked somewhat pleased at Colin's discomfort.

Ava gave Julian a hard, cold look. If he wanted her to trust him, he must be less of ... himself with her and her friends. Someone who could show normal emotion and compassion, even.

"More or less, yes," Julian said, shaking his head and giving Ava a nod that no one else seemed to notice. "For the Summer court, it's on the milder side."

As a look of relief spread across Colin's face, Ava gave

Julian a weak smile. It would take time to trust Julian and Geoffrey. But Ava wasn't sure whether Julian wanted trust or blind submission.

They took the conveyor to the Chamenon Ballroom on the nineteenth floor. Cascading drapery adorned the walls, forming an elegant, tented hallway. The halls grew increasingly more crowded the closer they got to the grand entrance. The clicking of heels, animated voices, and fragrant perfumes filled the air around them.

Students and instructors alike were dressed in breathtaking garments. Everyone, Tara included, buzzed with excitement as if this was the day they'd waited for all year long. Whether Tara was excited for the ball itself, the opportunity to dress up, or the potential headline for Arat Asoraled, Ava wasn't sure.

Ava joined the others in jumping off the conveyor outside two sets of floor-to-ceiling glass doors. Music wafted from the other side, more transcendent and grand than anything Ava had heard before. As the throng of instructors and students pushed through the doors, the harmonic, rhythmic tune washed out all other sounds.

Ava and her friends waited in the line to enter, their feet shuffling and then stopping, edging toward the entrance. The crowds split into two lines, a longer one toward the set of doors that led into the ballroom, and a shorter one toward the set of doors that led to a small staircase going up and to the right. The shorter line was filled with nervous students who looked out of place after they'd been separated from their friends.

"What's that all about?" Ava asked, the pit in her stomach returning.

"The left is for us common folk tonight," Duncan said. "The right belongs to you, Colin, and all the other Lost Ones —tonight's stars." He pretended to be awe-struck by their presence and fanned himself.

"You'll enter and sit separately from the rest of us during the speeches," Tara said. "Once they're done, you'll be introduced, one at a time, and greeted by your parents. The cameras like to capture each experience independently. Lazy, if you ask me. No finesse to it, unlike what I plan to write up."

Ava could practically see the wheels in Tara's head spinning.

"Well, this is where we leave you," Duncan said. "See you on the other side."

Tara pushed him along, giving Ava a lopsided smile as she rolled her eyes. She mouthed "You're fine," as she walked away.

"Are you two ready?" Ava asked Julian and Geoffrey. But the men stood in place and showed no intent to follow her. They did Ava's least favorite thing ever: whisper. Geoffrey glanced at the too-small watch on his meaty wrist.

"We've got business to attend to," Geoffrey replied. He looked left, right, and then back to his watch again.

"What business?" Ava asked. "I'm your business, remember?"

It wasn't that she wanted them to come, but she wanted to know why they—the same people who'd trailed her like bloodhounds—were suddenly so disinterested and willing to leave her unsupervised. Why here? Why now? On a night where all eyes and cameras would be not only on the other Lost Ones, but on her, the Impossible Girl. Wasn't that the most important thing they had to do? What they were ordered to do? She didn't like the timing of this.

"Trust me, you'll have plenty of eyes on you," Julian said in the same threatening voice he'd used the first time he'd met her, the slight progress in their relationship earlier that day gone. "Now, hurry along."

Ava turned. One step forward, ten steps backward. Every. Time.

Ava followed Colin up the stairs, glad to be wearing flats.

"So … are you ready for this?" she asked, desperate to distract herself.

"You sure that's what you want to talk about?" Colin said. "You look … frustrated."

Ava's mind raced with possibilities of what, exactly, Julian and Geoffrey could be up to. The only other time they'd left was at the press conference when the Resistance Riders appeared.

"I'm sure," Ava said.

"OK, then." Colin leaned closer and whispered, "I'm as ready as I'll ever be."

Colin's face mirrored how Ava felt: a mixture of nervousness, fear, and, to the smallest degree, hope. Hope for a life with their families that they'd given up on long ago.

"Same," Ava said, glad she wasn't alone in this.

To distract herself, Ava counted the steps as they climbed the stairs. Fifty-six steps, then a second flight of stairs leading to the right.

One hundred steps later, she and Colin reached a frosted, glass door. She turned the silver handle, drew in a deep breath, and pushed through.

They stepped into a large balcony, where several students were already seated in crystal chairs with silver cushions. The types of chairs that didn't allow you to slouch and forced you to look proper.

The balcony offered a great view to the events that unfolded down below, with a spiral staircase on the far end that led down to the main floor.

Ava approached the balcony's railing and stared down to the main ballroom. Along the far wall was an ivory table that matched the snow-like marble floors. It sat on a dais in front of a large door. The chairs at the table were even larger and grander than the chairs on the balcony. In the middle of the table were two larger chairs. One was occupied by Headmistress Astrae, and the other sat unoccupied. Other students and instructors mingled about the room and chatted.

Positioned throughout the ballroom were members of the press, their hovering camera bulbs flashing in every direction as they captured each attendee. Several scribbled away on notepads as they engaged with the guests. Everyone in attendance was dressed to impress.

Ava spotted Duncan and Tara at one table, chatting with Kailani and Mira. They looked like they belonged on the set of a movie.

Throughout the room, trays filled with drinks and food levitated, unassisted, and offered hungry guests delicious-looking refreshments. Once empty, they floated off to a door to the kitchen as a new tray flew out. The empty hands of her fellow Lost Ones made it clear the refreshments wouldn't make their way up to the balcony.

Ava stepped back from the edge as a camera flew up and tried to snap her picture. She was almost certain it had only been successful in getting an image of her as she turned. She looked forward to, after tonight, no longer being the center of attention. She'd meet her parents. They'd explain why she wasn't tagged. How it was all one big misunderstanding—and she'd no longer have her shadows and the whole world looking at her as if she'd committed some cardinal sin.

She sat next to Colin in the first of three rows and gripped the underside of her seat.

"Welcome, welcome, everyone!" Headmistress Astrae's voice boomed throughout the ballroom, and all other noises died down except for the furious clicking of cameras.

"Tonight marks our tricentennial Lost Ones Ball, and I am so glad to have you all in attendance," she said. When she smiled, her eyes shined as brightly as the sparkles on her floor-length lilac gown.

"It is with great honor that I introduce Ambrose to begin tonight's events."

Headmistress Astrae took her seat as the door behind her opened. Through it walked Ambrose, who looked as magnetic as ever. He was definitely one who liked a grand entrance. He flashed an electrifying smile to the applauding crowd.

Ava's fellow Lost Ones and Colin all clapped. She tried to follow suit with a small clap of her own and a forced smile. Even if the cameras were down below, they were still on them, on her, and she didn't want to give them a story tonight—other than the one that cleared her and her family's name.

With Ambrose's entrance, the excited guests stood, poised and gave him their undivided attention. The music crescendoed with his entrance and fireworks exploded above their heads.

"Thank you, Headmistress," Ambrose said in a booming voice that made Headmistress Astrae's seem quiet in comparison. "Wow, can you believe it? Three hundred years already. It seems like yesterday we held our first Lost Ones Ball—and let me tell you, it was quite the event with nearly one thousand Lost Ones in attendance!

"Even though we only have twenty-two Lost Ones this year," he continued, gesturing toward the balcony, "it still feels as grand as that first night as we welcome back our Lost Ones to their true home and to their families! This is a tradition we have kept in place and will continue to keep in place until there are no Lost Ones left to welcome home. A day I know we all hope to see soon."

Ambrose's eyes sparkled as he spoke, and the crowd hung on his every word.

"Without further ado," he said as he picked up what appeared to be a champagne bottle, turned it on its side, and ran a knife along its bottleneck. Champagne burst out of the bottle like a volcanic eruption. The adults on the dais applauded. Every instructor's flute was filled as the champagne bottle levitated above the dais.

"And don't think I forgot about all of you," Ambrose said

with a chuckle. "We have some of the finest cider for those of you underage."

He pointed in the direction of the kitchen, and at least one hundred additional bottles flew out, high above the dais. The same blade he'd used flew above them in one fast, swift motion, and opened all the bottles, which floated around the room, to everyone's delight, and filled the students' glasses.

"Now that everyone has been served, it's high time to get this party started," Ambrose said. "What do you all think?"

More cheers erupted from the main floor as well as several of the Lost Ones around Ava.

Ava tried to match the crowd's enthusiasm but couldn't come close to doing so.

"I want this to be over," Ava whispered to Colin.

"Me too," he said.

"All the parents of this year's Lost Ones were notified of their children's arrival and are somewhere in this crowd tonight," Ambrose said as he eyed the crowd with a mischievous look. "I'll be turning over tonight's events to our emcee, Barrow Morelli, who has so graciously taken time away from his duties as editor-in-chief of *The Daily Believe It or Nots* to host tonight's event for us."

A man with a head of white hair and an all-white tuxedo next to Ambrose, rose from his seat and made his way down the short steps to the center of the ballroom. He gave the audience a broad smile, flashing unusually bright buck teeth. Instead of using a microphone, he pointed his casting finger at his own throat.

"Thank you, Ambrose," Mr. Morelli said, his voice booming louder than any microphone.

He made his way deeper into the heart of the crowd, and the people around him dispersed. They created a wide berth around him.

"The reason we are all here," Mr. Morelli said, gesturing to the balcony, "is to welcome you home and watch as you are embraced by not only your parents but by all of Xarcadia and Linhollow. Without further ado … as I call your name, please make your way down the staircase and join us on the main floor. And parents, you know the rules: step forward only after I've had a moment to finish the welcoming ceremony."

"Welcoming ceremony?" Ava asked. "No one said anything about a welcoming ceremony."

Her heart rate rose and her palms, which were still clenched to the underside of her seat, began to sweat.

Colin shrugged. He didn't know either.

"Ms. Paloma Aperton, will you please make your way down?"

A girl, dressed in an opaque black dress from the fourth row, shot to her feet. With a giddy smile, she skipped to the edge of the balcony, waved, then proceeded to make her way down the staircase as all eyes remained fixed on her.

Ava could have sworn she'd seen her earlier, on their way in, but in a different dress. The stress of the night was playing tricks on her memory.

Paloma took her place beside Mr. Morelli.

"And, this is a first," Mr. Morelli continued, "but will a Thea Munro also make her way down?"

The attendees gasped.

Another girl, two rows behind Ava, rose with a meek smile.

She was the girl Ava had seen earlier, wearing a loosely fitting orange dress—and she was identical to Paloma Aperton.

"They're twins?" Colin said under his breath. "What's so unique about that?"

"I'm gathering, from the fact that they didn't sit together, that they didn't know about each other," Ava whispered back.

"Oh, okay, right."

Colin was easy to appease, which was good because Ava's

attention was glued to what happened below as Thea Munro also joined Mr. Morelli and Paloma.

The girls looked at each other. Each appeared uncomfortable to be staring at their own likeness.

"This is a tragic one, everyone," Mr. Morelli said. "These girls—twins, obviously—were separated after being sent to the mortal realm, each adopted by a different family. Up until a couple of days ago, they went their entire lives not knowing they were without their other half."

The man wiped what appeared to be a tear from his eye as the crowd murmured with disbelief.

Ava watched the twins, who didn't look like they were happy to be reunited. Thea looked upset, while Paloma sported a pageant smile and seemed to want to upstage Thea.

Tara pushed to the front of the crowd. She held a notebook in her hands and a pen in her mouth. She removed the pen and scribbled away furiously. Where she had kept that notebook on her, Ava had no idea.

"They're fairies, belonging to the Spring court," Mr. Morelli said. "And girls"—he placed a heavy hand on each of their shoulders—"it goes without saying that we are so sorry to hear of what took place once you left your safe home back in Xarcadia. We know that couldn't have been your parents' intent."

He removed his hands from their shoulders and pointed his casting finger toward the same door Ambrose had walked through.

It opened, by itself. Two female fairies with massive wings wearing beautiful gold dresses flew through the door, waved, and flitted across the ballroom to where Mr. Morelli and the girls stood. They carried a small table filled with a smoking cauldron and several silver goblets. They held it between them, landed without a sound, and placed it down. Afterward, they flew back through the doors as quickly as they'd come.

"While I'm sure we'd all love to discuss how your lives

have been forever changed, we do have a schedule to keep."
Mr. Morelli chuckled. "More to come on their stories later,
everyone. I'll personally be writing their story, and it'll be
released tomorrow."

Loud grumbles of disappointment filled the room. Mr.
Morelli ignored them and began again, "Girls, as part of your
being home, having come from the mortal realm, it is at this
time that you will pledge your allegiance to the High Court of
Magical Affairs—and to your fellow citizens in both Xarcadia
and Linhollow. Do you understand?"

One girl, then the other nodded.

"With your right wrists turned upward, for everyone to
see, please listen and repeat after me when requested. Do you
two solemnly vow to spend the rest of your days in Linhollow
or Xarcadia, forever forsaking the mortal realm?"

The cameras snapped almost as furiously as when
Ambrose had entered the room. This was an important part of
tonight's events, and it was clear that the moment would be
forever memorialized.

"I do," the girls said in unison, to Paloma's clear dismay at
sharing the spotlight.

"And you understand, should you ever attempt to leave or
break this vow, that you will be brought to justice upon being
captured?" Mr. Morelli said, waving his hand toward the crescent-shaped scars on the girls' wrists. A clear reminder that
they were always being monitored, never truly left to their
own devices. To their own free will.

How could they, or anyone on the balcony with Ava, say
no, with what was embedded deep inside of them? Even
though Ava had the scar, she didn't have what was supposed
to be there—but the threat was still there, as evidenced by
Julian and Geoffrey's constant presence as her watchdogs.

"I do," Paloma said in a rush, followed by Thea.

"Should this vow be broken, you will spend perpetuity in
Desmios, forever left to the devices of the sentinels who

oversee it—a fate so horrible you would most certainly wish you were dead."

A little less enthusiastically this time, Paloma and Thea agreed again.

With a steady hand, Mr. Morelli reached down and grabbed a ladle that had been left beside the cauldron. He dipped it into the cauldron's contents, scooped out a good-sized amount into two of the silver goblets, which begun to smoke with the addition of the liquid.

He handed a glass to each of the girls, who stared at the bubbling liquid with guarded curiosity.

Ava and Colin exchanged a tense look, glad to not have been called upon first.

"It is with great honor that I ask you each to repeat the following before indulging in your drinks: I, Paloma or Thea, hereby pledge my allegiance to the High Court of Magical Affairs. From this day forward, I solemnly swear to follow all laws, existing and those yet to exist, and to report and aid in the efforts of stopping any who should seek to destroy or endanger our way of life."

Paloma again went first and fumbled several times with the words. Ava imagined she desperately wished for a teleprompter by the beet-red color of the poor girl's face.

Thea went second and didn't stumble even once—which made Paloma's face redder.

After they repeated their lines, they turned back to Mr. Morelli with expectant expressions. He gestured for them to drink.

Paloma tossed the contents back in one big gulp, her eyes beginning to water. Thea finished seconds later and looked pleased the spotlight was about to be on someone else. The crescent-shaped scars on their wrists glowed a fiery red.

The girls gaped at their wrists.

"Absolutely wonderful," Mr. Morelli exclaimed as the crowd cheered. "Now for the moment we've all been waiting for. Will the parents of Paloma Aperton and Thea Munro, known at birth as Celeste and Camilla Appletail, please step forward."

The girls' eager eyes darted across the room.

In the far-right side of the room, the crowd shifted. An older woman with an elaborate updo and a forest green dress pushed forward. A much shorter gentleman in a forest green tuxedo followed her.

They rushed the rest of the way to the girls. The woman embraced Paloma while the man embraced Thea. They switched after a moment; tears poured down Paloma and Thea's faces like a dam had been broken.

"We've waited for this day for so long," the woman exclaimed.

"Not a day has gone by where we haven't thought of you and imagined how your lives have been," the man added with a tearful smile.

"So wonderful, everyone," Mr. Morelli added warmly.

Mr. Morelli pointed his casting finger once more, and another large dais rose from the snowy marble floors, creating a central platform with rows of seats.

"If you four will take a seat," he gestured to the newly formed dais with a polite dismissal, "we still have twenty other Lost Ones and their families eagerly waiting to be reunited."

Ava watched the happy family climb the steps with a pang of jealousy, the mother and father never letting go of their hands.

As more names were called, more of Ava's classmates joined their newfound families. Intermittently, Ava scanned the crowd to see if there was anyone out there with features similar to her own.

The students appeared to be at peace with how tonight's events were turning out. They even seemed to form an instant bond with their parents, which confused Ava as they hadn't seen each other in thirteen years.

The number of unmatched Lost Ones dwindled. Ava wondered if she would look joyous when her name was called.

Mr. Morelli directed a young male vampire who had been reunited with his parents. Then three more students were called, leaving only Ava and Colin on the balcony. The final two.

"I'm guessing I'm up next," Colin said.

"Why's that?" Ava asked, confused.

"I take it you're more the grand-finale type, what with all the press you've been getting." Colin seemed to sense that wasn't what Ava wanted to hear and added, "If it helps, the rumors I've heard are less about you and more about your parents…"

"After tonight, I hope the gossip stops," Ava said.

"Colin Arion, originally known as Aedan Ariti, please make your way down," Mr. Morelli's voice boomed.

"Told you—grand finale," Colin whispered with a laugh and winked at her as he got up.

Ava could tell he was nervous, more nervous than he wanted to let on.

Beneath the level of the balcony rails, where the cameras couldn't see, Ava grabbed Colin's hand and gave it a tight squeeze. "You've got this."

Colin smiled back at her for a moment before he turned and began his walk down the steps. The gold of his tuxedo shone even more brightly in the well-lit main ballroom than it had in the balcony. Everyone's eyes were fixed on him.

In a matter of days, Colin had come a long way from the boy who'd stood aloof and alone. He belonged to this world and her friend group, and she was glad to have been at least a small part of that.

Even so, this moment would be hard for him. Such a private, intimate moment of being reconnected with his parents turned into a public spectacle. The pressure to say and do the right thing was insane. With each passing moment, Ava knew that pressure would soon be on her.

"Young Colin Arion is a Summer fairy from Linhollow. He arrived days ago and, from the impressions shared by his instructors, shows incredible promise in his studies."

Mr. Morelli repeated the speech he had given nineteen times already that night. Colin nodded, repeated when prompted, and drank from his goblet. His scar, like the others, glowed.

"Will the parents of Colin Arion, known at birth as Aedan Ariti, please step forward."

A tall man stepped forward wearing an almost identical suit to Colin's. While his hair was the same fiery copper as Colin's, the man doubled Colin in height and was three times as broad. Behind him was a small woman Ava almost over-looked because of the large stature of the man taking giant strides toward Colin. The woman's long, blond hair cascaded down the elaborate black-and-gold dress she wore.

The man stopped in front of Colin. He looked him up and down, then, to Colin's apparent displeasure, picked him up off the ground like some sort of rag doll. He squeezed Colin before he placed him back down. Once back on his feet, Colin gave him a nod of acknowledgment and turned his gaze toward the woman, his mother.

"My baby, how you've grown…" she said as she embraced him. Tears pooled in her eyes and trickled down her face. "You'll tell us everything tonight." Her voice was shaky as she placed her hands on either side of his face and gave him a kiss on the forehead.

"Uh, sure," Colin said, blushing.

"I think he's a shy one, everyone," Mr. Morelli said with a laugh. "Give him time, Jarrah and Olea. He's had a lot to take in these last few days, and the night is still young! Please join everyone else as we finish our welcoming ceremony and spend the rest of our night dancing, celebrating, and learning more about each Lost One's journey home over an exquisite eight-course meal."

Before his dad could pick him up again, Colin darted in front of him and rushed up the steps, and took his place beside another family. His parents rushed to keep up with him. His mother, a little over four feet tall, stood on her tiptoes and whispered something in Colin's ear.

"Everyone, everyone, if you could please settle down," Mr. Morelli said. "While normally the news of sweet twin girls being separated at birth would be the talk of tonight, our next Lost One comes to us even more mysteriously. I've hosted this ball thirteen times in the last one hundred years, and I can say, without a doubt, that it is not something I ever expected to hear about, let alone see with my own two eyes. While I'm sure she requires no introduction—some of you may know her as the Impossible Girl, or some variation—please join me as we welcome Ava Jones."

Paloma Aperton scowled in Ava's direction.

Ava unclenched her fingers from the bottom of her seat and rose, thankful Rhapso had not given her a long gown or heels that would cause her to trip.

She tried to hold her head high as she gripped the banister and began her descent, her eyes fixed on each step in front of her. She'd tripped on a lot less in her life, and she didn't want to make any more of a spectacle of herself tonight than she already was.

She joined Mr. Morelli, focusing on him rather than the crowd of people whose eyes were locked onto her every movement.

"Ms. Jones, your journey to this point has been a highly followed and publicized one. Do you have anything you'd like to say before we begin?"

No one else had been asked this question. If they had, she would have spent the last hour trying to come up with her own satisfactory response.

She swallowed, then mustered her pageant decorum. "I'm happy to be here. I look forward to learning about my past and seeing how it helps to shape my future."

"What a wonderful response—and I know we all look forward to following your journey for years to come."

Great.

"Ms. Jones, with your right wrist turned upward, for everyone to see, please listen and repeat after me when requested. Do you solemnly vow to spend the rest of your days in Linhollow or Xarcadia, forever forsaking the mortal realm?"

This, she was prepared for. "I do."

"And you understand, should you ever attempt to leave or break this vow, that you will be brought to justice upon being captured?" Mr. Morelli again gestured toward the crescent-shaped scar on Ava's wrist.

Even though the man must have known Ava wasn't tagged, he stuck to his script and acted as if the warning held true.

"Yes," she said, trying to sound confident.

"Should this vow be broken, you will spend perpetuity in Desmios, forever left to the devices of the sentinels who oversee it—a fate so horrible you would most certainly wish you were dead."

Ava nodded, clearly the only acceptable answer.

The man reached in front of him and again picked up the ladle, scooping out what remained of the liquid and pouring it into the final silver goblet.

"It is with great honor that I ask you to repeat the following before indulging in your drink," Mr. Morelli said as he led her in the vow.

With the cup in her left hand, Ava repeated the vow. "I, Ava Jones, hereby pledge my allegiance to the High Court of Magical Affairs. From this day forward, I solemnly swear to follow all laws, existing and those yet to exist, and to report and aid in the efforts of stopping any who should seek to destroy or endanger our way of life."

She'd heard this so many times tonight, she recited it perfectly.

Ava held her breath and washed back the contents in the goblet. An acrid flavor with a hint of peppermint and oak, hit her tongue. It wasn't the worst thing she'd ever tasted, but it wasn't the best.

She stared at her wrist—nothing happened. Not surprising —since whatever was supposed to be there, wasn't. Still, it made the cameras flash with more frenzy, and the crowd murmured louder—as if seeing it with their own eyes somehow made it more real.

"Yes, well, that much was expected," Mr. Morelli said as he, too, stared at her wrist with disbelief. "Will the parents of Ava Jones, previous name unknown, please step forward."

EIGHTEEN

This was it. This was the moment Ava had waited for. Any moment, her mother and father would push their way through the crowd and make their way to her, and they would be reunited at last.

Even though she told herself she'd be furious with them, at this moment, she was filled with forgiveness. Everything that had happened, regardless of whose fault it was, she would move forward. She would go in with open arms.

She ignored all the other sounds from the crowd, all the other faces, and watched for her parents to emerge. For them to claim her. To explain everything to this hungry crowd who looked like this was the moment they'd been waiting for all night.

But no one emerged.

No one stepped forward.

"Again, I ask that the parents of Ava Jones please step forward," Mr. Morelli said for the second time, raising his voice.

Ava scanned the crowd. At any moment they would burst through to claim her. They'd not heard the question, obviously.

In the distance, Tara and Duncan stared back at her with sad looks. Layla and her group of cronies snickered. Others in the crowd began to whisper. Ava turned and looked behind her and met Ambrose's unfaltering gaze.

It set in. No one was here. Her parents weren't here.

Not only had they sent her into the mortal realm as a baby, but they'd also not been here for this pivotal moment in her life: to help explain away any of their supposed wrongdoing. To clear her name. To make this transition that they had set into motion any more bearable.

"Well, everyone, it would seem this makes for three firsts tonight," Mr. Morelli said, appearing unsure for the first time.

Mr. Morelli glanced back at Ambrose, who nodded, before he added, "Ms. Jones, dear, please take your place on the dais."

Ava tried to mouth some type of acknowledgment. She tried to nod, but it was all she could do to move her legs and walk the five steps up to the dais. She took her place beside Colin's family, next to two empty seats that should have been occupied by her parents. Ava remembered back to that first day when the envelope before the kelpie ride had teleported into her pocket.

Housing and food comped until after the Lost Ones Ball.

What would become of her with no one to claim her?

The dais had been cleared, the Lost Ones and their families moved to another room for the press to take their pictures before the ball began. First on the agenda, Mr. Morelli announced, was the father-daughter dance.

As soon as he'd finished with his press pictures, Colin found Ava.

"Are you okay?" he asked with a kind smile.

Ava stared back, numb. Out of all the possibilities she'd considered for tonight, this hadn't been one of them. Her mind, so filled with thoughts of the unknown, of what was to come after this, was unable to formulate the words to respond.

She was humiliated. She was broken. She was alone. The family she'd been promised never materialized.

"Ava, are you okay?" Colin repeated.

The minute she spoke, her voice would crack and tears would flow, so she shook her head in response.

"Let's find Tara and Duncan and get out of here," he said with a soft hand on her shoulder.

"Aedan, honey, we've got to get ready for the mother-son dance," Colin's mother called out. "It'll be after the father-daughter dance. Come on."

Ava managed to motion for him to go, for him to be happy. These people, his parents, had shown up for him. He didn't deserve to lose precious time with them because of Ava's problems.

"Ms. Ava Jones," someone called, "you're up next."

Family pictures. They expected her to do family pictures without a family. This was unbelievable.

"Let's get this over with, then we'll leave," Colin said.

Ava walked over to the photographer, who looked at Ava as if he had struck the lottery.

"If you could stand right there." He pointed.

Ava made her way around all the other families in the small room toward where the man motioned.

To her surprise, so did Colin.

"Young man, this photo is for families only," the photographer said. "Please step aside."

"Aedan, move it along," his father called with a huff.

"We *are* her family," Colin said, speaking to the other Lost Ones in the room. "We're *all* Lost Ones. We were all sent out into the mortal realm at birth with no one, no inkling of where we came from, where we belonged. And I guarantee, if any of you were in her place tonight, she would be where I am—so move your feet and join us in this picture."

Ava had never heard Colin sound so serious. The room fell silent. The photographer looked as if he didn't know what to do.

Several Lost Ones moved forward and took their place beside Ava and Colin. Thea Munro was one of the first to move forward. Paloma, after she saw everyone else join, also decided to get in on the photo.

"Okay, we're ready," Colin said. "Her family is all here."

Ava's heart swelled, and tears fell from her eyes. No one had ever done anything like that for her before. She hadn't expected it, and even more so, she hadn't expected everyone else to rise to action because of his words.

"Smile like you're going to be on the front-page tomorrow —because you will be," the photographer said.

Ava managed a weak but genuine smile as their photographs were taken.

"Are we done here?" Colin asked.

"I have everything I need," the photographer said. He smiled as if this was the biggest moment of his career.

Colin grabbed Ava's arm and led her out of the room.

"Aedan, you have to wait for us to be called back!" his father shouted after them. "There's an order to these things!"

"Don't worry about him," Colin said with a smile. "If I've learned anything from the mortal realm, it's that children get into plenty of arguments with their parents. This one shall pass. I'll be fine."

They entered back into the ballroom through the same door Ambrose had used. Duncan and Tara waited for them.

"Oh, Ava," Tara cried as she threw her arms around her. "It's terrible, just terrible."

"They're fools, whoever they are," Duncan added.

"What do you want to do?" Tara asked. "Do you want to go back to our room?"

"Tell us what you need," Duncan added as Colin nodded in agreement.

"What's worse—if I leave, or if I go back feeling and looking like this?" Ava asked, barely able to get the words out.

"She's right," Tara said. "If she goes back, like she's going to break at any moment, one of two things will happen. She's either going to break or she's going to do her best to act like she's not broken, and fool no one, really."

They were only a few feet away from the door, the music for the father-daughter dance beginning as the announcer called everyone back.

With thousands of guests in attendance, it was easy enough to slip through the throng of people without being noticed—until they stepped out into the main hallway to find Layla, her back turned toward them, holding court with a group of girls and blocking their perfect escape.

"Did you see her face?" Layla said with a laugh to her cronies. "Oh my gosh, my side hurts. It was so pathetic, and it's no surprise they didn't show. With a daughter like that, why would they?"

"She's tragic, is what she is," one of the other girls said. "And you know what, I hear she's a big part of the rise with The Resistance. She's not as innocent as she pretends."

"Oh, absolutely," Layla agreed.

Duncan cleared his throat, startling Layla and her friends. "Layla, you'll never look good trying to make someone else look bad."

Layla whipped around, clutching the sides of her black lace, high-low dress.

"Oh, please, Duncan, stop speaking for her like you know her," Layla said. "Those two"—she gestured to Tara and Colin—"I can understand. But *you*? Your father is on the Elder's Court. You're one of us, and you know better. You're the only ones she's fooling; how do you think that makes you look?"

"Here's a fun fact," Tara said with a wicked smile. "If you spent half as much time on improving yourself that you spent on gossiping and spreading nasty rumors, people may like you."

Layla laughed as the other girls around her joined in.

"I think it makes us look a lot better than you," Colin said with a cold stare. "I don't think green is your color."

"You think I'm jealous?" Layla said with a snort. "Of what? At least my parents didn't ship me off, happy to be rid of me, and then not even have the decency to show up on the one night they are called upon to be parents. Even they know she's bad news."

Ava stepped forward. "Move," she demanded. "We're done."

"Or what?" Layla said with a wicked laugh. "If I'm wrong, go back in. Face everyone. Maybe they got … delayed."

Ava's ears burned. She'd had the worst night of her life. All these thoughts already ran through her own mind, and she didn't need anyone else to add to them. She wondered how someone she hardly knew could hate her so much.

"I said MOVE!" Ava screamed.

What happened next was a blur. Rage mushroomed inside Ava: rage at Layla, rage at her parents, and rage at the whole spectacle that had been tonight. Ava had nothing left to give, no more ability to restrain herself. Elorise and Beatrice's level of nastiness didn't compare to Layla's.

Ava uncrossed her arms and pointed her casting finger in their direction. Her fingertip glowed with a golden light.

Layla flew backward to the end of the hall and landed with a loud thud. The other girls shot Ava looks of shock before scurrying off to help Layla, who screamed as she lay on her side twenty feet away.

"Ava, how—"

Duncan held up his hand and cut off Tara.
"Not now, and not here. Dorms."

"We're not allowed in your dorms," Tara said, for the umpteenth time. "Why don't we do this somewhere else where Priam or Evander won't find out and take away all our privileges?"

Duncan placed his wrist on the scanner outside the entrance to the freshman boys' dorms. Colin and Ava exchanged nervous looks.

"It's fine," Duncan said. "Everyone will be at the Lost Ones Ball for at least another couple of hours. Plus, this is the last place anyone will look for her, and that gives us time to figure out a plan."

"Fine," Tara conceded. "Point made."

"A plan?" Ava asked. Her head spun. "I didn't even mean to do it. I don't know how I did it. I was so angry."

"We know," Colin said, giving Ava a reassuring look. "And Layla's fine. Only her ego is hurt."

Duncan and Colin led the girls through the living quarters, up the stairs, and to the left, to their room.

"Wow, I thought living with girls was messy," Tara said, her jaw dropping at the condition of the room. "You guys do know those furnishings are meant to hold clothing, right? And the trash cans—not the floor—are for trash."

"You're more than welcome to pick up while we talk, if that's what you're thinking about," Duncan replied.

"Yeah, I could use someone to show me how those things work," Colin teased. "In the mortal realm, they don't exist...."

Tara rolled her eyes and ignored them. She and Ava pulled up two chairs from the corner and sat down.

"Okay, so what are we thinking?" Colin asked as he changed the subject, the seriousness of the situation seeming to set in.

"I'm thinking Layla hobbled her way back to the ball and told everyone some exaggerated version of what happened—of course, leaving out any part she had in it," Tara said.

Was it exaggerated, though? Ava had sent Layla across the room, but she had been fine. She'd made sure of it before they ran away from the ballroom.

Duncan nodded his agreement with Tara about how it may have played out.

"Julian and Geoffrey are probably off looking for Ava," he added.

Julian and Geoffrey.

Ava had forgotten about them. This was the one time they'd left her alone. The one time she could have gained their trust—and in turn, more freedom—if she didn't mess up.

"Well, we were all there," Colin said. "Clearly, it was provoked. She's, like, new at this and can't control her powers, right? Problem solved."

"I agree, it was provoked, but I don't know about the powers thing," Tara said. "Since coming into my powers, a couple months before Ava, I've never been able to do anything like that—and believe me, I've been angry enough to do so. It's not natural. We haven't even had offensive and defensive training yet."

"Ava, has anything like this ever happened to you before?" Duncan asked. "Before Healer Gwyn's apothecary?"

"I don't think so, I mean..." Ava paused, memories flooding back.

It *had* happened before. Even before she'd turned thirteen, strange things had happened even in the mortal realm. The hairspray that'd exploded. The twins losing their voices. Strange occurrences at the orphanage. Maybe they weren't so strange after all.

"Is it possible I had my powers all along, before my thirteenth birthday?" Ava asked.

"No, absolutely not," Tara said. "That's not how it works. Believe me, I spent years as a small child staring and pointing at a wall—at anything—to make something happen, to no avail. We all did."

"I don't know how to explain it, then," Ava said, bending over the wobbly legs of her chair and covering her head with her hands. "I don't want to end up in Desmios because of this."

"They wouldn't send you there for this," Duncan said. "It won't help the rumor mill and you'll—*we'll*, I mean—have to meet with the headmistress and possibly get a mark on our records."

"Doesn't sound bad," Colin said.

"It is, though," Tara chimed in "Marks affect what type of job you're able to be placed in after school. No one wants a journalist with a bad reputation."

Ava covered her face and groaned. She couldn't imagine her friends suffering the consequences for years to come for something she had done. "I'll make it right," she said. "I'll tell the headmistress it was all me because it was."

"Ava, it's—what was that?" Tara started and stopped.

The door to the living quarters opened, slammed shut, and carried with it loud voices that came up the stairs.

"The ball wasn't set to end for at least another four hours," Tara exclaimed, her eyes wide. "We can't be here."

"Colin, block the door for a minute," Duncan ordered.

"You want him to block our way out?" Tara asked, incredulous.

"Do you have a better idea?" he asked, frustration evident in his voice. "I don't know. Hide somewhere until we can sneak you out."

Ava looked around the small room. The beds, identical to theirs, were raised too far off the ground to be able to hide under. The large tapestries on the windows would not work; Tara attempted to hide behind them, but her feet and body were visible.

"Go under the beds, and we'll drape our blankets over. It's our best option," Colin said. "I can hear Theodore coming up the stairs with Triston."

Tara scurried under Colin's bed, but Ava froze and stared at the wall and the windows that overlooked Linhollow.

Something pulled her and nudged her closer. It didn't make any sense—and time was about to run out. But she walked over anyway and gestured for Tara to follow. She placed her palm against the wall's cold surface and closed her eyes. "Something's here that's not here," Ava said, her eyes still closed.

"Uh, Ava, that's great, but we don't have time for riddles," Colin said. "I'm about to forcibly keep this door closed, so can we talk about this later, maybe?"

"No, it's not a riddle. Give me a second."

Her friends' eyes bore into Ava's back. They probably thought she'd lost it, but she hadn't. She blocked it all out and focused harder than she ever had before. An image came to mind, an impossible one.

"There's a passageway here," Ava said, opening her eyes. "It leads throughout the entire castle. I don't know why I've never felt it before. It's so obvious."

"Ava, did you by chance take another fall?" Duncan asked. "There's nothing on the other side of that wall—look out the window."

"Avoiyw," Ava whispered, so quietly that she wasn't sure anyone else had heard her.

The solid wall dissipated beneath her hands and a door-like frame of shimmering gold materialized out of nowhere, shining so brightly that Ava shielded her eyes.

She peered her head in to find a rough, stone passageway

that extended, to the right and left, as far as her eyes could see.

Ava stepped back, smiling at Tara, Duncan, and Colin, who had their mouths hanging open.

Duncan and Tara peered out the window, which still showed the city of Linhollow on the other side. They then stared into the entrance of the secret passageway, which, when looking in, appeared to go right by the window, but only visible from the inside.

"What do you see?" Colin asked as he blocked the bedroom door.

"Hey, what's the deal?" Theodore hollered from the other side of the door and tried to push it open.

"We were all ordered to return to our rooms," Triston added, banging on the door. "The RAs are going to do a head-count to make sure everyone is accounted for, and I'm not about to have my head bitten off."

"One second," Duncan called. "I think it's jammed."

"Tara, let's go," Ava said. She stepped into the passageway as Tara followed close behind.

"We'll talk tomorrow," Ava whispered to Duncan as she placed her hand against the wall near where the entrance had been formed.

She closed her eyes again and focused. She pictured the wall closing back up. She opened her eyes to darkness, the entrance no longer there.

"Ava, please tell me the wall's still talking to you," Tara whispered. "Telling you how to get back to our room before Priam discovers we're not there?"

The cavernous tunnel, dimly lit and perfectly straight, was easy to navigate. The clap of their footsteps on the cobblestone floor sent a chalky dust in front of them. Obviously this tunnel was not a popular means of navigating throughout the castle. Symbols Ava couldn't identify lined parts of the walls. This tunnel had been used before.

"The wall did not talk to me," Ava whispered back, her voice reverberating against the sides. "I don't know. Something was there, behind the wall all along, but it wasn't until we needed it that I sensed it, you know?"

"Okay, well, can you try to visualize what way to go? You heard Theodore and Triston. Something happened, and everyone was sent back to their rooms! Priam will be in our room any minute."

It couldn't have been the incident with Layla, could it? They wouldn't shut down the entire ball—three hundred years of a tradition—for that.

But whatever had happened, it would look suspicious if

Ava and Tara were the only ones unaccounted for. With her eyes shut, Ava tried to picture the layout of the castle. The freshman boy and girl dormitories were on the same floor, on separate sides of the hall. "Okay, we need to go that way," Ava said as she pointed with her eyes still closed. "That should lead us down the hallway and in the direction of our room."

"How will we know when we're there?" Tara asked, still standing so close to Ava that they practically touched. "Are you sure you can form an entrance again? That was your first time doing that, and this type of magic isn't easy to tap into."

"When we're there, we'll know," Ava said. "We're fine. I promise. Now run!"

Ava grabbed Tara's hand and pulled her along. Ava wouldn't let Tara's future be affected because of her.

"Wait, wait." Tara stopped, removing her heels.

With her shoes in one hand, they continued down the cold, dim passageway. Their footsteps pounded on the stone floor.

Ava skidded to a stop. "We're close. See if you hear anything." She motioned for Tara to follow her lead and place her ear against the wall.

"I don't hear anything," Tara said, in a tone of defeat. "I have told you I'm claustrophobic, right? This is so not ideal."

"We're here," Ava said. "I can feel it."

"How can you be sure?"

"I am. It's hard to explain."

With both hands pressed against the wall, Ava closed her eyes again and pictured the wall opening.

A door again materialized, revealing their dorm room.

"Oh, thank goodness!" Tara exclaimed. "You're a genius, and I never doubted you for a moment!"

"Oh, yeah," Ava said with a laugh as she followed Tara through the opening and closed it back up.

Ava glanced around the empty bedroom.

"So, where is everyone?" Tara asked. "Priam should have been through here by now."

The door to their room flung open. Ava and Tara jumped, startled.

"Dang, I know we're all a little shaken, but chill, it's just us," Mira said with a bewildered look as she and Kailani walked in.

"Where were you?" Kailani asked. "Priam was in earlier, and we had to cover for you guys." She gestured toward Ava and Tara's beds, where the pillows and blankets had been arranged to look like the girls were already in bed.

Ava and Tara sighed with relief.

"You guys rock." Tara rushed over and hugged Mira, then Kailani. "I can't believe that worked on her. Whew."

"You're welcome," Mira said, giving Ava a sad look. "With the night you had, we figured you needed to be away from everyone for a while."

"Yes, I did," Ava said, blushing and grateful.

"So, what happened?" Tara asked. "Why did the ball end early?"

"You haven't heard?" Kailani asked.

Ava and Tara both shook their heads.

"Well," Kailani said, darting her eyes from side to side, "you'll want to sit down for this."

Kailani was serious and didn't look like she'd continue until they sat. Tara and Ava obliged and took a seat on their respective beds.

"Okay, so," Kailani continued, "right as everyone was about to sit down for dinner, a body was found! Layla stumbled upon the body on her way back from the lavatory—and her scream, oh, everyone heard it. It was bone chilling."

Kailani shuddered at her own words and covered her eyes.

"Who was it?" Tara asked, sitting up straighter and seeming to switch into journalist mode. The only thing missing was her notebook.

"A student," Mira chimed in. "A close friend to Layla, I heard."

"Was it … from natural causes?" Ava asked. She didn't know why she asked—part of her already knew the answer.

"Definitely not," Kailani answered without uncovering her eyes. "There was blood everywhere. I mean, today this girl was somewhere in our dorms. She was a freshman. It's so terrible. What type of person could do this?"

"Yes," Mira agreed.

Ava gazed at her hands folded on her lap.

For some reason, Julian and Geoffrey came to mind. The first time Ava met them in Healer Gwyn's apothecary, before Ambrose came, she thought they would kill her. Their sudden disappearance tonight was strange. Would they—could they— have been the ones to have done this?

"Wake up!" Tara exclaimed as she pulled the covers off Ava.

"You need to stop doing that," Ava grumbled, her eyelids still heavy.

Couldn't there be one day where Tara would let her sleep in before her alarm went off? Sleep hadn't come easy the night before. The confrontation with Layla and the mysterious death of Layla's friend cluttered Ava's mind, keeping her from a restful sleep. She also found herself grieving her parents' absence from the ball.

Out of everything that had happened, that had pained Ava the most—and she hated herself for it. She'd been awake until sunlight peeped through the windows and hoped no one had heard her sobs.

"Seriously, this time everyone's already up," Tara said.

Ava rolled over and opened her eyes to confirm Tara's story.

"I know you, uh, didn't get a lot of sleep last night, but I let you sleep as long as I could. I'm sorry."

"You heard me?" Ava asked. She wanted to hide her face for the rest of eternity.

Tara played dumb. "Heard what?"

She loved that about Tara. While she always dug for a story, she knew when to not push.

"Thanks," Ava said, grateful for Tara's friendship. She glanced at her alarm clock. "So why is everyone already up? Classes don't start for another two hours."

"Kailani and Mira mentioned a vigil this morning for the girl who was killed. Everyone at the ball was told attendance is mandatory."

Killed.

The word alone was enough to wake Ava up.

"Put this on," Tara said, tossing a black shirt and pants at her. "Rhapso must've been up all night; everyone had these in their drawers."

Ava expelled a deep sigh and dragged herself out of bed. She got dressed and tried to work a brush through her matted curls. Like her curls, her life was a mess. Once one was untangled, another, out of nowhere, tangled up—inflicting more pain the harder she tried to untangle them.

"I'm ready," Ava lied, as she gave up on her hair and her problems, and put up her curls in a ponytail.

Cromwell Hall had transformed overnight. Where light usually shone—dancing off the ebony walls and marble floors—the room instead appeared dark and ominous, with the large windows covered to block out the sunlight. Students and instructors dressed in black packed the hall, and thousands of candles floated high above their heads and tables.

Instructors waited on the dais for everyone to arrive. Beside them was a large portrait of the dead girl. She looked familiar, but Ava couldn't place her. Fairies flew above the girl's portrait, seeming to put the finishing touches on a floating floral arrangement of two hands cupping to form the shape of a heart. Some of the black-and-white petals fell and arranged themselves into a floral walkway.

Their fragrance wafted to where Ava sat at a table with Duncan and Colin to her left, and Tara to her right. They hadn't had time to discuss last night—what with too many listening ears in the room.

Headmistress Astrae rose from her seat and stepped over to an awaiting podium, resting her hands on top of it.

"Everyone," she began, and silence fell upon the room, "it is with great sadness we are all gathered here today. One of our own, a young vampire, was killed last night during the Lost Ones Ball. The loss of Tori Balfour will be greatly felt. By her family, by her friends, by her instructors, and by the impact she could have had on us had she not been taken so soon.

"I know a lot of you are grieving"— Headmistress Astrae glanced at one end of the freshman table where Layla sat and sobbed—"but I want to assure you, justice will be served."

The headmistress paused, looking off in the distance, seemingly at nothing in particular.

"This is supposed to be a safe place, and that was violated last night," she continued. "I know a lot of you are scared. Until the perpetrator has been apprehended, we will be implementing some security measures. Before we have a moment of silence and hear from Tori Balfour's friends and family, I would ask that you all listen as two of Ambrose's closest advisors take the stage and go over these new protocols."

Ava's jaw dropped as Julian and Geoffrey took the stage.

Headmistress Astrae stepped back, relinquishing the podium to Julian.

"Until further notice, all students must travel with at least one other student everywhere they go," Julian said. "No student can walk the halls alone. Furthermore, after six-o-clock, all students are to remain in their dorms. Lastly, if you see anything that does not sit right with you, report it. Does everyone understand?" Julian scanned the crowd.

With his hands on the sides of the podium, Julian's shirt sleeves rode up his arms. A bandage covered his right wrist—a bandage that had not been there the day before.

"Geoffrey and I will pass out the official list of rules that will remain in place until this has been sorted out," Julian continued. "Take one and pass it down, please. Headmistress…"

Julian yielded the podium.

"Thank you, Julian and Geoffrey," Headmistress Astrae said with a weak smile. "We are lucky to have you with us at this difficult time. Make sure, everyone, to read through your safety guidelines thoroughly. If you should see or hear anything, come to me or to them. Now, at this time, I would like to invite Margo Balfour, the sister of Tori Balfour, to the stage."

A tall, slender girl took the stage. Her eyes were red and puffy; clearly, she'd spent much of the night crying.

The guilt of Ava's own selfish tears last night flooded back. In the grand scheme of things, her loss, her hurt, couldn't hold a candle to this girl's grief.

"Thank you, Headmistress Astrae," Margo said, her voice cracking. "It is with great sadness that I stand here today. Tori was not only my sister but my best friend. She was so excited to begin her studies this year, to come to school with her big sister, and to set her path for the future. It is a loss to everyone she will not be able to do this. A loss that will never go unfelt. Our—my—parents couldn't be here today. They're shocked and broken by the loss of their youngest daughter, a loss that didn't have to happen. Whoever did this took a piece of all our hearts, and for that, they deserve whatever comes their way. It is with a heavy heart that I say…"

Margo turned her head away, unable to continue. Her shoulders heaved with silent sobs. She handed her note cards to Headmistress Astrae and rushed off the stage.

"It is with a heavy heart that I say goodbye to Tori today," the headmistress said, reading from the note cards. "She was taken much too soon, and it is my hope that whoever did this to our family is brought to justice."

Headmistress Astrae placed the note cards down. "Thank you, Margo, for your bravery in adversity. One other student has asked to speak today. Ms. Layla Lelantos, if you'll make your way up."

Despite Layla's expressed dislike for Ava, Ava's heart went out to her at this moment. She looked so vulnerable.

"Tori was not just a friend; she was a sister to me," Layla said. "A sister who was taken too soon. She will forever hold a place in my heart, and I will forever look back on the memories from our childhood with fondness. I know everyone is scared, and I know everyone is looking for the cold-hearted perpetrator responsible for Tori's death. The only solace I have today is that I know who took Tori's life last night."

Loud gasps escaped the mouths of everyone in the hall.

Headmistress Astrae rose from her seat and tried, and failed, to pull Layla away from the podium.

Murmurs throughout the room drowned out Layla's voice as she pointed and proclaimed, "It was Ava Jones."

va sat, frozen, as all eyes turned to her. At first, she'd thought she'd misheard Layla, but her name was on everyone's lips.

"I knew it."

"It makes sense, really."

All Ava could do was stare back at the stage at Layla, who was escorted off by Julian, who looked furious.

Geoffrey and Headmistress Astrae met them at the door behind the dais. Ava's eyes never left Layla until she could no longer see her. To think, moments ago, Ava had felt bad for Layla. Thought her vulnerable, even. But she had a feeling Layla was never vulnerable. Every word, every thought, every decision, was a calculated one. As Ava sat, in shock, Margo, Tori's sister, stormed toward her.

"How dare you come to her vigil, you sick murdering psychopath," she exclaimed as she charged at Ava.

Ava opened her mouth to respond. At the same time, Duncan and Colin jumped up from their seats and blocked Margo's rampage.

"Margo, I know you're hurt," Duncan said, trying to calm

her down. "I know how easy it is to hang the first person possible out to dry, to have closure, but I can say with certainty that Ava did not do this. I have no idea why Layla would say she did."

"It's true," Colin added. "She was with the three of us last night when it happened."

"Out of my way," Margo replied, not at all calmed down. "Now."

At this, several instructors, Mr. Viscardi, Ava's instructor from the History of Magic class included, rose from their seats, ready to intervene before things escalated.

Headmistress Astrae, who was back from escorting Layla out, beat them to it.

Even without the microphone, her voice rose enough for everyone at the vigil to hear her. "That is enough, thank you. Mr. Stavros and Mr. Arion, take your seats at once."

She turned toward Margo. "Ms. Balfour, I know you experienced a great loss, and Layla's accusation will be looked into," she said. "But that is all it is—an accusation with no substantiated evidence to support it. But this will not bring justice, only more chaos. If and until Ms. Lelantos' accusations have been confirmed, you will be wise to return to your seat. And all of you—you will save your condemnation until an official report has been made and the culprit named. Justice is blind. It does not condemn based on accusations and rumors, but rather on irrefutable facts. Mr. Viscardi will lead you all in a moment of silence. You will think of Tori and her loss as well as seeking the truth rather than the impertinence of trying to create your own."

Headmistress Astrae gave the crowd a long, hard glare to make sure everyone understood. After she seemed satisfied, she directed her attention to Ava.

Ava shrunk under her gaze. The headmistress' face was unreadable, her demeanor firm. Ava couldn't tell if she believed Layla's accusation or not.

"Ms. Jones, come with me."

Headmistress Astrae had not said one word to Ava since they'd left the vigil. She'd barely even glanced in Ava's direction after telling her she wanted to speak to her in her office.

As they made their way up five floors and toward an area Ava had not yet explored, the silence began to eat at her. Even if they didn't kick her out or send her to Desmios, Ava doubted she'd ever know every bit of the school—she doubted anyone, including the headmistress did. All Ava wanted to know was whether Headmistress Astrae believed Layla.

The headmistress led Ava down a long hall before she stopped in front of a large drinking fountain. Ava waited. The silence was bad enough, but now they stopped for a water break? As if her entire life, her future, didn't hang in the balance.

To Ava's surprise, the headmistress didn't drink any water. Instead, she placed her right wrist against it. The wall to the left opened at once.

Ava peered in, confused. She had to stop herself from asking the headmistress why she had led her to an empty room no larger than a linen closet. Headmistress Astrae pointed her right casting finger as a slight breeze filled the small, dimly lit room. Ava's eyes followed a small flight of stairs. At the top sat another door made of ice. An orange fox with pointed ears ran down to greet them. It rubbed against the headmistress' leg and let out a series of loud barks.

"Go, Dania, up the stairs with you," Headmistress Astrae said to the fox, who begrudgingly obliged. Once it reached the top of the stairs, it opened its snout and breathed out fire. The ice melted, and the door opened.

Ava walked into the headmistress' office and forgot why she was there. It wasn't anything like Ava expected. For starters, the room was larger than it appeared possible from the outside. Unlike Cromwell Hall, the light from the domed ceiling lit up the whole room. The walls were lined with portraits of people and landscapes. The shelves were filled with books that appeared rather old, some of which sneezed from the dust that covered them and some of which Ava could have sworn moved and watched her with great curiosity.

Headmistress Astrae sat behind her desk and gestured for Ava to take the guest chair. Ava's eyes darted to a candy bowl on the edge of the desk filled with candy from Polianne's. Her stomach growled.

Headmistress Astrae followed Ava's eyes. "Help yourself."

Ava grabbed a packet of gummy bears, which tried to punch their way out of the bag. She opened it—like Tara had taught her—grasping one before the rest got out.

After she'd finished chewing, Ava decided she couldn't take the silence or the headmistress' stares any longer.

"I didn't do it," Ava blurted.

"That's what we're here to talk about, isn't it?" Headmistress Astrae replied. "For the record, I believe you. If I didn't, you'd already be awaiting trial before the High Court, getting ready to be shipped off to Desmios."

She believed her.

Even though Ava knew she hadn't done it, she still harbored the feeling of walking through a metal detector that was about to go off. Pockets and bags empty, but taken away regardless.

"Thank you," Ava managed to say. She had no idea what else to say to someone who was, essentially, keeping her out of Desmios.

"However, you do have some explaining to do," the headmistress said. "While Layla admitted in the hall that she didn't see you attack Tori, she did have a compelling theory as to why you might have sought retaliation. Something along the lines of an altercation your two groups had earlier that night — an altercation that led to Layla being sent flying while you and your friends took off, running down the hall."

"That looks bad, I know," Ava admitted. "It was after the family portraits were taken. I was upset … neither my mother nor father showed up…" Ava kept her eyes fixed on the desk; she didn't want the headmistress to see her eyes fill with tears.

Headmistress Astrae remained silent and waited for Ava to gather herself and continue.

"I wanted to leave after that," Ava said. "We all did. But when we got to the door, Layla and her friends wouldn't move. And the things they said and laughed about were horrible. I … reacted. I didn't even know what I did. It just happened."

"Is that the first time something like this has happened?" the headmistress asked. She sat stoically as she scratched Dania's ear.

"No, there was one other time the day I arrived," Ava said. "I was scared. I didn't know what was about to happen. I thought a bunch of crazy people who believed in magic, in being tagged, were about to hurt me or worse."

Ava took a deep breath and added, "That time the impulse, my reaction, was bigger. As if my body went into self-defense mode and acted of its own accord, without me knowing how it did it."

"And there were other times?" the headmistress asked, alluding to before Ava arrived in this world, to when it was supposed to be impossible for her to even have any powers at all.

Ava nodded. She didn't want to lie to the woman, to one of the few people who didn't look at her like some sort of problem that needed to be fixed.

"Ms. Jones, you show incredible promise in your craft," the headmistress said. "More so than any student I've ever had during my tenure, more so than some witches and warlocks I know who have been at this for a few hundred years.

"With that said, your powers are volatile because *you* are volatile," she continued. "To stop more incidents, you must stop holding everything in. You must let yourself feel the pain, let yourself be healed from it. With any witch, emotions can play a large part in one's powers. Especially a young witch. In your case, it controls yours. The things that happened before, the things you've described, all have that in common. So, control it; don't let it control you."

Ava nodded and tried to take in the headmistress' words. It was easy to feel empowered in her presence. It was easy to feel as if what she'd spoken was as easy as turning on a light switch.

Ava reached for another gummy bear and accidentally dropped the bag. All the bears escaped onto the desk. Dania, the fox, jumped from the headmistress' lap at once and tried to catch them with her paws.

"Don't fret—she will get them all," Headmistress Astrae said with a laugh before folding her arms on her desk. "Now, in my two hundred years, I have been wrong about little, and I can say with certainty that I am not wrong about this. About you. You have a bright future ahead of you; one your parents, I'm sure, will be proud to see, wherever they are."

"Thank you, Headmistress. That means a lot coming from you." Ava paused and thought for a moment before she asked her next question. "But what of the rumors? What Layla said … it won't die down, will it?"

"After your friends have corroborated they were with you, an official statement will be released. Both to the students and the press—whom, I assume, has caught wind of this. The folly of anyone making an accusation with no proof can be damaging. But you and those closest to you know your truth better than anyone. Own it and hold your head high."

Before Ava could ask a final question that had weighed on

her, Headmistress Astrae rounded her desk and placed a heavy hand on Ava's shoulder. "No one is making you leave, child. Your housing and food will continue to be comped. Wipe away those tears, and go give them a better reason to call you the Impossible Girl."

TWENTY-ONE

Ava and Tara scurried through the secret passageway, down the long hall, and back toward Duncan and Colin's room.

Tara had thought ahead and had slipped the boys a note after the vigil, telling them to make sure no one was in their room that afternoon. It was easy to do since all classes had been canceled for the week. Before the curfew, everyone wanted to spend as much time outside their dorms as possible.

"Okay, we're here," Ava said. She placed her hand against the wall with more confidence this time.

Whatever this was, whatever power, whatever gift, it became easier to control. It was nice, especially with all the things Ava didn't have control over.

On her way back from Headmistress Astrae's office, Ava had found the halls filled with students, in groups, as the new rules had instructed. A handful of students had screamed out "murderer," as Ava walked by, while still others had rushed away from her as if frightened for their lives. Like if she *had* been the killer, she would do it again, right then, in front of a room full of witnesses. It was ridiculous.

After Ava opened the passageway, she stepped back. On

the off chance Triston and Theodore were in their room, she didn't want to risk another public shaming.

"Guys," Tara whispered. "Come on, now."

Duncan and Colin joined them, grim looks on their faces. Ava closed the passageway and took a steadying breath. Here, in the silence and security of the secret tunnel, it'd be easier to hear whatever they had to say.

"So, since you're here and not being shipped off to Desmios, I'm guessing Headmistress Astrae found Layla's outburst as ridiculous as we all did?" Duncan asked.

"Yes," Ava replied. "Layla admitted she didn't see me with her own eyes but claimed I was the most likely to have done it because of our … incident with them last night."

"She knew what she was doing," Tara added. "Even at a vigil, she'll do anything to steal the show and throw anyone she considers an enemy under the bus, proof or no proof. And she's had it out for you since the kelpies."

"She's bloody crazy, is what she is," Colin added. "They don't make them like her where I'm from. She's a few sand-wiches short of a picnic."

"She's what?" Tara asked, looking annoyed that she didn't understand Colin's reference.

"You know, like, she lacks common sense."

"Right," Tara said, satisfied with his answer.

"What happened after I left?" Ava asked "How was Margo?"

This wasn't the most urgent issue Ava had to contend with, but her heart hurt for the girl and her family. They were all in such a fragile state. A state made worse by Layla's outburst. If Ava lost someone she loved, she'd be just as eager to learn who was responsible, her judgment clouding because of her grief.

Her friends' faces told her it wasn't good news.

"Well … she was upset," Tara said. "After the vigil, everyone gathered around her in the hall. Margo said she would take this to the press, promising if Headmistress Astrae wouldn't give her family the justice they deserved, she'd make sure someone else did. I think Headmistress Astrae's speech about justice upset her, like she expected you to be taken into custody right then and there."

"Wonderful, just wonderful." Ava's head began to pound. The day wasn't even halfway over, and again, she'd be the center of every news story out there.

"If it makes you feel any better, Arat Asoraled is writing an article tonight that is sure to be in every paper this time tomorrow," Tara said, giving Ava a consoling look. "While we can't undo what's already been done, we can try to control the narrative and make sure both sides are heard. The truth will prevail."

"Thank you, Tara. I don't know what I'd do without you guys—and Arat Asoraled," Ava said with a chuckle.

"Do we have to do this?" Ava asked the next day. "I'd rather be back in our room, away from all the stares and whispers." She gestured to everyone around her as she chased after her friends down the stairwell toward the castle's main entrance.

Despite Tara's article, which had been in nearly every paper this morning, there had been twenty others that condemned Ava and called for her head. One was even titled, "The Impossible Girl Does the Impossible—Commits a Murder and Gets Away With It."

"Yes, we do," Tara said. "Only guilty people hide away in their rooms."

"Plus," Duncan added, "this is going to be awesome."

"What's so 'awesome' about trying out for the Assembly Games, anyway?" Colin asked.

"A fairy *would* ask that," Duncan said with a chuckle, obviously trying to lighten the mood. "You guys have no chance. Gavin, a senior, was the only reason you guys took it last year!"

"I don't know what you're laughing about, funny guy," Tara said, turning defensive. "The vampires aren't taking it this year, either."

"They canceled classes, but they're allowing *this*?" Ava asked. It didn't make sense.

"*This* is a three-hundred-year-old tradition," Tara said. "One of the few I am actually on board with. Plus, after something as dark as a murder, it's good for morale. I think it helped with their decision when Margo mentioned to the press that Tori had wanted to compete this year. They've dedicated this year's games to her and her family."

"Okay, spokeswoman Tara Delarosa." Ava decided to make the best of today and even managed a smile. "I've been convinced."

Even though she'd fought them tooth and nail—Tara had to physically drag Ava out of her room—she couldn't argue the fresh air wasn't what she needed. She'd forgotten how much she'd missed being outside, close to nature. While the castle was magnificent and full of wonder, nothing compared to the fresh air and wet grass beneath her feet.

And there was also the fact Tara had forced Ava to spend the previous night with her nose buried in books. To study casting, herbology, and whatever else might prepare them for the challenges they'd face—the challenges they'd have to conquer to qualify past the initial tryouts. The upperclassmen had the upper hand not only today but in this whole competition, their knowledge greater than the younger students.

The freshmen who did qualify would be placed in teams with their fellow magites, but Ava doubted the freshmen would be able to contribute much to their teams with only two weeks to prepare.

They approached a massive stadium, where the tryouts

would be held, near the outskirts of the school grounds by a beach. Ava stole a quick glance over her shoulder. Julian and Geoffrey followed, ten feet behind, inscrutable expressions on their faces. She glanced down at the bandage still on Julian's right wrist.

As if he sensed her gaze, Julian pulled down his sleeve and swung his arms behind him as he walked. How had he gotten the injury and, more importantly, where had Julian and Geoffrey been that night? Ava didn't like to think they were capable of having killed a young, innocent girl, but the thought wouldn't leave her mind, no matter how much she wished it would. The one thing she was sure of: she wouldn't be like Layla. She wouldn't accuse Julian and Geoffrey of anything until she had evidence to support her suspicions.

Ava slowed her pace and fell a couple of steps back from Colin and Tara. Duncan, too, hung back.

"You really think they could have done it?" Duncan asked.

"Ugh, you have to stop doing that," Ava said. "Isn't there a way to turn it off or something?"

Ava looked around to check no one else listened in on her private thoughts. She'd been studying up on ways to close it off. No such luck yet.

Maybe she should confide in Colin and Tara about her suspicions of Julian and Geoffrey.

"If it makes you feel any better, it is harder for me to listen in," Duncan said. "And I try not to, except when you start to hold everything in. I doubt anyone else has been able to since you started to put the wall up. It lowers around me because we're friends."

"Thanks," Ava whispered. "And I'm not sure if they did or not. It's too convenient, the timing—but Julian was hurt that night. He's had a bandage on his arm ever since."

"Well, you can't figure it out on your own," Duncan said. "Let's bring Tara and Colin in on it, and we'll figure it out together—discreetly."

"Okay."

"Guys," Tara called. "Hurry up, it's about to start."

Ava stared up at the looming stadium, covered in crystals that sparkled brilliantly and reflected every bit of sunlight from above. Its beauty filled Ava with warmth and hope.

"Are you ready to qualify?" Ava asked Duncan, excited for the first time.

"I was born ready," Duncan joked, then immediately turned serious. "Really, though, because of who my dad is. Failure's not an option today."

Ava couldn't imagine the type of pressure Duncan was under, what with his father on the Elder's Court. To his credit, he did look ready. As if he had no doubt he would qualify, move on to the finals, and help his fellow vampires take home the win.

"I believe you *will* qualify. I just don't believe you'll take the win. Not with the Impossible Girl ready to represent." Ava straightened her shoulders. She felt ready too. She was ready to change the narrative around her nickname as Headmistress Astrae had suggested.

Duncan chuckled. He elbowed Ava in the ribs as they hurried to catch up to Tara and Colin and make their way into the stadium.

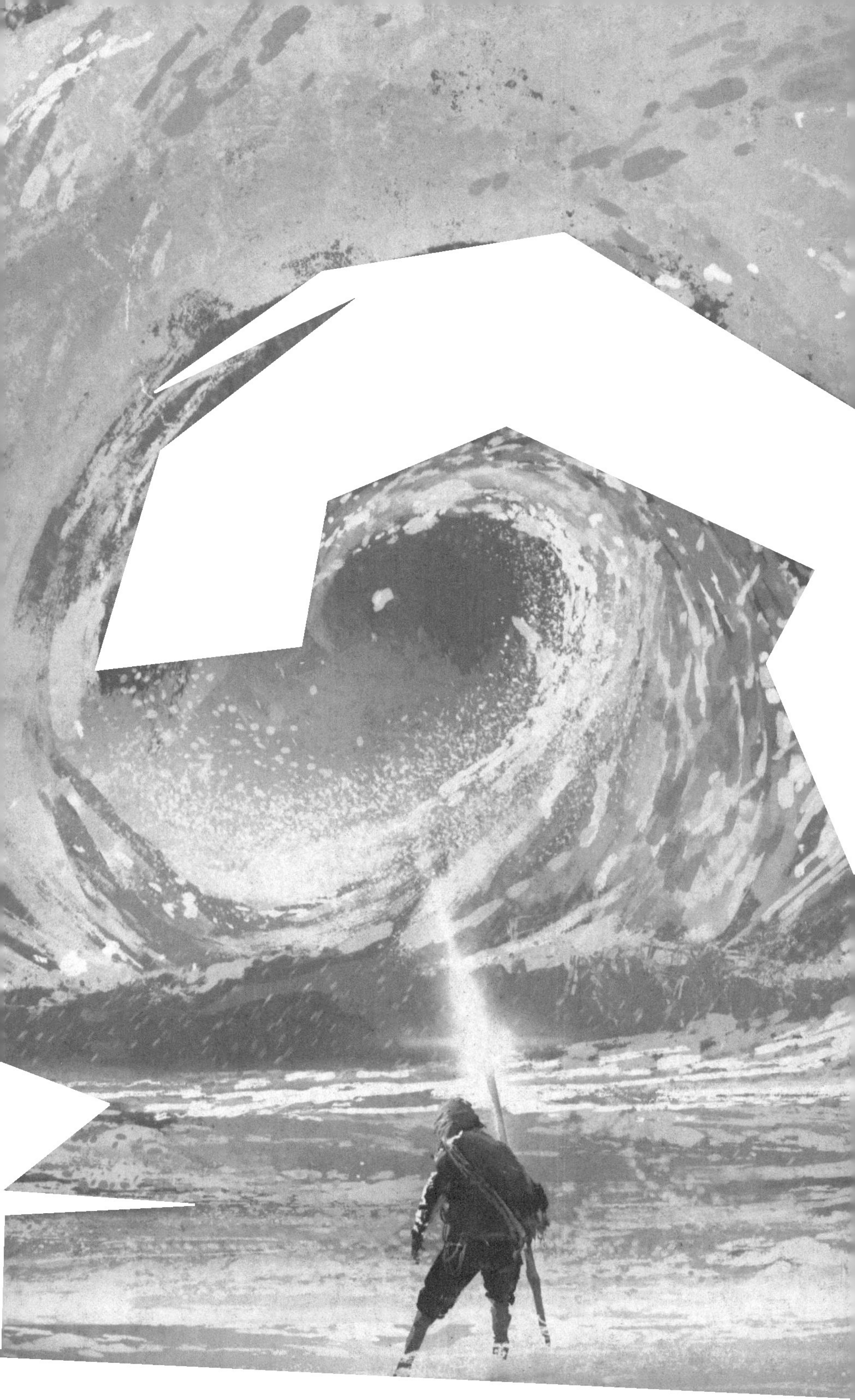

TWENTY-TWO

The stadium resembled a Roman colosseum, but instead of stone and marble, it was covered in crystals and iridescent gems that seemed to sparkle brighter than the sun. Ava shielded her eyes as she followed her friends into the open-air arena that appeared to be double the size of a football field. The main entrance led into the center of the oval-shaped stadium with a grass-covered field stretching from end to end.

When Ava turned to look around her, she drew in a sharp breath. Tiered rows of seats rose high above them toward the cloudless blue sky. The seats were made of sparkly crystals like the exterior, with plush cushions in vibrant colors.

"How many people can this place hold?" Ava asked, amazed by the sheer size of it as Tara, Duncan, and Colin claimed their seats near the bottom.

Tara, always quick with an answer, replied first. "About sixty-five thousand."

Ava settled next to Tara and was surprised to find her seat as comfortable as a feather pillow despite being made of hard crystals.

"Did everyone miss the memo or…" Colin asked, looking around in confusion at the nearly empty stadium.

"No," Duncan said with a laugh. "They'll be here, just not for the tryouts. Only the press and—now—the extra security is allowed at this stage. They'll publish feature stories on the forty who make it past the qualifiers. It'll be all everyone talks about until the Games."

"That'd be a nice change." Ava hoped it would prove true, sensing the eyes of the few students already in the stands on her back. Maybe they should have picked seats higher up, away from the prying eyes.

Layla and her friends entered the stadium and made their way up the stairs toward a higher tier. As they passed Ava, Layla whispered into one of the girl's ears; the girl laughed and scowled in Ava's direction.

Colin rolled his eyes. "I'm surprised she's even allowed to be here today," he said.

"There's no way she would miss this," Tara said. "She's told everyone she intends to get the highest score among all the freshmen today. "

While Ava had no control over whether Layla advanced, she did have control over whether Layla got the highest score. If anything, she would at least do better than Layla.

Let her try that on for size.

Beside Ava, Duncan smiled.

Mira and Kailani, who had become good friends, waved as they entered the stadium and took seats in front of them.

"Break a leg," Mira said with an encouraging smile. She turned back around in her seat just as Headmistress Astrae walked onto the field.

In those few moments, more students entered the stadium and filled the stands around Ava.

"Good afternoon, everyone," she said with a broad smile, her face beaming on the crystal jumbotron on the opposite end of the field. "It's a beautiful day, is it not? I'd like to welcome you all to the start of our tricentennial Assembly Games! For our Lost Ones who have just arrived, this has been an annual competition since our world's inception. It's a light-hearted competition where one magite comes forth the victor, as well as an incredible bonding experience and source of pride for everyone here, whether you advance or not. Each year, it fosters the magical advancement of all those who participate … while also earning them some bragging rights, I assume."

She chuckled as she took in all the faces around her.

"It is a fair competition that puts everyone—regardless of their powers—on an equal playing field to face some of the greatest challenges they've ever yet faced," Headmistress Astrae continued. "It is with great pride and honor that I bring Mrs. Avilasa onto the field to go over the rules. Listen closely, and let the Games commence!"

A loud bell rang somewhere in the distance. Above them, hundreds of fairies rose from the highest seats in the stadium. Sounds of horns, trumpets, and other musical instruments Ava didn't recognize filled the arena, causing adrenaline to course through Ava which made her feel like she could do anything.

Mrs. Avilasa stepped onto the field. Several witches and warlocks flew high up in the sky. A light show shot out of their brooms, spraying sparkly particles onto the students and the field.

"Alright," Mrs. Avilasa said, adjusting her large-rimmed glasses, which tried to make a break for it. "I know you're all anxious to begin, so listen up. Each magite and their class will be called upon, one at a time. If you're interested in trying out, you'll walk down onto the field and meet whichever instructor is waiting for you. Your names"—she pointed up at a large, digital game board that had been divided into two columns—"will appear there. To start, you'll have zero points and be on a level playing field. As you face different obstacles, you'll be scored. There are one hundred points available. One male and one female from each grade who score the most points will advance to the finals, which will be held in two weeks. Your three judges will consist of Headmistress Astrae, Mr. Viscardi, and Healer Gwyn filling in for Keeper Sable, who is dealing with an unexpected creature on the loose. Everyone ready?"

Everyone, Ava included, cheered that they were. Members of the press released their cameras, which flew off to snap photos of the crowd and the judges. Ava was nervous about Healer Gwyn serving as a judge; Ava wasn't sure if this helped or hurt her chances.

"Okay, then, at this time, I am pleased to turn everything over to our alumni, Jorina and Derrien, who are returning for their fifth year as gamecasters for the Assembly Games," Mrs. Avilasa said, gesturing upward toward luxurious box seats at least forty rows above and taking a seat in her own field-level box beneath the judges.

The jumbotron zoomed in on Jorina, a witch with wild, strawberry blond hair, and Derrien, an athletic-looking werewolf with jet black hair, who both flashed toothy smiles and waved to the crowd. Personal microphones levitated inches away from their faces.

"Alright, alright, let's get the fun started," Derrien bellowed. "All freshman vampires wishing to try out, please make your way down."

Feet shuffled in all directions as excited vampires rose from the stands.

"First one up, you know what that means?" Colin asked.

Duncan flashed a confident smile as he made his way toward the aisle. "Yeah, it means everyone else will copy how I got to the top," he said.

"Nah, they're putting you guys up first because you have no shot this year," Tara said with a smirk.

"Ouch," Duncan said, grabbing his chest.

Ava reached out and gave Duncan's hand a tight squeeze. "Good luck."

"Don't need it," Duncan said. He pulled away and made his way onto the field. "But thank you anyway."

The field filled up fast. It seemed everyone in Duncan's class wanted to try out. If all the other witches and warlocks from Ava's class also tried out, the statistical likelihood of her advancing decreased quite a bit. Ava squared her shoulders and shook the thought away.

"Enjoy watching how it feels to make it to the top, ladies," Layla said with a giggle as she passed by and joined the other freshman vampires on the field. She edged her way toward Duncan and whispered something in his ear.

"She's certifiable," Colin said, shaking his head.

Two tall, pale instructors Ava didn't recognize separated the competitors into different groups. The female instructor, a dark-haired woman with alabaster skin, had the female students line up in front of her. The male instructor, a blond gentleman with almost translucent skin, had the male students line up in front of him. The students were given instructions that Ava and the others in the stands couldn't hear. Several of the students nodded, while others seemed to scout out their competition and only half-listened.

"All right, everyone," Jorina called down. "We're in for a long and exciting day! Hold on to your seats, take note, and enjoy the ride!"

"For our first of three challenges, we begin with the all-important speed and agility test," Derrien said.

As he spoke, the competing students moved to one end of the field. Several stretched, while others tried to edge past the imaginary starting line ever so slightly.

"On our mark, our contestants will have one simple challenge: making it from one end of the field to the other," Derrien continued.

"Seems simple enough, Derrien," Jorina said. "But it's not, is it?"

Headmistress Astrae pointed her casting finger toward the

field. Sprouting up from one end of the green grass to the other was a cross between a maze and an obstacle course full of large metallic objects, metallic structures, and random balls of fire throughout the field.

"It wouldn't be much fun if it was as simple as it appeared, would it?" Derrien said with a hearty laugh.

"Are those *silver* crucifixes?" Ava asked, confused as she stared on. The fastest route, straight through the middle, was riddled with crucifixes, random waterfalls, and billowing flames.

"Silver crucifixes, silver horseshoes, silver chains, and fire —you name it," Tara said, shaking her head. "Most of them won't make it even halfway."

Ava stared at the impossible maze. The obstacles manifested vampires' worst nemeses.

"That water that's coming down—that's holy water," Tara added as she pointed at the waterfall.

Ava followed her gaze. Sure enough, dozens of fairies and witches hovered above the field blindfolded, pouring water from wooden buckets. While the competition hadn't started yet, Ava was sure they did so as a warning to the students—a reminder, even—to pay close attention to the path they chose.

"At the start of three, your time begins," Jorina announced.

Derrien and Jorina counted in unison: "One, two, three!"

Only two students leaped forward, each taking a different route. The other students remained at the starting line, looking down the field, up above, and at the other two students who had sprung ahead, trying to determine their best course of action.

One student wiped the sweat off her brow with a terrified look, then stepped back from the starting line and returned to the stands. She plopped back down in her seat and folded her arms across her chest with a pout.

Duncan stood stoically and studied the field. He seemed

unconcerned by the other students or the buckets of water above him. Ava hoped to be that focused when she took the field.

Several students took their first steps.

"And we're off, everyone!" Jorina called.

"You'd think the easiest way through would be straight down the middle, but we'll be surprised if any attempt that today," Derrien said.

"True," Jorina added. "It's well-known that the crucifixes ward off vampires. The intense pressure they feel in their presence can be all-consuming."

While everyone else around him moved forward, Duncan remained at the starting line, deep in thought, staring aimlessly ahead.

"Do you think he's stuck?" Ava asked, hoping she was wrong. "Like that other girl, but too embarrassed to make his way off the field?"

Regardless of how confident, how nonchalant he'd been about making it past the tryouts, Duncan would be devastated if he not only failed but came in dead last—which could be a good possibility.

"Or maybe I got in his head," Colin said. "I was jostling with him. I wasn't serious. He has to know that, right?"

"Oh, you two, calm down!" Tara said. "If there's one thing I've learned growing up and seeing him in the spotlight, it's that the boy always has a plan. I'd still put Aurum shekels on him winning the male spot."

Ava hoped Tara was right. From the looks of it, Colin did too.

A few feet ahead of Duncan, Layla appeared to be making better progress. She edged her way around a ring of silver horseshoes. Two other freshmen followed close behind her, and Layla scowled back at them, apparently not happy about them trailing her. She inched forward with careful, deliberate steps. She went to great lengths to avoid silver particles that floated up from the grass. The announcers had called it "Silver Mine Lane," with certain parts of the grass containing more silver particles than others. Stepping in any of those areas resulted in a cloud of silver smoke, which seemed to drain the competitors.

With ten minutes elapsed on the game board, no one was more than twenty feet down the field.

A short male vampire stared at some silver chains in his path. He appeared to be forcing himself to put one foot in front of the other with a great deal of effort. He lifted his thick leg to step over the chains, but he tripped and fell on top of them.

Gasps erupted from the stands. Tara even jumped to her feet.

"Well, that's not good, folks," Derrien said matter-of-factly.

"No, no, it is not," Jorina added. "We have to see if young Melvin has the strength and determination to recover here or if someone will stop and help him."

Ava glanced at the game board. Melvin's name had dropped, points taken away when he fell. He was near the bottom, but still higher than Duncan, who remained at the starting line.

Another boy skidded to a halt and appeared as though he might help Melvin. But instead, he tapped Melvin with his foot, then walked over his back.

The crowd burst into laughter.

Melvin's body pressed harder against the chains, smoke billowing from where his face made contact against the silver, and the poor boy writhed in pain.

"Well, we have our answer, folks," Jorina said, no judgment whatsoever in her voice. "It looks like young Melvin has only himself to pull this out."

"Oh, wait, look at that!" Derrien called out.

With great effort, Melvin moved his left hand into his left pants pocket.

"I see that too," Jorina said. "It looks like we're about to have our first signal. If he commits here, he'll be helped off the field and be disqualified."

Melvin struggled but managed to pull out what resembled a flare gun. He shot it upward, his arm barely able to turn it upright. A white flag with his name on it shot into the sky and signaled he was done.

Several instructors, Mrs. Avilasa included, rushed onto the field. They picked Melvin up and carried him off toward a stretcher, where several healers waited. The burn marks on Melvin's face disappeared. No trace of his injury remained. Still, the boy appeared out of it and was unable to walk.

"It's always a shame, Derrien, to see someone out so soon," Jorina said, "but, I suppose, it is a double-edged sword."

"True, Jorina. On the one hand, you want to see everyone succeed, at least making it past that finish line. But, on the other hand, with the competition only growing in difficulty from here, it's best anyone who can't push through gets out early and avoids any personal injury."

Ava turned toward Tara. "Do people get hurt?" she asked. "Like seriously hurt?"

It seemed an obvious answer, what with the large group of healers on the sidelines. But Melvin hadn't appeared injured. Rather, he'd appeared physically drained, what with his skin healing as soon as he'd been lifted off the chains.

"Oh, you know, there's been some broken bones and scrapes and bruises over the years, but it's nothing the healers can't handle," Tara said with nonchalance. "No one's ever died, if that's what you mean."

"So, nothing I haven't already experienced back in the mortal realm *and* here," Ava said with a laugh. "It's like this competition was made for me."

"Well, I've never broken a bone, and I don't intend to today," Colin said with a look of determination.

"You'll be fine," Ava said. "We have an advantage: We can fly, and they can't." Ava hoped she was right.

Twenty minutes had elapsed, and Duncan had still not moved one iota.

To Ava's great displeasure, Layla had gotten around the silver horseshoes and stared down at a moat filled with fire, which kept her from advancing. Every few seconds, the fire would disappear, then return. Layla's lips moved as if she was counting, maybe trying to time its pattern, as she waited to make her move.

Ava glanced up at the game board. Layla's name was high on the list of the female competitors.

"What if no one finishes?" Ava asked, hopeful that even if Layla's name was at the top, she'd be disqualified if she didn't make it all the way through.

"Someone always finishes," Kailani chimed in before Tara had a chance to respond.

"Oh, everyone, our last starter may be about to make his move," Jorina called. "Duncan Stavros has passed the starting line!"

The crowd buzzed with excitement, and every competitor on the field glanced back.

"Yeah, the real question here is whether or not all that planning paid off and whether he'll be able to catch up," Derrien added. "All that elapsed time could have cost him this whole thing."

To everyone's shock, the announcers included, Duncan didn't steer left or right, but forged straight ahead. He ran toward the crucifixes and the downpour of holy water. While this was the fastest way through the obstacle course, it also was the most treacherous.

"He's crazy," Tara said.

"I think all that time he wasted got in his head," Colin said, sounding happy that it hadn't been his fault like he'd thought.

A handful of the other competitors turned back at the

announcer's comments. Once they'd confirmed with their own eyes Duncan had chosen the quickest path, they began to speed up. Unfortunately, their haste also caused several of them to make mistakes. More white flags flew into the air moments later as a result.

Duncan's name began to rise on the game board. He'd received thirteen points when he chose his path and was dead in the center with his other competitors. Thaddeus Dumville was a mere five points ahead of Duncan and about ten feet in front of him on the field.

With bare feet, Duncan jumped over and around an array of crucifixes that lay in front of him. He was able to avoid most of them but tripped on one, causing blue flames to burn his leg. But still, he continued, even as the flesh on his feet bubbled. Ava imagined it did the same on his legs, underneath his pants.

Ava held her breath. She couldn't believe Duncan was still able to walk.

From above, a blindfolded fairy poured her bucket directly over Duncan. The contents barely missed him as he dodged out of its way at the last moment.

Duncan's score increased by five points.

Duncan swiveled to his left, where a puddle pooled on the ground. He stepped on the final crucifix to get past it, but more flames shot up his legs.

Duncan passed everyone else, including Thaddeus Dumville.

Three more points.

"Well, would you look at that," Jorina exclaimed with excitement. "Young Stavros has made it through the crucifixes and holy water and is leading the pack. I'm sure Elder Stavros will be pleased to hear that not only was his son the only one to take the most direct path but also was successfully able to execute it, moving to the final leg of the course."

"I'll be honest, Jorina," Derrien chimed in. "I didn't see it playing out like this. Not only would most young vampires his age be warded off, but they wouldn't have been able to withstand those blue flames. I don't want to jinx anything here, but I'd wage Aurum shekels that if he gets past this next portion, he'll be moving on today."

The other competitors paid little attention at this point, all too wrapped up in their own challenges to give any focus to Duncan or the announcers.

A creature shaped like a large bird with the face of a human dived down from the sky. It weaved through the course, causing several competitors to dodge out of its way. A tall girl with crimson hair, who had not moved fast enough, was snatched up and dropped back at the starting line. She tossed her hands up in the air and yelled at the creature, then stormed off toward the stands. She obviously did not want to start all over.

"That makes two, everyone," Derrien announced.

"With so much time having elapsed, things are about to escalate, and that number will increase," Jorina called. "The rest of the competitors are on a time clock, the competition never going past sixty minutes."

The blindfolded creature flew high above and circled the course, searching for its next victim. The competitors crouched low to stay off its radar.

Duncan was halfway down the field, his full focus on the flames that blocked his final obstacle and the finish line. The flames shot at least ten feet in the air before they retreated seconds later back into the earth.

Ava counted—just like Duncan was probably doing—how much time elapsed before the flames shot back up again. Tara and Colin must have had the same thoughts that Ava did.

"It's five seconds," Tara said.

"I counted four, but then three one time," Colin argued.

"I think you're both right," Ava said. "I think it counts

down and gets shorter each time. All he has to do is wait until it's at five seconds again and make his move."

They watched and counted out loud to confirm Ava's theory.

"Okay, okay, I think you're right," Colin said, excitedly.

"Let's hope he figured that out as well," Tara added.

If ever there was a time Ava had wished for Duncan to read her mind, it was now. She waited until the final flame disappeared for about one second and thought, as hard as she could, she focused on the word *now*.

Duncan jumped. The crowd went crazy as he made his way toward the final obstacle.

Ten points.

Duncan was now at the top of the game board.

"Absolutely wonderful, just wonderful!" Derrien cheered.

"It's important to remember these Games are not all about brute force, but also about one's deduction and reasoning skills—and Mr. Stavros proved he has these in spades," Jorina said.

All that stood between Duncan and the finish line was an elbow-to-elbow line of ipotanes, with Alastair at its center.

Each creature held a pointed spear, which rested on the ground and reached their shoulders. In unison, the ipotanes turned their spears sideways and indicated they wouldn't let him pass.

"What's the play here?" Ava asked.

"I'm not sure," Tara said. "They never repeat an obstacle. While certain aspects will show up again, it's always for a different reason."

"You think they want him to fight them?" Colin asked, puffing his chest out like *he* was the one on the field.

"Unlikely," Tara replied.

With Alastair's spear still turned, locked with the other ipotanes' spears, he glared at Duncan.

Ava considered Duncan's options. He could try to fight

them, but there were at least thirty that stood shoulder-to-shoulder. He could try to run and jump over them—but those spears. Ava wasn't sure if they were for show or if they were a warning.

Duncan did neither of those options. He locked eyes with Alastair. Time seemed to slow. Five more minutes elapsed, and still, Duncan remained, his eyes never wavering from Alastair's.

"If Duncan doesn't hurry, he's going to have more to worry about," Tara said, gesturing toward three male competitors who were almost finished with their final obstacles, Thaddeus Dumville included.

For the female competitors, Layla led the pack and approached the final obstacle. Ava had been so focused on Duncan, encouraging him in her mind, she hadn't paid any attention to anyone else's progress.

Then the most amazing thing happened. Alastair moved aside, allowing Duncan to pass and cross the finish line.

The crowd went crazy. Ava, Tara, and Colin jumped to their feet, screamed, and hugged one another.

"While there's no wrong way to pass the finish line, choosing to 'glamour' your way through shows some finesse, wouldn't you agree, Derrien?" Jorina said, sounding impressed.

"Oh, absolutely," Derrien bellowed. "I look forward to seeing which route the rest of the competitors take—although the freshman male spot has been filled by young Stavros!"

The press moved onto the field at once to surround Duncan, whose wounds were examined by the healers.

"I can't believe it," Ava said, beaming.

"Told you," Tara said. "We should've placed a proper wager. Next one?"

Immediately after Duncan claimed the male spot, several students shuffled off the field in frustration. Others had forced themselves to finish despite minor injuries. Tara said it hurt the students' chances for next year if they walked off before time ran out because the judges would remember their lack of determination.

Ava's joy for Duncan had been short-lived. After he'd finished and the press had taken the same photo at least one hundred times, Layla moved on to the final obstacle with one other girl. The game board said the other girl's name was Cynna Wormald. While Cynna was barely five feet tall, she had a fierce look about her. The announcers said her older brother had been a large part of the vampires winning three years back.

Ava hoped, prayed even, Cynna would beat out Layla.

At first, both tried to glamour the ipotanes, like Duncan had done. But after five minutes and little time left on the clock, they gave up on that idea. Cynna's confidence seemed to waver at that point. When she noticed Layla was about to run and leap over the ipotanes, regardless of the spears—Cynna tried to copy her strategy.

Cynna soon realized her mistake. Layla had at least six inches on her. Cynna had jumped first, and this had turned all the ipotanes' attention to her, ensuring Layla was able to jump over unscathed and secure the spot for herself.

Ava was determined to not only get past the tryouts, but to play a large part in helping her kind win this whole thing. There was one downside to her plan: To do so, she must also beat Duncan.

After everyone cleared the field, Headmistress Astrae pointed her casting finger and her voice boomed throughout the stadium as she said, "Exafanizomai."

Everything disappeared off the field, and a new course replaced the previous one. The witches and fairies flew up and took their seats in the uppermost levels.

The fairies began to play music again as the announcers called for any freshman witches and warlocks who wished to compete to make their way to the field.

Ava had hoped to be able to talk to Duncan after his win, to get encouragement from him, but he was led off the field and didn't return to the stands.

Ava and Tara approached the starting line. Mrs. Avilasa rattled off the rules for engagement. A flare appeared in Ava's back pants pocket, feeling like it weighed a million pounds. The mere idea that she would need to use it made her throat tighten.

"Madge, if you will, please add sixty minutes to the game board," Derrien said. "We'll begin in two minutes."

"That's right, our second match of the day is about to go down," Jorina added. "We're in for a long day, and I suggest everyone in the stands stretch their legs and get comfortable as this is sure to be one you won't want to miss."

"The committee who designed this year's tryouts have outdone themselves," Derrien said with a laugh. "I'd suggest the competitors also have a good stretch." He sounded glad not to be on the field himself.

To Ava's surprise, Tara hadn't opted to stay in the stands. Ava assumed Tara would want to mentally take notes and prep for whatever story she planned to write next.

Instead, Tara joined her in the competition with a fierce expression. She even postured up to another girl, who rolled her eyes and turned to converse with her friend.

Ava felt guilty. Guilty that she had assumed she'd be the one to move on today. Tara wanted this for herself, but if Ava failed today, there was no one else she'd rather fail to. Either way, their kind would have a strong addition to their team.

"Are you ready for this?" Tara asked, eyeing the obstacle course as she stretched and touched her toes.

"As ready as I'll ever be," Ava replied.

She took in her surroundings. It now appeared that practically every student and instructor packed the stands and watched their every movement. At least twenty members of the press surrounded the field, all at different angles, taking furious notes. Their cameras flew and snapped pictures. A shoelace could come untied, and the press would know about it before the competitor did.

Ava was thankful Julian and Geoffrey had remained in the stands. It was easier to forget the implications of where they'd been the night of the ball—to forget their existence momentarily—without them hovering over her shoulder.

A second loud bell rang from somewhere in the distance. Ava was still unsure about the whereabouts of this bell and squinted in all directions to no avail.

The competitors around her readied themselves as the announcers declared the start of the second competition.

She exchanged a smile of encouragement with Tara, the only competition that mattered.

Ava redirected her gaze in front of her and focused on the thing that would matter for the next sixty minutes: the obstacle course. A maze of stone pillars rose from the grass in varying heights, some seeming to reach all the way up to the sky. Several lurched up and down, constantly in movement. They seemed to change with every second that passed.

Going around them on foot wouldn't be an option, but neither was flying, unless she could get her hands on a broom.

Ava stood there, perplexed. "They mean for us to fly," Tara deduced and sounded as though she wished she was back up in the stands, where she had control.

Everyone around them had similar looks on their faces. All remained motionless. Tara and Ava were the only competitors talking to each other.

Ava inched up to the first pillar. It wouldn't be an option to move it. There was no hidden passage, no hidden button to lower it to get to the other side.

"With three minutes on the clock, it would seem all our competitors face a similar dilemma—what to do next," Jorina said.

"It would seem, perhaps, they should look *up* for the answer, wouldn't you say?" Derrien said with a laugh, providing a valuable clue.

Everyone on the field, Ava included, tilted their heads up to discover a plethora of brooms. They floated at least one hundred feet above them. They were all different styles, sizes, and materials.

"Oh," Tara said. "They mean for us to bring them down to us. That's not even something we've practiced yet, though, what with classes having been canceled yesterday!"

Tara's brows furrowed.

"True," Ava whispered. "But it is something *you* made us study last night."

From what Ava had read, to move an object at all, she had to focus intently on the object and speak the word "Erchomai." The book, *An Introductory Guide to Casting*, had mentioned things like orbs, fruits, and other small objects—not a broom suspended high up in the air.

Ava tried her best to lock her casting finger onto a broom with a metallic handle and gold birch twigs, then proceeded to try to pull the broom down with her mind, voice, and finger working in unison. Unlike with flying, Ava kept her eyes open as she focused on the broom. She pictured the broom moving, coming down, and landing in her right hand, which she held open. This expectation of success was said to be key. If you thought you'd fail, you would.

The broom lowered a little but then pulled to the left unexpectedly. Ava followed the direction it had moved, her finger still locked. Despite having dozens of brooms to choose from, one of her competitors had locked onto the same one.

Great. Just great.

Ava had been there first, as the moment the other girl had locked on, she'd felt it. She could redirect her attention to another broom, but she refused to do so.

With her teeth gritted, Ava turned her gaze back to her prize and focused as hard as she could. The broom moved closer to her. She could still feel the resistance—the pull—from the other competitor, who clearly could feel Ava's pull but also chose not to move on to another broom.

Not now, not today.

They refused to start this competition in surrender, but only one could claim this broom, and Ava intended it to be her. "Erchomai," Ava uttered, much more loudly than she'd intended.

With inhuman speed, the broom fell out of the sky and landed into Ava's open palm, as she had envisioned it.

Her competitor glared at Ava with a mixture of frustration and embarrassment. For a moment, the girl still tried to will the broom to come to her as Ava tightened her grip. Finally, she gave in and turned with a flip of her curly brown hair.

From the looks of it, Ava was the first one to have achieved this feat, although she couldn't make out what everyone else around her was doing.

The game board eased her mind—five points appeared next to Ava's name. The only points on the board. Ava wanted to stay ahead of the curve, so she mounted her broom and prepared to take flight.

"Ms. Jones, our first competitor to bring her broom down, appears to be about to show us why so many have speculated she's the one to beat today," Derrien called out to the crowd.

"She's going to have to keep a fast pace, what with several of her competitors about to get their hands on a broom," Jorina added.

Jorina was right. Several other competitors were close behind Ava, with several brooms bobbing up and down toward the ground.

Ava tried her best to focus on her own actions and hoped Tara would be the next to join her.

"See you on the other side?" Ava said to Tara.

"See you at the finish line," Tara said with a smile. Her grin turned into a frown as her concentration and incantation had broken and sent her broom higher into the air. Ava kicked herself internally for interfering but said a thankful prayer as Tara's broom began to lower once more. Screams and whispers of "Erchomai" were the only things Ava could hear.

Ava could win. She felt invincible as she flew into the air and glanced down on everyone else. She stopped her ascent and took in the maze of pillars which had risen with the start of the competition. Logically, she tried to rise higher, to fly high enough to skip the pillars. As she flew higher, though, it was like she had slammed into an invisible wall. The impact nearly caused her to lose her balance as she clutched her head, which throbbed.

"That feature was designed by Herbert Dublin himself," Jorina said.

"He's had a heavy hand in this year's design and made sure there's no easy way for the competitors to bypass any one obstacle," Derrien added. "You'll all be happy to know, he'll be joining us later today for the final leg of the competition."

Ava steadied herself and tried to brace for whatever other surprises awaited her.

She regained her bearings and gazed down, trying to determine the best path to the finish line.

For three minutes, she remained in place, studying the movement of the walls. If she didn't time it right, she could be knocked down. She'd have several broken bones from a fall from that height. Healers waited on the sidelines, their gurneys already prepped.

By now, Ava was almost certain of the right path: two pillars directly in front of her, then a quick left, then back to the right, and, finally, through the center and she'd be through. She flew forward and tried to remember the pattern in her head. She couldn't stop. If she did, she'd fall. Doubt wasn't an option.

She flew past the first three pillars effortlessly and according to her plan.

As she swerved back to the right, she narrowly missed the impact of the hard, stone pillar which had begun to rise again. The rough edges grazed the heels of her feet.

Two more to go.

Ava's heart beat out of her chest. The memory of her fall when she'd flown to the heart of the city came flooding back.

She did her best to push the images out of her mind. But she couldn't lie to herself and say she didn't look forward to her feet being planted firmly on the ground in a few moments —if she could get past the last two pillars.

The ground welcomed Ava as she passed one more unmoving pillar.

One more to go.

The last pillar, to her horror, rose against the pattern—or, more likely, she had taken more time than she'd thought to get past the first four. She swerved out of its way as it rose again, which allowed her to avoid a head-on collision.

Noise carried from the crowd, as the announcers' warped voices echoed in Ava's ears. Something was wrong. All she could hear, all she could comprehend, was the sound of her heartbeat as it begged her to hurry up, figure out a new plan, and end this.

She needed a new path—and fast. The original pillar she'd chosen didn't lower, and she was sure the one she hovered over was one of the ones that *had* moved moments before.

Left or right. Backward or forward.

Ava's mind raced with all the different options, and she prayed she'd make the right choice.

She didn't have time for logic or reason. She didn't have time to calculate the pillars' movements again. All she had was her gut—and it had gotten her this far.

So, against everything she and Tara had talked about regarding strategy, Ava went with the first thing that popped into her head: *left.*

She flew as high as the invisible barrier above would allow and veered to the left, then flew forward. She locked her eyes on the last pillar which separated her from either an embarrassing, painful, and public fall *or* the second challenge.

"I want to make it known to all you other competitors," Derrien boomed from somewhere above Ava, "I do not advise this strategy and recommend more time be taken to study the pillars, to memorize their patterns, before you embark on this challenge."

"Yes, I concur," Jorina added. "This is either going to be the end of Ms. Jones's journey or a fascinating piece for the press, who'll be asking how she had the confidence to almost certainly fly smack dab toward a pillar which hasn't moved once."

Hasn't. Moved. Once.

Those words repeated on a loop in Ava's head. She closed her eyes as she was within a couple of feet of the final pillar—which had still not lowered.

"Well, I'll be!" Derrien called.

Ava took the comment—and the fact that she was still airborne—as a good sign. She opened her eyes and found herself past the final pillar and with an additional ten points on the game board.

"With everything circulating in the press, she needed this win, if only for herself," Jorina said to a half-booing, half-cheering crowd.

Ava was unsure if this was meant to be a dig or an encouragement. At that moment, though, she didn't care. All she cared about was the ground. Her heart still pounded as though it might beat out of her chest. After this was over, she would need the taffy from Polianne's to calm her poor heart.

Ava's feet touched the ground, and she dismounted. She loosened her grip on her broom, allowing it to fall to the ground. She could again see her way to the finish line, although she hadn't the faintest idea what the second challenge might be.

No fairies flew above her, no ipotanes blocked her path. It seemed as though there were no other challenges.

What lay ahead of her in the center of the field was a deep, calming stream surrounded by bushes and trees. Visible beneath the water were colorful pebbles.

Ava approached the water's edge as cheers erupted from the crowd.

The reason they cheered, Ava realized when she turned around, was that a handful of other competitors were gaining on her. The girl who'd fought Ava for her broom was included in that group.

Ava scanned the pillars, hoping to see Tara up there with them, but she didn't. With a deep breath, Ava again faced the stream and its tranquil waters. She wanted to keep as much of a lead as possible, even if she didn't understand what she was supposed to do.

She kneeled, peered into the waters, and saw nothing but her own reflection and the pebbles, which didn't strike her as a challenge worthy of this competition.

How was this the start of the second challenge?

Ava placed her hands into the stream's cool waters. She cupped her hands and raised a palmful of water closer to her face, looking for a clue. Something that said, "*This* is what you're supposed to do with me."

As she did so, though, Ava began to feel disoriented. Her knees weakened beneath her as she fell over onto her side.

From their box, the announcers continued with their incessant chatter. Murmurs from the crowd echoed throughout the stadium. Cameras flew onto the field and snapped all around Ava. But she couldn't move her head, let alone her limbs, to confirm this. She could no more move any part of her body as she could speak. It was like every muscle had been paralyzed.

No healers rushed onto the field, despite Ava needing them to. She had no ability to reach into her back pants pocket to send up a flare. To surrender.

Ava's eyes became heavy. They had been the muscle she *could* control, but that control left her. She had no idea what had happened. What had gone wrong. The last thing her eyes saw before they closed was a pair of black boots that stepped in front of her.

TWENTY-FOUR

Ava opened her eyes to find herself lying in the same position in a small, poorly lit room—alone. Her muscles no longer felt paralyzed. Her mind, no longer foggy, only confused. She got to her feet, her eyes darting around her. There were no windows or doors, no secret hatches up above. She could think of no logical way she could have gotten here; let alone how she would get *out*.

Ava bubbled with anger. Anger that she had been in the lead and had forfeited the entire competition. The press and all the students who'd believed Layla at the vigil had probably loved that. Ava's face was probably already plastered in every newspaper.

She had no idea how long she'd been unconscious. Or how she hadn't woken up when she was moved. Most importantly, she had no idea why she'd even reacted the way she did and how she'd ended up in a room like this, all by herself. It made no sense. One minute she was fine, the next she had lost consciousness.

She would've at least liked to know what the challenge had been and why she was here, not in a room that appeared to be run by someone like Healer Gwyn. Goosebumps formed on

Ava's arms, and when she glanced down, she could see why. She no longer wore the outfit she'd started the day with: white pants, an aquamarine long-sleeve shirt, fur-lined cloak, and tennis shoes. Someone had changed her and placed her into an itchy, gray, short-sleeved shirt and matching gray pants. On her chest was a white embroidered emblem. It said "AJ267839" in black letters.

She took several deep breaths.

There was probably a logical explanation for all this.

"Hello!" Ava called. "Is anyone there?"

The walls were thick, made of a gray stone that matched her outfit. It was hard to imagine anyone could hear her through those walls, no matter how loudly she screamed. Still, she tried again.

"What does AJ267839 mean? Hello?"

Ava's voice echoed around the room. Panic seized her and covered her in a cold sweat. The room was a cell of some sort. But why? Had it not been an accident? Had someone— someone higher than Headmistress Astrae—decided she was guilty of Tori's murder?

This had happened after the announcer had brought it up. Had it been a signal of some sort? No trial, no plea for her innocence, just locked away, never to be let back out. Maybe that was why she had reacted the way she did on the field— because someone had forced her to with magic.

And now, what? She was in Desmios with no way out. Never to see her friends again. Never to learn why her parents had not come for her, which would have allowed her to bypass all this. Never to experience what this world had to offer— what she had to offer to it.

She had just started to acclimate. She had learned the rules and become a person with purpose. Building a life of her own, rather than watching others live out their lives, as she had done back in the mortal realm.

Ava started to hyperventilate. She collapsed to the ground,

her back against the wall—her arms colder for it—and put her head between her knees as tears escaped her eyes. She hated crying. Hated being weak. But here, with no one to see, it didn't matter. After her eyes had run dry, the knees to her pants soaked, she raised her head if only for some air. Something caught the corner of her eye. Something she was sure hadn't been there a moment ago.

In the far corner of the room was a manila folder filled so tightly with paper that it couldn't close.

Ava ran to it and picked it up. She hoped for answers. Hoped for hope, ironically.

She squatted back down and opened the envelope to find article after article, which had all been written about Ava.

"The Impossible Girl in an Impossible Place—Forever," "Justice Served, a Murderer Serves a Life Sentence in Desmios," "Parents of Ava Jones Step Forward—Now That She's Behind Bars," and, the worst, written by none other than Arat Asoraled, "A Master of Manipulation: Why Ava Jones was Never Truly a Friend to Anyone, With a Shocking Confession by Duncan Stavros."

The papers fell from her hands, as Ava slumped back, speechless and broken.

Tara and Duncan, of all people, had known her better than anyone. They'd known this wasn't her, that it couldn't have been her. But, like with her entire existence, Ava had been tossed under the bus at the first sign of trouble. Her parents hadn't wanted her. She'd never been close to anyone at the orphanage, her adoptive family had been horrible, and now, the people she considered friends had turned on her.

And Ava's parents? An article said they stepped forward *after* they were assured of never meeting her face-to-face. While she had no desire to read any of the other articles, she did need to read that one.

She could barely make out the text as tears fell and wet the piece of paper.

Her parents told the person doing the interview that they were relieved Ava was locked up, that everyone was safe. That no one so evil, without being properly tagged, should ever be allowed to exist outside Desmios, and they'd known this since her birth, which was why they'd sent her away and been reluctant to step forward. Instead, they said, they wanted to let her true nature play out for itself.

Ava's hands shook, and she dropped the article on top of all the others.

Maybe perpetuity alone would be easier. There'd be no one left to hurt her.

A speck of an idea tugged at the back of Ava's mind, though.

None of it made any sense. Headmistress Astrae had assured her that, if she was a suspect, she'd be brought before the Elder's Court. Then, she'd have the opportunity to plead her case.

So why, in all this, hadn't that happened?

Unless, this *was* the challenge.

Ava clutched her amethyst amulet and prayed that was the case. Prayed her friends hadn't turned on her. That her parents, wherever they were, didn't believe her to be evil.

In class earlier that week, Ms. Damia had mentioned the different herbs and plants and their powers when combined with certain elements—like water!

But what was the challenge?

To break out of an impenetrable room with no exits? To be forced to read horrible things about herself? She hoped she hadn't lost her mind after only being in solitary for a short time.

With sixty minutes on the clock—ten of them having elapsed before she'd completed the first challenge—Ava didn't have a lot of time left. Ava was unsure of how long she'd been unconscious, and because of the sheer size of the manila envelope and the number of articles that had been stuffed into it, she was certain being forced to read them all wasn't the challenge.

But it had tempted her and probably was meant to throw her off course. Time continued to elapse, and the competition with it if she didn't act fast.

Ava hoped she was right as she got to her feet with determination and pressed her fingers into every crevice in the walls. There had to be a way out, something she hadn't seen yet.

After she'd checked every inch of the wall three times from top to bottom, or as high as she could reach, she knew with absolute certainty three things: there was no hidden door, no hidden button or lever, and no way out. It was a challenge, though. It'd be too easy if all she had to do was to find something hidden, something already there.

So, what, then, was the challenge?

She'd already had her worst fears play out in front of her. She'd already read headlines of all the things she knew people to believe about her. To have been put into a place—a state— that she was so fearful of…

Fearful. Fears.

In this room, Ava had faced her greatest fears. She had faced each one, one at a time, and somehow had summoned the wisdom to know it wasn't real.

Again, she hoped no one could see, or hear her, as she screamed, at the top of her lungs. This time, the only person she wanted to hear it, to believe it, was herself.

"This ISN'T real! I am not in Desmios, and I have not been abandoned by my friends!"

For a second, Ava wondered if she was crazy. If she had misinterpreted the challenge, perhaps. She knew in her gut, though, she hadn't. As soon as she reminded herself of that and pushed away her last shred of doubt, a flash of brilliant white light started to fill her vision. The room faded away, and the hard stone ground beneath her disappeared.

The goal had never been to find a way out; it had been to realize she already had it all along, within her.

When her eyes opened again, Ava was no longer in the cold, dark room all alone. She lay on the field, her hair sprawled in the stream, drenched.

As she pushed off the ground with her elbows, any feelings of disorientation gone, she discovered three more things. The first was that she was surrounded by other competitors who stirred and laid unconscious on the ground, facing their own greatest fears. The second was that behind her, other competitors still struggled to get past the first obstacle. The third—and most important—was that no one had yet completed the challenge. Her name was still in the lead with thirty additional points added.

"We've got a live one, everyone!" Derrien announced, as if he'd grown tired of calling a match with little action, what with most of the people who still had a shot to win the competition passed out cold on the ground.

"Ms. Jones, welcome back!" Jorina called. "How was it?" She seemed to find great amusement in this challenge.

Ava shaded her eyes and glanced up, giving a thumbs up with a wide smile. She turned her attention back to the field and toward the finish line. She was delighted to see Tara not far from her. Tara *would* finish this, and Ava would take solace in that.

For a moment, Ava considered what Tara's greatest fear was. What she faced. It took all the strength Ava could muster to turn away, unable to help. She hoped Tara would figure it out soon. It was not a place anyone should dwell in for long.

With a second, quick glance at the game board, Ava realized she'd been unconscious for thirty minutes. Nineteen minutes remained. Whatever this third obstacle was, she'd have to complete it fast. After she'd already faced her greatest fears, the final challenge had to be easier.

She made her way around the other competitors, making

sure not to step on anyone. She leapt over the stream with confidence. While the second challenge was over, she was weary of the water and whatever ran through it and did her best to avoid it. She was a couple hundred feet away from the finish line.

A commotion drew Ava's attention behind her. Three of the other competitors had regained consciousness, including the girl who'd fought her for the broom.

Ava ran, full steam ahead.

"Four competitors are about to face the final obstacle, people—things are heating up," Derrien called.

Her only true competition was the other girl. The other two were boys and didn't worry Ava, since she was vying for the freshman female spot on the team. She ran, grateful her drenched hair countered the beads of sweat that ran down her brow. Ava hoped the third obstacle would be like the second. Either way, she tried to keep her wits about her as she ran.

She was within one hundred feet. Within minutes, she'd be across that finish line. She continued to put one foot in front of the other and paid no attention to the sounds behind her. Then, the field again transformed.

The place where she should have landed, effortlessly, rose beneath her feet. Ava fell backward from at least a five-foot height and smacked her head against the turf. She pushed off the ground and regained her balance at the same time as the fierce winds began to blow. They pushed her back, keeping her from advancing. Her hair flew in every direction and blocked her vision. The ground beneath her continued to move, and Ava had to focus to stay upright.

What had been a flat field had morphed in moments into hills that rose and plateaued, throwing white and blue powder into the air.

Closer to the finish line, the hills grew impossibly taller.

Unable to move, Ava could only laugh.

"Do you see this?" Ava asked a boy a couple of feet behind

her. She laughed and clutched her side, all while she tried to remember to breathe.

"It's wild," the boy called back, the wind drowning out his voice. He was in hysterics as he collapsed to the ground and shot back and forth like a ping pong ball between two small hills.

Ava took a couple of steps forward and ran into a wall of turf, which sprouted before her.

"This stuff, this stuff is incredible," Ava called to no one in particular. With her hand outstretched, she tried to grab some of the blue and white particles around her.

You're supposed to be doing something, a voice in the back of her head reminded her.

That voice—that voice was so funny. What was there to do when all Ava could do was laugh, run into walls, and fight the wind? All she *could* do was enjoy herself. After what she'd been through, didn't she deserve it?

But no, she didn't deserve it—not yet.

That voice in her mind agreed. It told her to move her feet, to drag herself to the finish line.

For a third time, she pushed herself against the wind's current and placed her hands on the top of a knoll and tried to pull herself up.

"Competitors, you have ten minutes," Jorina reminded them.

"At this rate, I wouldn't be surprised if anyone from the freshman class finished," Derrien added.

Finished.

She needed to finish.

Ava waited for the hill in front of her to lower enough before she ran forward. She laughed still at the irony of it all.

First, she'd faced her greatest fears, scared to death of what her future held—and now, she could barely advance without tumbling over in laughter.

More dust particles blanketed the air. She was sure it was

the dust particles doing this to her. Against her mind's protests, she unraveled her scarf and covered her face as best she could. She hoped it would act as a mask and keep her from inhaling the particles.

After a few moments, the effects seemed to wear off, although Ava couldn't get over the fact a ladybug flew by that seemed to smile at her.

Ava did her best to shake the strange thoughts. To time when to move and when to remain still. The way the hills rose and lowered was easy enough to time, although it proved difficult to keep her balance. The winds made every step she took more difficult.

Ava struggled to climb higher on the ever-moving hills. A fall atop them would result in broken bones, no matter what direction she fell. With every second she kept her nose covered, she continued to regain more and more of her composure.

At the first sign the hill was about to lower, Ava ran, pushing through the wind that slowed her down. As two hills in front of her receded, the finish line revealed itself. The game board said there were four minutes left. She didn't have time to think, she had to move—and quickly.

The first hill had been easy enough to pass. As she scaled the final hill—the thing that separated her from the finish line—her stomach turned. She was at least thirty feet off the ground, having landed on it as it had risen again. Her legs buckled underneath her, and she struggled to keep her balance. The wind made things worse.

The hill began to lower, making Ava's balance more precarious by the second. She wouldn't be able to stand like this for much longer. She was sure about that. Any second, she would fall and end up being tended to by a healer. She wished she had her broom, wished she could fly her way to the finish line. But it was so far behind her, Ava couldn't attempt to look for it.

She didn't have any other options, though. She closed her eyes and held out her hands and whispered, "Erchomai." With her mind's eye, she tried to picture where she'd let it fall. Tried to picture it coming to her. In the distance behind her, it pushed against the wind and then it was there.

Her broom.

She'd never been so thankful to see anything in her life. It landed in her palms as the hill rose again.

Ava grabbed the broom with both hands, but she was unable to mount it properly. She closed her eyes, leaped, and hoped for the best.

Ava held on for dear life.

Work, just work.

To her amazement, she was still airborne on top of her broom—something she couldn't manage days ago.

"Unconventional, but it'll work," Jorina called out from her boxed seat high in the stands.

Ava was above the finish line. She approached the ground. Her hands gripped the broom's handle, her fingers numb. Once on solid ground, she continued to clutch the broom that had saved her from an embarrassing fall and glanced up at the game board.

Thirty-five points added.

She smiled, grateful. With a few more steps, this would be over.

A loud buzzer sounded and startled her back to reality.

"One minute left, everyone," Derrien called.

"That's right, move or regret it until next year," Jorina added.

Ava dashed across the finish line as the final seconds of the competition ticked away.

With five seconds left on the clock, the male competitor

she'd talked to during the third challenge while under the effects of the strange blue particles tumbled down from high above. While he finished and would move on, he was a mess.

He didn't smile. He didn't celebrate. His leg bent in a way it shouldn't have, his face contorted in pain as he screamed. Upon closer examination, Ava saw why: Not only was his leg twisted in the most awkward way, but a large bone protruded from the middle of his thigh. Blood pooled at his feet.

The sight of his blood made Ava woozy.

The initial cheers that had resounded upon the boy crossing the finish line died down as the announcers commented on his state. A camera zoomed in and flashed embarrassing images of the writhing boy on the jumbotron for all to see.

Several healers rushed toward the boy, a gurney in hand. When they moved him, his screams intensified. They filled everyone's ears until he had been carried off the field—in a different direction than Duncan and Layla had gone.

Ava stood, alone, surrounded by the press who had rushed onto the field. They'd captured every moment of the boy's victory and injury and now turned their attention to her.

"Tell us, what fears did you face during the second challenge?" one member of the press asked, her eyes wide.

"How does it feel to stand here, not only after seeing your fellow champion, Evan, carried off but what with the accusations you face?" Ambrosia, the woman from Ava's press conference, asked as her microphone glided toward Ava's face.

Ava smiled but remained silent. She let them get her picture—which she couldn't control—but wouldn't give them a sound bite. That, she could control.

Ava stepped around their endless barrage of questions, knowing they would follow.

She wanted to find Tara and to make sure her friend was okay.

The field had calmed down, the hills no longer bobbed up and down, making it much easier to see.

In the distance, several of her competitors still lay unconscious. Healers with smelling salts of some sort woke them, one by one.

Tara regained consciousness, looking shaken as she rose to her feet. She pushed her bushy hair out of her face and met Ava's gaze. She gave her a weak smile before she followed the healers off the field and went back into the stands with the other competitors in tow.

The girl who had been Ava's biggest competition, the only other girl to make it to the final challenge, strolled past with a sneer.

"It was *not* stated in the rules that we could use brooms or other objects if they weren't provided to us," she said with a huff, shooting Ava a nasty glare, making sure the cameras caught her words and her disdain.

A boy, who appeared no older than six, pushed his way through the press.

"Come on, Ava," the young boy said. "We have to stop by the judges' table, and then I'll escort you up to the winners' box."

Unlike everyone else, he didn't seem to judge Ava. Too young to understand the politics that took place.

She followed the boy to the judges' table.

"Headmistress Astrae, your victor," the boy said with a grand wave of his arms.

"Thank you, Matthias. Well done." The headmistress turned her attention to Ava. "Quick thinking with the broom, and despite what Carey said, it was not against the rules."

"Thank you, Headmistress," Ava said as pride rushed over her.

"Well done, Ms. Jones," Mr. Viscardi said. "Be sure to pay more attention to timing, though, before the finals. Every second counts, and you and Evan barely made it in."

"Glad you didn't reinjure that arm, dearie," Healer Gwyn added. The woman seemed uncomfortable around Ava after the headache she'd caused upon her arrival.

"You and me both," Ava said and meant it. The adrenaline still coursed through her veins and kept her on high alert.

"All righty," Matthias said. "We are off. More competitions to take place, and we've got a schedule to keep."

"True, Matthias," the headmistress said, amused by the boy's seriousness as he grabbed Ava by the hand and dragged her away.

Before they'd gotten out of earshot, Mrs. Avilasa whispered to the headmistress, "Changing the flying curriculum this year paid off, no?"

Unable to hear any response from Headmistress Astrae, Ava peeked back to a smiling Mrs. Avilasa, who nodded at Ava.

Matthias led Ava off the field and up a set of stairs.

"Am I allowed to ask how much farther?" Ava joked, half-serious.

Her legs ached to sit; her mouth yearned for a drink of water.

"Not much," Matthias said. He clearly enjoyed being the one in the know.

As they rounded a third corner, he announced, "We're here." He turned the knob to a large, frosted-glass door and led them through.

Inside were four people: Duncan, Layla, Julian, and Geoffrey. The men didn't bother to peer up from their papers as Ava entered the room.

"Congratulations again," Matthias said. "Can't miss the start of the next match. Gotta go."

Matthias ran back down the steps.

Now that tryouts were over—and rest and refreshments were in her future—Ava's adrenaline started to die down. She caught her breath and glanced about the room.

To her left was an enormous fountain. Its base appeared to be filled with vanilla-flavored ice cream; root beer poured down over it.

Duncan jumped up from his lounge chair and ran over to Ava, pulling her into a tight hug.

"Congratulations," he said. He followed Ava's gaze back to the fountain.

"Polianne supplied that," he added.

"Congratulations to you too," Ava managed, all the air sucked out of her by his too-tight embrace.

Duncan stepped back and blushed. "Sorry, I guess I forget my own strength sometimes."

Duncan steered Ava away from Layla and toward the buffet-style table, which was filled with sweet treats. "Come on, plate up," he said.

"You don't have to twist my arm," Ava replied. She stacked everything in sight onto her plate and made herself a root beer float before following Duncan toward a corner of the room.

She sank down into a leather chair, which molded to her body, and a tray popped out for her spoils. "Best feeling ever," she said.

"So, what'd you have to do, and where's the other champion?" Duncan asked.

"He was carried off by the healers," Ava said. "Weren't you able to watch?" She glanced around the room again and realized there was no television or monitor that displayed what was happening on the field.

A third bell sounded from a distance.

"Nope, we wait," Duncan said. "The tryouts take a little more than eight hours or so, so you have tons of time to fill me in as we're forced to remain here with an endless supply of food and good company." He gave Ava a crooked smile and clinked Ava's root beer float with his own.

Over the rest of the day, new champions continued to trickle in, two at a time. Only Evan was hurt badly enough to be carried off to the healer's apothecary.

Ava didn't recognize most of the other competitors, although all recognized her and steered clear of her.

With more numbers, Layla, who had remained silent, turned boisterous.

"I'm surprised she didn't murder someone else to secure her spot," she said in a voice loud enough for the entire room to hear. "Maybe Evan's broken leg wasn't from the fall."

At those words, Julian and Geoffrey glanced up from their papers, as if expecting an altercation. Duncan was ahead of them and placed a heavy hand on Ava's shoulder to force her to remain seated.

She could take Layla.

Ava hoped Duncan would hear *that* one.

He nodded but kept his hand on her until the tenseness in Ava's body melted away.

Duncan had helped her a lot today. He'd let her vent about the first and third challenges for hours. Drone on about Carey, who couldn't get over losing to Ava.

He hadn't even pressed when Ava refused to discuss the second challenge, although she was certain he had a pretty good idea of what had taken place from her thoughts alone.

She didn't know if she'd ever be ready to talk about it out loud. Part of her felt ashamed by what her fears had been. Ashamed she'd let herself believe her friends would turn on her.

Ava did a quick headcount. "What is that, only two champions missing?" she asked, the room near maximum occupancy.

She was eager to get back to her room and pass out until Monday rolled around.

After he'd scanned the room himself, Duncan nodded. "It should be any minute, then we'll meet our team captains and be set free," he said, not seeming to be in the slightest bit of a hurry.

"I see," Ava said, playful. "I'm sure the concession speech you guys give will be gracious and well written, what with you having two full weeks to work on it."

"Funny, funny," Duncan said. "But we'll see. It's not so easy when you're up against everyone. Different advantages and disadvantages come into play. You'll see."

Before Ava could quip back, the door opened as a tired Matthias escorted the final two champions in and left again.

A few minutes later, the boy returned, out of breath. He instructed them all to follow him back onto the field to join their team meetings.

Ava was thankful to have gone second, as her legs, head, and stomach had time to recover from the challenges. It would have been nice to see the other tryouts play out, to have seen the competition she would be up against.

The last two champions, who'd just plated their food, grunted and rolled their eyes. Sweat still dripped from their brows as they shoveled whatever they could fit in one bite before washing it down with a gulp of the root beer float and following everyone else out.

Once back on the field, all forty champions were instructed to line up, shoulder to shoulder, for one long photo taken by a fairy who flew high above.

"I'll never get over their wings," Ava whispered to Duncan.

Those in earshot shot Ava strange stares. Maybe she should have *thought* the words instead of saying them out loud.

Once the fairy was satisfied with her photo, everyone clustered into their original cliques.

Headmistress Astrae gave her closing remarks. Ava wasn't sure about the rest of them, but she was too distracted by the fireworks that lit up the dark sky, as well as the fairies and witches who flew and sprinkled confetti onto the field.

Duncan nudged her as five instructors approached, one for each magite.

Ava instinctively knew she was with Mrs. Avilasa.

"Work on that concession speech," she yelled to Duncan as she ran to join Mrs. Avilasa and her fellow witches and warlocks. "You'll need it!"

TWENTY-SIX

It was a little after eleven, the living quarters silent. Julian had used his wrist to let Ava into her room, and she did her best to sneak in. She didn't want to wake Tara, Mira, or Kailani who were likely physically drained from the day, the challenges, as well as mentally defeated, knowing none of them would move on and represent their kind in the final competition.

Ava was exhausted. Her team meeting had drawn on for three hours, with practice scheduled for the next morning. All she wanted was for her head to meet her pillow. To be enveloped in the warmth and comfort of her blankets before she had to do it all again tomorrow.

As she made her way through the inner bedroom door and tried to shut it behind her, Tara whispered from across the room, "Don't shut it. Let's go downstairs."

Ava kept the door ajar and glanced toward her bed, vowing to return shortly. Tara pulled her back out the door and down the steps.

"Let's go in the game room," Tara whispered.

Ava shut the doors of the game room and turned on the light.

"Why are you still awake?" Ava asked. "Aren't you exhausted?"

"Clearly," Tara said. She rubbed her eyes, then readjusted her ponytail to capture the stray hairs. "I'm up because this couldn't wait. This came for you while you were gone—it says it's from Ambrose."

With a yawn, Tara used tongs to hold up a small, wrapped parcel.

"I'm surprised you didn't tear this open already, let alone read the note," Ava said.

"Are you kidding? Ambrose is definitely one who pays a healthy amount of Aurum shekels for special shipping. I'd be terrified that scorpions would crawl up my arm."

"Oh. Right. Forgot about that."

Why would Ambrose send Ava anything, let alone write to her? Ava stared at the name card, half expecting it to have been for someone else, only to confirm it was her name elegantly scribed on it.

"Note or package first?" Ava asked as she weighed the box in her hands.

"Definitely the note," Tara said, a tad more alert.

Disappointed by Tara's choice—but not in the least surprised—she dropped into a chair, opened the envelope, and read the note aloud:

Dearest Ava,

I wanted to formally send you my regrets for not being able to attend today's tryouts. Especially since I hear congratulations are in order!

I had meant to speak with you after the Lost Ones Ball, and then again today, but I have had my hands full.

There has been a disturbing rise in attacks from The Resistance.

This radical group wishes to profit from your arrival, making the pain you've had to endure some sort of political symbol from which they can gain traction. Their true means are to destroy our way of life. To destroy the peace we've enjoyed for three hundred years.

I personally wanted to ease your mind and assure you that members of the High Court and Elder's Court do not hold you responsible for any of this, despite what your arrival has seemingly brought down upon us.

While The Resistance does not have the purest of intentions, nor peace in mind, I want to assure you, personally, that we are continuing the search for your parents.

It's a working theory of mine that these radicalists are responsible for why you were not tagged, why there's no record of you being born, and for your parents not showing up to the ball.

It would seem they've had this plan in place for some time.

I will update you as soon as I have further information, and I look forward to seeing you compete in the Assembly Games in two weeks.

Until then, I ask you to keep this information to yourself to avoid showing our hand, but I felt you deserved to know the truth.

Please accept this present as a promise to bring you peace in the weeks to come, as well as good luck for the Assembly Games.

Congratulations again,

Ambrose

"Please don't tell me you want to keep this off the record, as he suggests," Tara pleaded. "He means to keep everyone in the dark as he continues this witch hunt, when, in reality, how do we even know these attacks are from The Resistance?"

"*If* there's even the slightest chance he's right, publishing anything along these lines could endanger my parents," Ava said. "You can't."

Ava's fingers squeezed the parcel, as angry tears filled her eyes.

"Ava, I didn't—I didn't think. I'm sorry," Tara said. She

came over to sit on the edge of Ava's chair and wrapped her arms around her. "We'll do this your way. In your time."

"Thank you."

Ava opened the parcel, sleep and thoughts of happier things heavy on her mind. If it was just her there, she would leave it for tomorrow, but she knew Tara would be hard-pressed to let her do so.

Ava removed the wrapping paper and stared down at a mahogany box inscribed with her name.

She opened it and found three black amulets.

Saturday night, Ava tossed and turned in her sleep. Dreams of The Resistance—of her parents being attacked and held by this radical group—haunted her.

Throughout the night, she had woken from her sleep countless times, drenched in a cold sweat, her heart racing from the inevitable bad that had been coming her way. Her mind spiraled in the darkness, where the real world and her dream world seemed to collide.

She woke to screams from downstairs.

At first, Ava thought it was another nightmare and tried to lay back down, her hands over her ears.

The day had been filled with training exercises and her body still ached from the six-hour session Mrs. Avilasa had put them through.

Sunday was Ava's one day to sleep in before classes and training resumed Monday morning. She had even bribed Tara, with some of her candy from Polianne's, to bring her back some breakfast so she didn't have to leave the dorms. Didn't have to look into the eyes of those who still called for her head

—including some of her teammates, who treated her with open disdain during practice.

Regardless of her troubled sleep, every inch of her body fought for more. Demanded more.

As Ava's mind tried to drift off, more yells erupted from downstairs. Frantic, hysterical. This wasn't a dream. This was real.

Ava bolted up in her bed and came to terms that her plans to sleep in were a wash. She glimpsed around the room to find no one else was there. The door to their room stood wide open.

Ava jumped off her bed as shouts still floated up from downstairs.

Ava was a sound sleeper, once having slept through an evacuation drill at the orphanage, but even she couldn't have slept through this. Still in Tara's too-short pajamas, Ava tossed on an aquamarine robe, which Rhapso had sent as a present for qualifying in the Assembly Games.

Ava sprinted down the stairs to find everyone surrounding Dana, a girl from her casting class. Only the girl's face was visible, the rest of her blocked by the bodies that surrounded her. From the look on her face, she was distraught.

While the girl appeared upset, Ava could hardly understand why it had been worthy of screams and yells and regretted getting out of bed for this.

Ava edged closer and navigated through the crowd. Only then did Ava realize Dana slumped in a chair and her clothes were covered in blood.

The room fell silent, save for Dana, who mumbled incoherently to herself. Her eyes were bloodshot and swollen, her hands shaking violently.

Tara knelt by the girl and spoke first. "What happened?"

"Blood. So much blood," Dana mumbled to herself more than to Tara. She proceeded to repeat those four words over and over.

"We sent someone to get Headmistress Astrae," Tara said. "But you need to tell us, Dana, were you attacked? Are you okay?"

Tara tried to check Dana for wounds, but the girl shuddered and pulled away, screaming as if she was scared for her life. Tara pulled back at once, hesitant to push any further.

"Blood. So much blood," Dana repeated.

"Okay, this is getting us nowhere," Layla's voice chimed in. She made her way toward Dana, practically pushing Tara out of the way as her cronies—Paloma Aperton being the newest member—followed her into the living quarters from the hall.

Layla placed her hands on the arms of Dana's chair, leaned down, and stared her dead in the eyes. "If there has been another attack, you need to stop your blubbering and let us know what you saw—and more importantly, *who* you saw," Layla demanded, shooting a sharp look toward Ava.

Ava had already seen the way people stared at her, already promised herself she wouldn't get involved. That she would only observe and make sure Dana was okay.

But, like Layla was good at doing with so many, she managed to get a rise out of Ava. "You're kidding with this little act, right?" Ava challenged, shaking with anger but trying to keep her voice steady. "You're going to go there again; the truth matters so little to you? Instead of trying to choose the assailant yourself, maybe he or she would have already been caught if you weren't busy steering everyone in the wrong direction. You ever think of that?"

Layla scowled back at Ava. "Oh, stop with the crusader act," she said. "I'm going where everyone else's minds have already gone." She turned back to the injured girl. "Dana, was it her? Did Ava do this?"

Layla's voice lowered—vibrating ever so slightly—like she was trying to *lull* Dana to agree.

Dana's mouth began to move, but the door to their dorms swung open wider.

"That's enough, Ms. Lelantos," Headmistress Astrae snapped. "Back away from her *now*. She's traumatized, and an interrogation or apparent glamour attempt is the last thing she needs."

"I wasn't going to—" Layla couldn't get her objection out before the headmistress directed her to move.

As she complied, Layla glared at Ava and whispered something under her breath Ava couldn't make out.

"Everyone, to your rooms," the headmistress ordered. "The show's over."

"Don't we have a right to know if the killer has struck again?" Layla insisted.

"You have a right to information once there is some to share," the headmistress shot back. "You do not have a right to watch this girl, in a fragile state, go over how she got here. I will *not* ask again."

As everyone shuffled out, Layla whispered to her cronies. Ava overheard her instructing them to go to Layla's dorm, insisting they needed to regroup and figure this out themselves if they didn't want to be next.

Sunday had come and gone, much too quickly after the incident with Dana. The girl was taken away and had yet to return, no information released about her whereabouts. The students were placed in lockdown in their rooms. Haphazard goblins delivered food and drinks, sometimes not in the proper prepared states, while the instructors patrolled the halls outside the dormitories.

The stir-craziness that ensued from being confined to their living quarters made everyone assume the worst.

Monday morning finally came, and they were allowed to step out again into the light of a new day.

"What if another person was killed?" Ava whispered to Tara, making sure to keep her voice low as they headed to their first class. "What if members of this Resistance are on campus? You saw Ambrose's letter. He said their attacks have been growing in intensity."

Ava's usual shadows followed a few feet behind her. When Ava first spotted Julian and Geoffrey, she took in their appearance and searched for new wounds or injuries that could corroborate her theory that they were somehow involved in the attacks.

"Members of The Resistance aren't violent," Tara said, sounding defensive. "It's propaganda, Ava. Whoever's doing this, it's not The Resistance."

With the tension still lingering from Saturday's events, Mrs. Kataros's casting class was a welcome distraction. It was clear Ava's classmates felt the same way.

Ava wasn't particularly confident in the paper she'd turned in, having spent only thirty minutes on it, but she tried to clear her mind during the forty-five minute lecture about different gemstones and metals used in casting rings and then spending the rest of the time moving objects up, down, left to right, even successfully casting water for a few seconds.

The instructor assigned another paper due the following week as well as hands-on practice homework of their craft. One thing became clear to Ava: Balancing friendships, classes, assignments, practices, and all the chaos would be difficult.

Even Mrs. Kataros had seemed different today—strained. After she'd collected their assignments and sent them off in groups, she spent the rest of the class at her desk, never raising her head to monitor them. Her cat, Gregory, did the same.

After class and lunch, Ava and Tara walked with Duncan and Colin to their shared history class.

"You guys hear anything?" Ava asked, hopeful for even the littlest detail as they took their seats in Mr. Viscardi's class.

Much like Mrs. Kataros earlier, Mr. Viscardi seemed downtrodden that afternoon.

Ava was certain they knew something. Tara and the others seemed to also notice, which only intensified the unrest the students already felt.

Ava decided to bite the bullet and ask Duncan a question that burned in her mind since Saturday night.

"Can you read his mind?" Ava whispered, her voice so low even Tara and Colin wouldn't hear. "Just to figure out what's going on, I mean. That's not some unspoken rule between vampires, is it?"

Duncan started to chuckle, but stopped as soon as Ava punched him in the leg.

"Vampires can't read other vampires' minds—and before you ask, any instructor with defenses low enough for me to read wouldn't be an instructor here at all."

"It was worth a shot," Ava mumbled. She gazed back at Mr. Viscardi, a man who probably had all the answers but wouldn't share them.

"Ladies and gentlemen, welcome," he said with a meek smile. "Today we'll veer from our syllabus and go over the history of shadow souls, the shadow court, and dark magic. Due to recent events, Headmistress Astrae feels it's appropriate for you to learn these topics sooner rather than later, in the unlikely event that any of you feel the curfews are too severe."

"Does that mean you have information on what happened—with that girl?" a werewolf in the back asked, showing just how fast word traveled.

"When information becomes available, it will be delivered by the headmistress herself, I assure you," Mr. Viscardi said. "Until then, I advise everyone to take a deep breath and keep your imaginations in check."

"Easier said than done," Colin whispered, loud enough for those around him to hear.

"Now, moving on," the instructor said. "If you would all be so kind as to take one and pass it down."

Mr. Viscardi handed each row a heavy box filled with books.

"Once you receive your copy, open to page two hundred and thirty-two."

"What are these?" Ava asked, taking a book and letting it fall open to a blank page made of crystal and bound with silk. "There's no writing at all, just page numbers."

"It's an immersive lesson," Tara replied. "It allows the user to be transported back to a time when a significant event took place. To view it but not alter or interact."

"Only the most respected of magites are asked to donate their memories for these lessons," Duncan said, excitement evident in his voice. "I've wanted to try it for years. He's trying to buy our silence here, and it's working."

Ava flipped through the pages.

"We begin our field trip in three, two, one … Eisago." Mr. Viscardi's voice faded away.

Ava was in the mortal realm. That much, she was sure of. But it felt … different. It was like seeing a familiar face—one she'd seen before but couldn't quite place.

She stood in a small village off the coast, the cool night breeze sending shivers down her spine. Nearby birds chirped and animals scurried off to the bushes. The clearing was eerily still, no sounds but from those of the animals. Everyone, it seemed, was asleep, the nocturnal animals the only ones keeping her company.

Mr. Viscardi hadn't told the students much about this immersive lesson, or what to expect. She didn't know whether to stay or wander off to find everyone. She didn't even know if she *could* find anyone or if this was meant to be a one-on-one experience.

In the distance, from beyond the tree line, the sound of marching feet grew louder. The feet stepped in unison, like a practice drill of soldiers.

As their footsteps neared, Ava became uneasy. It was like something deep within her knew something bad was about to happen. Her instincts told her to run and find safety. To find the others.

Even though Mr. Viscardi had said they'd be observers, unable to interact one way or another, she couldn't shake the feeling that she needed to move. And *now*. She bolted to her right and hid behind a Sitka spruce tree that resembled the Cathedral tree.

That's why it felt familiar.

Here, now, the tree still promised to serve as a refuge for Ava. If she needed to, she could climb it, to get high enough out of reach from the approaching footsteps. It was silly, considering if they were magites and not mortals, it wouldn't matter how high up she was.

The footsteps grew closer, but no voices joined them. There was no danger, she reminded herself, as she peered around the tree to find a small army marching toward the village.

It was an army filled with members from all magites, but they weren't like the magites she knew. They were dark and ominous. They wielded or concealed weapons, which they seemed eager to use on whatever unsuspecting people they were about to awaken. Several of the soldiers were missing limbs.

They continued their way toward the village, elbow to elbow, footstep to footstep. Once they arrived, a tall one in the middle, whose face Ava was unable to make out, sent them off in every direction to the various homes. Once the soldiers were positioned, he raised his hand in the air and lowered it back to his side, signaling for whatever was about to take place.

The tall man remained in the clearing, while all the other soldiers stormed into the homes. The clearing filled with screams, cries from young children, and people pleading for their lives. It lasted for five minutes before silence returned to the town.

The soldiers rejoined their leader, one by one. The final person to return was a young vampire, covered in blood. Behind him, two men carried the weight of an unconscious man.

The leader examined the man from head to toe. He stared at him for what seemed like an eternity before he nodded and signaled the soldiers to bring him with them.

They retreated as quickly as they'd come, heading back into the trees, to whatever lay beyond.

The leader suddenly stopped short. He turned in Ava's direction, toward the Sitka spruce she had ducked and hid behind. Surely, it was too dark for him to have seen her. No, it was *impossible* for him to have seen her. Duncan had assured her of it.

With the knowledge she was safe, Ava drew in a breath and peered around the trunk of the tree.

The leader's black eyes glistened in the moonlight as he smiled back at her, his face visible.

TWENTY-SEVEN

Ava screamed. She sprinted away as the leader pointed in her direction, and his soldiers charged after her. Her legs weren't fast enough, she was sure of it—although she was too scared to turn around and confirm this. The wind pounded on her skin, the dark night making it hard to traverse the forest floor. She ran, ran as fast as she could, then—she was back in class. Mr. Viscardi and her classmates gaped at her.

"Ms. Jones, I know the trials of the shadow souls, shadow court, and all dark magic users can be disturbing, but are you okay? Do you need to step outside for a moment?"

Ava didn't respond; she shot up and ran down the steps toward the classroom door, drawing laughs from Layla's cohorts.

She collapsed in the hall. Her heart still raced, her eyes darted back and forth, looking for the man who had come for her with his army. The door to the classroom opened, and Ava tried to scurry off before she realized it was Tara.

"Ava, are you okay? What's going on?"

"After dinner. Passageway." Ava returned to her feet and

headed into class before Tara could demand more. There was no way she would tell what she saw twice.

For the remainder of the class, Mr. Viscardi lectured about the trials he'd shown the class—the part of class Ava missed—about the sentencing of the shadow souls, witches and warlocks who had used their powers for evil, and about the members of the shadow court and other dark magic users. They had all been sent off to serve an eternal sentence at Desmios. Mr. Viscardi assured the class that all such members had been tried and convicted. That whoever was responsible for the recent crimes at school probably operated alone. That even if the first attack hadn't been a freak accident, dark ones would never return to their former numbers.

Since Ambrose brought about order and peace, no such activity had taken place in their world—but the security measures instituted at Linhollow were necessary regardless.

Mr. Viscardi seemed to want to put the students' minds at ease. His tactic seemed to work; the students around Ava relaxed their shoulders and leaned back in their chairs.

But Mr. Viscardi couldn't explain away what Ava had seen. That man who had commanded an army with a simple wave of his arm, sending them to slaughter an entire village and then to chase after her. Something that wasn't supposed to even have been possible. A man like that, a man who could see what wasn't supposed to be there?

Could that man—whoever he was—have been brought to justice, no longer a threat to her or anyone else?

Ava was lost in her thoughts as Mr. Vicardi dismissed the students at the end of class—in pairs, per the new guidelines that had been implemented.

"Six hundred words by next week," he reminded the students as they packed up. "On my desk and in that bin as soon as you get in. Not a second later."

Ava gathered her things. She stuffed everything into her bag and hurried to catch Mr. Viscardi before he left.

Duncan, Colin, and Tara followed behind her.

"Mr. Viscardi, do you have a minute—"

He held up a hand before Ava could finish.

"I'm sorry, but I don't," he said, cutting her off. "Office hours are Saturdays and Sundays between twelve and two. Feel free to see me then."

"Okay," Ava replied, her eyes darting to the papers on his desk as he turned his back and packed up his own bag.

On a small piece of white paper scribbled in a sloppy handwriting were the words "Tonight. Cromwell Hall. Midnight."

Mr. Viscardi turned around and startled at Ava still standing there. "Did you need something else, Ms. Jones?"

Ava tried to think of something, to cover for the fact that she was snooping. "Are there any other books on these trials that I can read over before next week's class?"

At that, Tara rolled her eyes. She knew full well Ava was slammed already and had complained about how little free time she had this week.

"Sure, always happy to help a history enthusiast when I see one," Mr. Viscardi said with a smile. He bent down and opened his bottom desk drawer and handed her two large, dusty books.

Ava tried to feign excitement as she took them.

"Sorry about that," he said, coughing at the dust. "Not many students request additional reading."

"Thank you, Mr. Viscardi," Ava said.

"You're welcome. Bring them back next week, and I'll have some new ones for you."

"Oh, great," Ava replied, already hating herself for this white lie.

"What was that all about?" Duncan asked as they exited the classroom.

It annoyed Ava when Duncan chose and chose not to read

her mind. He always seemed to miss the opportunities when she would have welcomed it the most.

"And why'd you go all psycho during class?" he said. "It was a boring trial filled with geezers, Ava. You're a champion. Nothing should scare you."

"I'll explain tonight," Ava said as she checked over her shoulder to make sure Julian and Geoffrey couldn't hear. "No more talk about it until then. Eleven o'clock. In your game room. It's risky to do this when others are around—asleep or not."

"Our leader has spoken," Tara said, jokingly.

She didn't seem to understand why Ava shuddered at the playful nickname.

For the rest of the day, Ava did everything she could to keep the conversation from what had actually happened. She stuffed her mouth with food and laughed at Colin's bad jokes —anything to avoid the topic that paralyzed her mind. The other students who usually stared at her with guarded apprehension stared at her now as though she was a lunatic.

Later, Ava fidgeted in her room, watching the clock and counting down the minutes to eleven. She decided to take a break from Tara's questioning gaze and flipped through one of the books Mr. Viscardi had given her.

"You read this one," Ava said, tossing the other book behind her and hoping it wouldn't hit Tara in the head.

"All right, but you have to talk at some point."

"In one hour," Ava replied, staring back up at the clock.

"What am I looking for, anyway?"

"Their *leader*," Ava said. She didn't like the taste of the word in her mouth.

She flipped through the pages and was disappointed not to find anything about who led them. About what happened to him. Even though Ava had visited the past, she couldn't shake the feeling this man existed in the present.

Why he had wanted her, of all people, was a complete mystery—and one she would soon discover, after she investigated what Mr. Viscardi was up to tonight.

Ava navigated her way through the secret passageways that began to feel more like home as she and Tara met up with Duncan and Colin. They settled on the floor of the boys' game room in silence.

"He couldn't have seen you, not really," Tara said.

"Are you sure there wasn't someone from the past nearby? He could have been looking at them, not you," Colin added.

"I was there. I'm sure."

"So, what now?" Tara asked. "You think this unidentified man is somehow responsible for the attacks?"

"I … I don't know," Ava said. "That's what we have to find out. But to do that, we need more information. And they're not giving it to us, so we have to at least try and see why a history instructor would be meeting someone at midnight."

"Okay, lead on," Tara said.

Her word choice sent shivers down Ava's spine.

"Poor choice of words, sorry," Tara added with a sheepish grin.

The more time Ava spent in the passageways, the more she could visualize what lay on the other side. A sixth sense, maybe. She led them down several flights of stairs and through the hall to what should be the first floor near Cromwell Hall, although the stairs did continue down. If they weren't pressed for time, she would have gone down and seen where it led—it was the one direction that left her with a question mark.

Ava opened the wall, and she and her friends stepped out.

"If we get caught," Colin whispered, "this looks suspicious."

"You want to go back?" Duncan teased. He knew full well Colin was as curious as the rest of them as to what Mr. Viscardi was up to.

The light from Cromwell Hall shone as bright as day, the doors ajar.

Ava peered in, surprised to see Mr. Viscardi with Headmistress Astrae, Mrs. Avilasa, and a handful of other instructors she didn't recognize.

Ava gave her friends a thumbs up and backed away. She signaled them to copy her and place their ears as close as possible to the open door without making a sound.

"Thank you for coming," Headmistress Astrae said. "I know this is unorthodox, but these are not normal circumstances. With Mr. Burrow's body having been found and young Dana being stuck in some sort of trance all in the same night, it's wise to keep our circle tight."

"Headmistress, if I may," Mr. Viscardi's interjected, "the students were uneasy today. The immersive lessons helped, but we need to let them in on what's happening, if only to keep them alert."

"I disagree," a female voice Ava didn't recognize chimed in. "To tell them will cause more chaos. No. We wait until we've apprehended the assailant, until we've determined what dark magic is at work and whether The Resistance is behind it."

"Keeping them from the truth is not why I brought you here, Meave," Headmistress Astrae said. "I will release something brief about Mr. Burrow's murder and Dana's current state. What we're here for is to—"

Colin slipped and collided face-first with the door.

"What was that?" Mrs. Avilasa asked.

A few chairs scraped back on the marble floor, before Mr. Viscardi offered, "I'll check it out."

Ava and her friends bolted, rounded the corner and tucked themselves into a small alcove, hoping Mr. Viscardi would look outside the door and not go any farther.

As his footsteps grew nearer, Ava whispered to Duncan, "You've been working on glamours, right? Try now!"

"It doesn't work like that—I've only done it once or twice."

"Do it again. *Now*."

Duncan's face became strained as Mr. Viscardi's footsteps rounded the corner. The instructor slowed his pace and took more deliberate steps down the empty hallway, stopping in front of their alcove. Before he turned around, he turned to the left—to where Ava and her friends stood, crammed against each other, frozen and holding their breaths. To where hopefully he saw a blank wall.

He turned on his heel and retraced his steps. "False alarm, we're all clear," he called out. "Must have been Mrs. Kataros's cat. Loves to run the halls, the little fiend."

The doors of Cromwell Hall shut behind Mr. Viscardi with a loud bang.

"Oh my goodness, Duncan, you did it," Tara whispered.

Ava and Colin let out a loud sigh.

"I literally felt my heart beating out of my chest," Colin added. "I thought we were done for."

Ava smiled up at Duncan and patted him on his back.

Duncan's face remained grave. "It didn't work," he said. "He saw us."

Duncan had no trouble convincing everyone to head back to their dorms without trying to listen in on the rest of the instructors' conversation.

Ava wanted to protest. She needed to know more. Needed to know whether The Resistance or her parents would be mentioned, but she'd been outvoted. For whatever reason, Mr. Viscardi had let them go, and no one wanted to stick around to understand why.

Ava sat in Mrs. Avilasa's flying class with Tara the next day, and she couldn't help but sulk. Not only hadn't they discovered more about the assailant, but their worst fears had also been confirmed: Another person had been murdered. This time, an instructor named Mr. Burrow, and the whole thing was somehow connected to Dana's episode. There was no rhyme or reason to the attacks, but it seemed nobody was off-limits. And Dana, who had still not returned, was in some sort of trance, traumatized by the whole thing.

Ava was no closer to uncovering the truth, and after yesterday's disaster of a history lesson, she was scared. Duncan was so sure Mr. Viscardi had seen them, but it made no sense. Mr. Viscardi, an instructor of all people, had no reason to lie for them, a bunch of nobody kids.

Then there was the fact they couldn't share any of the information they had learned last night, unable to answer how they had gotten it without digging themselves into a hole Mr. Viscardi had kept them out of.

Ava studied her *Department of Flying Vehicles* handbook and tried to focus on her class, but it all seemed irrelevant in light of the events that plagued the school. She wanted to do some-thing besides act as if everything was fine. She didn't want to witness someone else falling victim—and, if she could, she wanted to find a way to help her parents.

"All right, class," Mrs. Avilasa said, pulling Ava away from the abyss that were her thoughts. "Close your books and continue whatever you haven't finished on your own time.

Now, I know you'd all rather be on the grounds, flying high as you look down on this classroom rather than sitting in it, but who can tell me something they've learned that will help prepare them for when we do that again next week?"

Tara's hand shot up, as usual, along with a few other students.

"Ms. Jones, what have you taken away from today's lesson that will help prepare you *and* also help you in the upcoming Assembly Games?"

Mrs. Avilasa seemed to don her coach's hat as her eyes bore into Ava and willed her to say something of substance, something that would show she was a champion.

"I learned how to close my broom and make it small enough to fit in my pocket, which would have come in handy during the tryouts—provided I have the proper permits," Ava said.

"And Mr. Cawthorn, what about you?"

Her fellow champion, Evan, blushed when all eyes turned toward him. "Personally, I'll look for a broom that better suits me and my flying style. What it's made of and how I respond to it. There were a lot of options during the tryouts, and had I gone another direction, I could have made better time."

"Wonderful," Mrs. Avilasa said. "I want you all to think of three things you would have done differently after you finish your reading for the week and be prepared to put it into action next week. Now, before you head off to lunch, I want to inform you that Headmistress Astrae will be making a statement, so don't be late."

"It is with a heavy heart that I stand here before you today," Headmistress Astrae said, acknowledging the students who packed Cromwell Hall with a slow nod. "While we are all grateful Dana Pennington survived her attack, she remains in an agitated state and under strict observation. At this time, she cannot provide any details as to *what* took place. Furthermore, that same night, we lost another: Mr. Burrow."

The headmistress gestured toward a portrait that two fairies had flown down and placed on a wooden easel.

Mr. Burrow.

The instructor from the kelpie ride who had treated Ava so poorly. Ava hadn't even known his name but now recognized him.

"While the dead cannot cry out for justice, we will, and justice will be served," the headmistress said, before pausing to take a deep breath and forcing a weak smile. "We will now hold a moment of silence for Mr. Burrow."

The headmistress' remarks left everyone shaken, and none of the students finished their meal.

Even though Ava and her friends knew the gist of what would be announced, they had been just as surprised as everyone else upon finding out whose life had been lost.

Somehow it made it worse that it was, again, someone Ava knew. Not that she would wish it on anyone else, but she couldn't help but see a pattern. First, Tori, a girl Ava had indirectly gotten in an altercation with, and Mr. Burrow, someone Ava had a fleeting negative encounter with.

If someone targeted people she knew, why go after them? Why not her friends? The people she was closest to?

A dark part of her wondered if maybe whoever was responsible didn't intend to hurt her, or those she cared for, but targeted people with whom Ava had issues with, no matter how small. As if they wanted her to know they did this for her.

The first thing that came to her mind was The Resistance, the group Tara was so certain wasn't responsible for everything that had happened but was somehow everywhere. The recent attacks had even pushed the release of the profiles on all the champions to the back page.

Speculation about the group was everywhere Ava looked; all anyone talked about.

If any of this was done for Ava's sake, a beacon for some sort of a resurgence of a political ideology, Ava needed to think of ways to fight back, and fast.

"This is the worst practice," Evan whispered to Ava. "I'm about to fall asleep. If she makes us sit here and listen to this for a second longer, just end me."

Ava laughed. Evan started to grow on her. Despite his ability to only have a superficial conversation, he was one of the few champions for the witches and warlocks who didn't treat her like a pariah.

Ava's other teammates for the Assembly Games also seemed to be close to nodding off in Mrs. Avilasa's classroom as she droned on with her lecture.

"Something funny back there?" the instructor asked. "You two won't be laughing this time next week if you aren't prepared for whatever is thrown at you. Now, I understand this isn't as fun as some of our other practices, what with you confined to this classroom, but you will thank me later. So, listen closely."

Ava wiped the smile from her face and sat up straighter.

Mrs. Avilasa was right. It was important to know how to deal with the various creatures she listed off that may or may not appear in the Games. But it was hard to try to take in so much information after already having been in class all day.

These training sessions started to become the only time she

could work out her aggression, which was hard to do sitting behind a desk or with her feet firmly on the ground.

Everyone wished they had more time to train—especially after the profiles on some of the other champions had been released—but Ava felt ready. Over the last couple of days, she'd even devised a plan on how she would counter The Resistance's attempts to use her as a pawn.

Mrs. Avilasa had mentioned earlier in the week that whichever magite won and took it home for their kind would have the opportunity, however briefly, to make a statement the whole world would hear. Typically, this would be something along the lines of, "We're so honored to have been able to do this for our kind," or "It was a team effort, one we are all grateful for having been a part of this year—and hopefully next year as well."

Ava had a different idea for what she would say, one she hadn't told anyone about yet. One that relied upon her winning. One she planned to discuss with Duncan after Mrs. Avilasa released them for the night.

That night, Ava watched the clock and waited for the time when Tara, Mira, and Kailani would be fast asleep, letting her slip out unnoticed to go and meet with Duncan.

Per a note to Duncan at lunch, he knew the plan and, after he'd read her face and possibly her thoughts, had agreed without any questions.

"I don't understand how Harold Sharp was listed as this year's person to watch," Kailani said for the third time that night. "He's a sophomore and hardly holds a candle to Leith Tullius, the person I know will bring us home the win this year."

"Can you really say that with Ava right there?" Tara asked. "Where is your loyalty?"

"Ava, I'm sure you'll do fine," Mira said. "But Duncan and the others have this on lock. I've watched the practices, and what I'm trying to say is you're all wrong." She gave a toothy smile.

"These profiles are going to be the death of me," Ava said, throwing her pillow over her face. "I can't believe we're all obsessing over them like this. Put me on the field, and I'll deliver."

"Oh, you're mad because you didn't like that they mentioned all the rumors, that they called you a dark horse that shouldn't have been allowed to compete," Kailani said. Seeing Ava's face, she added, "Clearly I don't agree with them, but I do think you're being prejudiced here."

Ava feigned fatigue and pulled the covers up to her neck. "I'm going to sleep. I have practice again tomorrow. You'd all be wise to follow my example."

"We haven't even discussed the rankings yet, Ava!" Kailani said, as though she wanted to get a rise out of her. "That could take hours!"

Ava lay there and pretended to be asleep for what seemed like hours. The others finally climbed into bed and shut off their lights. Ava didn't stir again until she was sure they were all asleep.

Ava pulled back her covers and tiptoed out of bed, praying no one would wake up. She left the door to their room open a crack and made her way to the game room.

Once inside the secret passageway and the walls had closed behind her, she let out a sigh of relief. That had been more difficult than she thought, and the good sleep she feigned would not be hers tonight.

Ava raced to where Duncan should have been waiting for her. She listened against the wall for a moment before she knocked three times, then waited for him to respond.

To avoid getting caught, they had devised a secret code.

Duncan responded with four knocks of his own.

When Ava opened the passageway, she was surprised to see Colin step in with Duncan.

"He caught me as I tried to sneak out—said he'd sound the alarm if I didn't fill him in," Duncan said. "Rather annoying, he is."

Duncan sounded like he was only half-joking.

"Okay, fine," Ava said. "But if either of you tells Tara before I do, she will have all our heads and then some."

Ava now wished she had filled Tara in. She didn't want her friend to feel like the odd one out. A feeling Ava knew all too well.

"Fine," Colin agreed.

"Understood," Duncan added.

"I got this letter from Ambrose after the tryouts," Ava said, taking the letter out of her back pocket and handing it to Duncan. "He mentioned The Resistance and how they're trying to use me—that the organization may be the reason my parents didn't come to the Lost Ones Ball."

Duncan took the letter and gave it a quick read before he handed it to Colin, who did the same.

Once they finished reading, Ava began again, "I think this is all connected. The attacks, they're all against people I've had an issue with, even Mr. Burrow. It can't be a coincidence."

"So, what are you thinking?" Duncan asked. "Someone in The Resistance is eliminating anyone you've had an altercation with? Why? What does that do for them?"

"Or it may be someone who wants to make it look like someone from The Resistance is responsible," Colin said. "It could be that, considering the majority of magites are against them."

"It's not enough to go on, especially when last week, you thought Julian might be responsible," Duncan added. "He's not The Resistance, and Ambrose would never sanction that.

My dad and the other Elders would never be on board with killing for political gain."

"It's a feeling I can't ignore." Ava grabbed the letter from Colin and folded it up. "And this isn't going to end until someone—me—stands up and makes it end."

"How do you expect to do that?" Colin asked, baffled.

"For starters, I'll win the Assembly Games and have my moment in the spotlight to draw them out, to come for me."

"Two things," Colin said. "First, it's a little cocky for you to assume you're not only going to beat my kind but also our boy Duncan here. Second, that's insane, Ava. You can't invite someone going around, undetected by the instructors and seekers sent by the High Court, and challenge him or her to come for you."

Ava turned to Duncan. She wanted him to tell her it would work. That her plan would end the violence.

"It'd be a death wish," Duncan said, avoiding her eyes.

"It's what I have to do, and you can't tell Tara," Ava said. "This is my life. It's my parents who are missing, my name that's on the line, and people I've had issues with who are being murdered. I can't sit by and do nothing. I've done that my entire life, and I won't do it now."

Duncan and Colin exchanged a nervous look.

"Well, you're not doing it alone," Duncan said.

"Yeah," Colin chimed in.

"And you're not doing it until we've talked it out more," Duncan added, with a sternness to his voice Ava had yet to hear from him.

"Okay," Ava said, a grateful smile creeping across her face that brightened the dim passageway in the darkness of night. "Deal."

TWENTY-EIGHT

The next morning, Ava woke again to screams—and more troublesome news. Another student had been attacked, although this time they'd survived. It had been Carey—and in her own room. A room in the *same* dorm as Ava. What had everyone in a complete panic was the fact that someone had gotten past the seekers, who had replaced the instructors stationed outside their dormitories, navigated through the building unnoticed, and attacked the girl so quietly, even those who slept a few feet away weren't awoken by it.

For days after, Ava couldn't help but wonder if the assailant had snuck through the living quarters at the same time Ava had left or returned from meeting with Duncan and Colin. If she had missed him or her by mere minutes or seconds. If she could have prevented this. It was a secret she, Duncan, and Colin shared and wondered about in the days that followed.

The boys tried to console Ava—out of Tara's earshot—saying she couldn't have prevented this latest attack. But Ava didn't believe them. Not if they were connected. Whether it was The Resistance or Julian, she could have stopped it. She knew that much, even if she didn't know how she would have stopped it.

The next few days, Ava waited until Tara, Mira, and Kailani fell asleep, then snuck down to the living area to wait. To watch. To guard, even. Whenever she wasn't in class or at practice, she was there. Sitting in the living quarters, waiting. She'd do her best to not fall asleep, to stay alert. But at some point, Tara would always come down to wake her, surrounded by the books she'd pretended to have fallen asleep studying.

Initially, Tara had been suspicious. She knew Ava valued her sleep and relationship with her pillow. After a few days, her curiosity had been appeased as she'd seen Ava continue with the pattern.

It pained Ava to lie to Tara, but she'd already involved too many people and she couldn't drag Tara into this, knowing about her grandma and everything she had gone through. The unwarranted house checks, the strange looks she'd received on the street—no, Ava wouldn't tell Tara of her suspicions until she had proof. Or until after The Assembly Games. Whichever came first.

With the Games only a day away, Ava's roommates had urged her to get a good night's sleep. Ava pretended to be on board with this plan of action, but as soon as they'd all fallen asleep, she'd gone back down to the common area, not closing her eyes until the sun rose.

"Ava, *seriously*?" Tara screamed, shoving her awake as she glared at Ava in frustration. "Today is *the* day, and you didn't even have the thoughtfulness to keep your promise and sleep. You're not only messing with your chances but *our* chances as well."

Tara meant the witches and warlocks taking home a second win in three years.

"I'm good, I'm ready." While Ava's body screamed at her that this was a lie, her mind felt alert, ready to tackle the day head-on.

"I hope so," Tara said. "This means a lot to us. Go get ready."

Despite her body's resistance, Ava was dressed within minutes. It was incredible what the mind could overcome when the stakes were high enough.

The only thing the uniform for the Assembly Games had in common with their school uniform was the color: teal. But instead of denim for the pants, Rhapso had changed the game uniform to a black, spandex-like fabric that would allow the participants to move freely without being hot. The teal tank top was made of the same material and clung to Ava, making her uncomfortable.

Ava and Tara met up with Duncan and Colin, as planned, and made their way to the stadium. Geoffrey, the only one to greet her that morning, had even wished her good luck—although he didn't sound sincere.

When they arrived at the stadium, Ava became uneasy. Her whole plan hinged on winning this thing with her fellow teammates. From the sounds that emanated from the stadium, the number of people in attendance was much higher than the tryouts.

As they made their way in, Ava's suspicions were confirmed. The stadium was packed, every row appeared to be filled. Men and women paced the aisles, hawking items from Polianne's Parlor of Tricks or Treats. The energy from the crowd was palpable as everyone awaited the start of today's events with excited chatter.

Before Ava and Duncan said their goodbyes to Tara and Colin, Ava leaned in and whispered to Tara, "I'll explain everything after."

To her surprise, Tara nodded and asked no questions—a first for Tara, aka Arat Asoraled.

"Are you ready for this?" Ava asked Duncan as they made their way to the edge of the field to take their places next to their respective captains.

"Since your whole plan hinges on you winning, you better hope I'm not," Duncan joked, taking the steps two at a time and forcing her to do the same to keep up. "You sure about this?"

"I'm sure." Ava smiled. She wished she felt more confident than she sounded.

Headmistress Astrae and Ambrose exuded the regal bearing of a king and queen as they smiled at the attendees from their luxury box seats beneath the announcers. A camera whizzed and stopped in front of them, flashing their faces on the jumbotron, their microphones floating in front of them.

"Hello, hello, how's everybody doing today?" Ambrose boomed into the mic. "Let's make some noise!"

The crowd erupted into cheers.

Ava kept her head down next to all the competitors on the field as Matthias handed out emergency flares.

"It's a beautiful day for the three-hundredth anniversary of our Assembly Games," Headmistress Astrae said when the cheering died down. "With all the heartache we've experienced these last few weeks, today's Games are about honoring those we've lost. It's about showing whoever's responsible that they can try to steal our joy, try to steal what connects us, but they will never win."

Headmistress Astrae relinquished the floor back to Ambrose.

Ambrose looked straight at the press this time and added, "We have several leads on the perpetrator. In fact, I can assure you all by the end of the day—with the help of my team—we will not only celebrate this year's champions but also the assailant being taken into custody."

This appeared to be news to Headmistress Astrae, who did her best to mask her surprise.

"Without further ado, I'd like to commence this year's Games at the top of the hour and turn the casting over to Derrien and Jorina," Ambrose said. "Enjoy, everyone! We're all in for one heck of a ride."

Ambrose smiled and took his seat next to Headmistress Astrae and the other members of the faculty.

Mrs. Avilasa turned and faced Ava and her team of witches and warlocks. "Okay," she said, "you've all prepared for this moment. Over the last two weeks, we've gone over every imaginable thing that may be thrown at you today. Do your best to take everything in stride, not panic, and, most importantly, to work as a team when it's called for. Your greatest weapon in this isn't your magical powers, but your ability to work together as a unit."

All eight of them nodded in agreement as they watched the game clock count down.

"Alrighty, competitors," Derrien called out from his box seat high above. "Say goodbye to your coaches, and take your places because whether you're ready or not, this thing begins in two minutes!"

The music from the fairies above intensified as the competitors said goodbye to their coaches and followed Derrien's instructions. Fireworks exploded from the flying witches' and warlocks' brooms overhead that spelled out, "Three Hundred Years and Still Going Strong!"

Ava glanced around her, at the same people she'd spent so much time observing in the winners' lounge two weeks earlier. From her observations, there was a handful she considered serious competition, having also caught glimpses of them during training and through their profiles in the papers.

Ava directed her attention to Ambrose, seated near the finish line as he laughed and spoke with the press, and tried her best to read him.

He seemed calm enough, as though this would all be over today. Perhaps she wouldn't need to make the speech she'd written with Duncan and Colin last night. She wouldn't need to reopen Tara's deep wounds and jeopardize their friendship. Perhaps Ambrose would even have good news about her parents.

Perhaps they were here.

With so many new developments, Ava's mind raced as she turned her attention again to the timer, which counted down the seconds.

Ava was prepared for anything. One way or another, this would end today. She hoped Duncan and Colin were wrong. That she wouldn't place a target on her back—but close a dark chapter to embrace the light of a new one. That she'd meet her parents. That she'd know more about herself. That the leader who'd sent so many after her was all in the past.

"Champions, we are ten seconds away," Jorina said. "Please take a ceremonial knee."

The competitors dropped to a knee. Ava kept one hand on her knee that was still raised, ready to push off at the bell's ring.

She peered at Evan, who nodded encouragingly to her, and then to Duncan, who stared straight ahead. He appeared focused and determined, probably more so because of the pressure of his father watching him from the stands.

"And we're off!" Derrien screamed.

Headmistress Astrae again pointed her casting finger as the entire field transformed before everyone's eyes.

To Ava's delight, the first obstacle was like the tryouts.

Large, moving pillars blocked the competitors from continuing forward; the best option again being to go over.

Ava and her fellow teammates gazed up to find four brooms hovering overhead for the eight of them. She and three others pulled them down and gripped them tightly.

"Okay, who's going with who?" Ava asked with a smile. Out of the corner of her eye, she watched the merpeople ascend the pillars. Their scale-like skin stuck to the rocks as they pulled themselves up. The fairies, to their right, already had their wings extended and began to rise from the ground, one after the other. The werewolves and vampires, on the other hand, took a different approach. Due in large part to their incredible strength, Ava suspected, they seemed to be preparing to toss their teammates up the wall. They'd be forced to then run across the tops of the pillars, jump, and weave to get to the next challenge.

"I'll go with you," Evan said.

With two to a broom, they caught up to the fairies, who had been in the lead.

Ava was in the driver's seat and did her best not to pay too much attention to anyone around her. She flew as high as she could and tried to find a pattern again. A way through that wouldn't result in getting toppled, needing to use their flare guns, or being tended to by the impressive number of healers who waited by the sidelines.

"There," Evan whispered, trying to keep his voice out of earshot of the other competitors with enhanced hearing. "Go straight ahead, to the right, left, and straight again."

Ava scanned the path Evan had chosen for a minute or so and agreed it was their best option. The first and last walls seemed stationary, unlike the others.

Ava flew back to her teammates and laid out their plan. After everyone agreed, they decided they would go in order of seniority and flying experience, with Ava and Evan going last.

If anything should go wrong with the path, the older students had the best shot at recovering.

The first pair, Nestor and Zoe, who were senior co-captains of the team, took off and sped ahead as some of the fairies did the same.

Above the field, blindfolded fairies and witches flew about and dropped various objects meant to slow or take out the competitors. From their hesitancy, it was apparent they hoped they wouldn't take someone out from their own kind.

"It looks like we're about to see some action, everyone," Jorina said. "Buckle up and be glad you're sitting in the stands, because this may become really bumpy."

Ava ignored the announcers as they nervously waited for the second and third groups to go after the first had made it through. All of them had avoided being hit. Now it was Ava and Evan's turn.

She'd done this before. She'd done this before.

With Evan's arms wrapped around her, Ava took off and flew straight ahead. After they'd cleared the first pillar, Ava hovered for a moment before she sped ahead to the right as a pillar began to lower, then to the left, then straight ahead toward the last, unmoving wall.

"The witches and fairies have all cleared the first challenge!" Derrien called out to the crowd.

"Not surprising when you consider they had a significant advantage," Jorina added. "But it's important to note that of the four challenges our champions will face today, each will have a challenge that has been tailored to their strengths—so don't consider anyone out yet."

Ava landed past the finish line and stole a quick glance behind her as she and Evan dismounted. Countless merpeople, vampires, and werewolves were atop several of the pillars, waiting for their moment to jump. A handful were already across.

Ava closed her broom and placed it in the opposite pocket

to her flare gun, which she hoped none of them would have to use.

"Ouch, everyone—it looks like our first champion has fallen," Derrien said. "Jaelyn, a merwoman, missed a jump and is being escorted off the field."

"So early on to have anyone out, this could prove catastrophic for their team as the challenges only grow in intensity from here," Jorina added.

Ava felt for the merwoman who had fallen, but it also meant her team was one step closer to victory.

Zoe pulled Ava's team away from the distractors on and off the field and gave them a pep talk. "I know your nerves are setting in, but this isn't my first rodeo. I've competed before, and you must stay diligent about what's ahead, not what's behind. If you don't, it'll be you who will be carried out next on a stretcher."

They all nodded, taking in the full weight of her words.

They pushed forward as the field transformed again in front of them. Gasps resounded from the spectators as well as the competitors on the field.

In front of them, separated into five spaced-out groups, lay countless bodies—bodies of people they recognized—Tara included. Friends to family members. They laid unconscious on the field and showed no signs of stirring as walls of boulders sprouted up from the ground around them, rising high into the sky and trapping them inside.

"A challenge we haven't seen before incorporating those off the field as well as those on it!" Derrien exclaimed.

"You're right, Derrien," Jorina added. "Each of our champions will have to find a way to get inside those giant boulders to rescue their closest friends and carry them to safety. All the while, lightning birds above them will do their best to make sure that doesn't happen."

"Oh, and here's the catch," Derrien added. "The unconscious friends have all been given an undisclosed potion, which requires an antidote. The champions not only have to rescue their friends, but do it in time to save their lives!"

The spectators exploded with wild whoops and hollers, the added pressure on the competitors only intensifying the audience's viewing pleasure. Chants erupted throughout the stadium, although they were hard to make out.

Flying wasn't an option. Not really. While Ava's broom could hold two people—which her team had proven in the first challenge—it would be impossible for Ava to fly the broom *and* carry an unconscious passenger on it. Even the fairies seemed to have ruled out flying and, instead, tried to move the boulders in their own station to make their way into the center.

The massive boulders refused to budge even the slightest bit.

"We're going to have to try to move them another way," Nestor screamed above the noise.

"You mean levitate the boulders away, one by one?" Zoe asked.

"Yes," he replied. He didn't look happy about the time it would take to do so. He turned to the lowerclassmen. "You've practiced this before. Do your best, but it's up to me and Zoe to carry the load here. We have the most experience."

Nestor turned his back to them to face the boulders, which were stacked twenty feet high. Everyone followed him, looking at the challenge with fierce determination, wanting to free their friends and to get them the antidote before time ran out.

Jorina had said, "Two of them have been given a lethal dose of the potion."

Ava concentrated, along with the others. She pointed her casting finger toward the rocks at the top. Her mind tried to visualize them moving with a mere flick of her finger. The weight of the boulders required an immense amount of effort and concentration, causing Ava's hand to shake.

Around her, the other magites had different ideas.

Some of the vampires and werewolves climbed to the top of the boulders and attempted to topple them. The merpeople, again scaled up and did the same—only much slower. All were careful to avoid pushing the boulders inward where their friends and families lay.

The fairies were split between creating wind gusts to move the boulders and shooting fire and ice from their hands to break the boulders to tiny pieces. Their wall began to shrink as, one by one, the rocks were moved or broken.

Ava started to get the hang of it, regardless of only having practiced on much smaller objects. Every part of her body burned as if she physically moved the rocks. Her mind felt drained from the pressure and the fear that Tara would be the one of the two people to have received the lethal dose. Ava hadn't even been honest with Tara that morning. Once Ava got her out, she planned to never hold anything back from her friend.

"It's taking *too* long," Zoe yelled. "We're not even halfway."

The vampires and werewolves had one-fourth of the way to go.

Ava let her hand drop, much to the frustration of everyone else on her team.

"Quitting already?" Cecelia, a junior teammate, yelled a couple of feet behind her. "I know this may not mean anything to someone like you, but it does matter to us, you impossibly selfish girl. Everything they said about you is true." She turned away and focused once more, and no one else dared to say a word in Ava's defense to incur Cecelia's wrath.

Ava stepped closer to the wall. Zoe screamed at her to move out of the way as boulders continued to fall—some not where they were supposed to land. Ava ignored her, coming face to face with the lower boulders, placing her hands against them. They were rough and smooth at the same time, cold and solid.

Ava was unsure if this would work like the walls in the school, and she also was unsure if she wanted anyone to know what she was capable of, but she had to try. For Tara.

With her eyes closed, Ava pictured the boulders shifting and creating a path that would lead inside.

The boulders moved beneath her hands, and a shimmering gold entryway materialized.

"Well, that's something you don't see every day, right Jorina?" Derrien said, in shock.

"Indeed, that type of magic is rarely seen except in the most gifted of witches and warlocks," Jorina replied. "It's not something even taught at this school, and it's even more likely to be a gift she didn't realize she had."

Ava opened her eyes. She met the gaze of Cecelia, the girl who had berated her, who now placed a firm hand on her shoulder and nodded her approval.

Ava stepped in first. She ran over to Tara and tried to drag her out. Even with Tara's petite frame, Ava struggled to move her more than a couple of inches at a time. She continued to pull her, little by little, until she made it back out the stone wall. Cecelia ran in next to retrieve her friend.

"There's about five yards between us and where we need to take them, I reckon," Nestor said. "We're going to have to get creative."

"We'll levitate them, like with the boulders," Ava said, more out loud to herself than to Nestor. "The boulders have to have weighed more than any of them, I'm sure of it."

Ava and her teammates used their casting fingers to raise the bodies of their unconscious friends off the ground and carry them through the air. They made their way toward the sidelines, where the healers waited to administer the antidotes. The witches and warlocks in the stands burst into cheers and wild applause.

But before Ava and her teammates could reach the sidelines, lightning struck the field ahead of them. The rumbling of thunder followed, shaking the ground under their feet. Three large birds, sporting the iridescent plumage of a peacock, circled overhead. Before their eyes, the birds' bodies morphed into one long lightning bolt before they struck again.

Ava and her teammates quickened their pace, trying to avoid another strike from up above.

"And we have our second group about to do their best to catch up with the witches, with the vampires on their tail," Derrien called out.

"Yes, and with their speed and strength, we expect the vampires to pass them in no time," Jorina added.

Another lightning bolt struck the ground inches away, and Cecelia lost her casting hold on her friend. The girl dropped with an uncomfortable thunk.

"You have to keep going," Ava yelled above the sound of more thunder. "If you leave her here, she will get struck."

"I know, and I can't do it," Cecilia shouted back. "I can't risk it." She reached into her back pocket and pulled out her flare gun, shooting it upward.

Cecilia's flare sent a shockwave throughout the stadium. She was the first person to willingly quit, instead of being forced to quit.

A small part of Ava wondered if that was the smart thing to do. To put your friend before your own victory, but Ava knew she could do this. She knew she could get Tara the antidote in time.

A few more feet, and they'd be home free. Most of the other vampires had already carried their friends over the sidelines to the healers, and their friends had received the antidote and recovered.

"We didn't need her, not if she's going to crumble under pressure like that," Nestor said. "There's too much on the line for anyone to show that kind of weakness, so if any of the rest of you wants to quit, do it now before one of us is relying on you later."

No one said anything.

Flashes of light filled the sky and hit the field again just as Ava's team was about to cross to safety. The lightning bolt hit the girl Nestor had been levitating. She convulsed from the electricity as the smell of burnt plastic filled the air.

Nestor rushed across the sideline, and the healers immediately tended to his friend. The crowd grew silent. The healers administered the antidote, but after a few moments of tense watchful silence, they carried the girl off the field on a gurney.

Nestor stared after her as they took her away. He appeared conflicted. He seemed unable to decide whether to follow her. As co-captain, he was in a terrible place of having to choose between staying with his team or following the healers to be by his friend's side when she woke up.

Before he could make a decision, Zoe addressed him. "She'd want you to finish, you know that."

With an anguished look, Nestor turned back to watch his teammates' friends receive their antidotes and wake up, one by one.

"What happened?" Tara mumbled as she came to.

A tremendous wave of relief coursed through Ava. "Nothing, absolutely nothing," she cried, hugging Tara. Ava felt re-energized and ready to tackle any other challenge, knowing her friend was safe.

"I can see that," Tara said, appearing confused by the chaos on the field. She then bolted upright in a panic. "Hey!"

"You're fine," Ava urged. "Don't worry."

"I know I am—but *he's* not."

Ava followed the direction Tara pointed, all the way to the field where Duncan carried Colin over his shoulder.

Ava's gaze continued upward to where three birds circled around him.

TWENTY-NINE

Duncan sprinted at a speed Ava didn't know he was capable of. At a speed she didn't know *anyone* was capable of. Even so, she feared Duncan wouldn't be able to outrun all three birds—which morphed between their plumage-peacock and pure lightning forms as they circled above the stadium—especially carrying the limp Colin over his shoulders. The birds streaked downward, connecting their bodies into one long lightning bolt headed straight for Duncan and Colin.

Duncan gazed up after hearing gasps from the announcers as well as the crowd.

Without thinking, Ava pointed her casting finger toward the streaking birds, sending them tumbling back, their super-sized bolt going with them.

The lightning—which had touched down—split the field down its center and sent flames into the air. Out of nowhere, seven alicorns with feathery, beautiful wings filled the sky and navigated around the lightning birds with grace. Their spiral horns glistened with every color of the rainbow as they carried, in their mouths, buckets of water, which they poured over the roaring flames.

"It looks like Mr. Stavros was spared a *very* unpleasant end to his journey here, thanks to Ms. Jones, a competitor on a different team," Derrien said.

"It says a lot about their chances this year if they already need to be rescued this early on and not even from a fellow teammate," Jorina added with no sympathy in her voice.

Duncan sped across the field and toward the healers on the sidelines before the birds regrouped. They were left to go after the werewolves, fairies, and merpeople, who clamored across the unstable field.

"Ava, you can't help other teams like that," Zoe said with a look of frustration.

Ava whispered to Tara, "I'll do it every time I can, and she'll have to deal with it."

Duncan locked eyes with Ava, a mix of shame and gratitude in that brief connection, and delivered Colin to the awaiting healers to get the antidote.

Ava's group moved on to the third challenge.

"I'll be watching," Tara yelled after Ava. "You'll do great! *Hermanas por vida.* Sisters for life."

Ava hoped so. She hoped she didn't lose Tara's friendship.

This time, the grassy field plunged deep into the earth to form two horizontal channels of water that ran from one side to the other. The water in the channel closest to them was calm while the second channel beyond the first appeared strong and turbulent.

After the tryouts, there was no way Ava would let any part of her body touch the waters. Ava pulled out her broom and restored it to full size.

"We'll fly over. Easy," Felix, one of the sophomores, said

with confidence, but a twitch in his eye made it clear he didn't believe it would be that easy.

As they mounted their brooms, wanting to maintain their lead, something shot out from the depths of the water. It splashed the entire field and temporarily obstructed their view.

When the water settled, they saw it.

A creature with six long necks and grisly heads with twelve dangling feet.

Within each of the creature's six mouths, three rows of razor-sharp teeth snapped in their direction. The noise the creature made sounded like a pack of a thousand angry dogs.

Its reach stretched from one end of the water to the other as well as high above. With the necks not even fully extended, they towered halfway up the stadium. With the necks fully extended, they would stretch the entire height of the stadium.

The witches and vampires were neck-and-neck as they discussed within their groups how to go about the challenge. The werewolves were close behind, followed by the fairies, then the merpeople who would have a significant advantage here.

"It's either flying or getting in these death traps!" Felix said, pointing toward the wooden boats that sat at the waters' edge. They appeared no sturdier than a piece of cardboard when compared to the beast.

"Then we're flying," Lucian, the other junior, said.

"Agreed," Ava said.

Ava raised her broom, mounted it, and gestured for Evan to climb on behind her.

The vampires, not surprisingly, started to make their way to the boats. Ava watched Duncan. Every fiber of her being willed him to make it to the other side unscathed. Not only because he was her friend, but also because she knew his dad sat somewhere in the crowd, judging his son's every move. Something she knew weighed on him. What he'd told her after the tryouts while they'd waited for everyone else to finish had been horrible. The reason he'd been able to push forward—to push through the pain that day. Since he'd come of age, his dad tested him nonstop with personal challenges to toughen him up. She wondered if his dad also had prepared Duncan for the scylla.

As she and Evan flew into the air, Ava tried to push her worries aside but her hands trembled. She tried instead to remember everything she could about offensive and defensive protection magic. Although they hadn't covered much in class, Ava and her teammates had practiced for the past two weeks. They'd pored over every book Mrs. Avilasa gave them in their spare time.

Only a couple hundred feet stood between them and the final challenge.

No clear path was visible. Unlike the first two challenges, the creature spanned the entire width of the field. It threatened any passersby with its teeth, legs, and sheer size.

"Give the vampires a head start," Nestor said. "Let the beast distract itself with them and some of the others."

They waited several minutes, watching as the vampires, then the werewolves, began to move forward. The merpeople and fairies followed afterward. To Ava's surprise, the merpeople dove into the waters and dodged the creature at incredible speeds.

It took every ounce of self-control for Ava not to follow them. To wait, allowing others to get ahead, was unbearable.

As the creature began to direct its attention everywhere else, Nestor and Zoe took off, leading the charge.

Ava and Evan followed on her broom, and Ava was grateful she had not eaten a heavy breakfast, what with the way her stomach churned. Every part of her told her to turn around, to go the opposite direction of the beast.

She ignored her mind and charged straight ahead.

As they bobbed and weaved, trying to take advantage of the distracted beast, they did their best to get through its interlocked appendages, which seemed to stretch everywhere. It was like she flew through a maze; one wrong turn and they would be in the waters, unable to continue.

As she navigated, the creature began to direct its attention to those in the water as well as those in the air. The number of magites around it seemed to infuriate it more. The high-pitched yelp that came out of its mouths hurt her ears.

Out of the corner of her eye, Ava saw the creature knock down a fairy from the sky. She'd fallen into the water and was no longer visible. Her teammates peered down for a moment, probably trying to decide if they should continue without her.

"Don't look down, only up," Zoe called, flying close by, her voice barely audible above the sounds that escaped the creature's grisly mouths.

Ava tucked her chin and called for Evan to offensively cast a shooting fireball as they approached one of the creature's unmoving necks to avoid crashing into it.

Evan obliged and burnt the creature's skin enough for it to move out of the way at the same moment they would have collided.

But just as Ava and Evan flew past the creature, *another* creature emerged from the depths of the stronger channel.

The announcers called it a charybdis. The scylla and charybdis went hand-in-hand—but they were two creatures Mrs. Avilasa had not prepared them for.

This whole time, it had lurked in the water below, not showing itself until they were directly above it.

The second creature—the charybdis—appeared to suck in the water, belch it out, and create a large whirlpool. Dangerous waters rose high above where they flew, and the competitors were unable to go any higher to avoid the waves.

The creature inhaled a boat and pulled the inhabitants deep into the water, but not before several flares shot up at once.

By trying to avert the charybdis, Ava and Evan were

locked into its whirlpool, which threatened to also pull them down. Ava tried dodging to the left, but almost ran into torrential waves. She tried dodging to the right, but the waves shifted in that direction. She tried going straight—but a wall of waves shot up ahead of her too.

They were trapped in the eye of the storm.

Ava tried to fly straight up, only to hit the invisible barrier to Linhollow. She and Evan tried to part the waters by casting an attack toward the creature below.

The waters closed in, engulfing them. They tried anyway, and moisture sprayed on their faces and shot up their noses.

"Ava, we should shoot the flare. We should end this before—"

"No!" Ava yelled and pushed his hand down. "This is not over!"

Beneath her, the creature's body revealed itself again. She cast a striking spell, hoping to burn the creature, and create a way out.

The charybdis rose above the water—thrashing with anger—and created a path for them to fly under.

They passed unscathed, breathing heavily, as the water tried to engulf them and steal what little oxygen they had.

Ava and Evan landed on the ground and collapsed, light-headed and terrified.

Ava took several deep breaths. Five of her teammates remained—Lucian and Lena, the second sophomore, were gone.

"They sent up flares," Nestor said.

They had quit. They had abandoned the team as Cecelia had done earlier.

"One more challenge," Ava said as she got to her feet. "We can do this, whether it's the five of us or eight."

A handful of the other competitors had also completed the challenge, and every team seemed to have taken a hit. Ava searched for Duncan as she followed her teammates forward, but she couldn't locate him. Instead, Ava locked eyes with a furious Layla.

"We are on to the final challenge, everyone, twenty minutes still on the clock," Derrien called out.

"With the witches and warlocks again leading and everyone else close behind, it's important to note this is still anyone's game," Jorina added. "This last challenge will prove to be the most difficult."

A new maze materialized on the field. The walls, made of perfectly trimmed hedges, rose so high, Ava was unsure if the people in the stadium could make it out. Beyond it, a final stone wall that stretched hundreds of feet into the air was the only thing Ava could see from the maze's starting point.

Ava and her team entered the maze and were immediately presented with the problem of whether to split up or face the challenge together.

Ava and Evan decided to go to the left, Nestor, Zoe, and Felix opted to go to the right. Their plan was to meet up in the middle and communicate through fireworks in the air: whoever found a clear path first would cast sparks toward the sky and thus alert the other party to backtrack.

"This isn't spooky at all," Evan said, following Ava down the first straight stretch to their left, nervously rubbing his head.

"We're minutes away from winning this thing—we'll be fine." As Ava said it, multiple sets of heavy footsteps seemed to approach and run all around them.

They jumped and searched for the source.

"It's our imagination," Ava said. She prayed she was right and hoped no one could see within the maze to observe how badly the sounds had scared them.

More footsteps echoed behind them, this time those of their competitors who were on their tail.

"Ignore them," Ava said. She did her best to follow her own advice.

They approached a junction where they had to make their next choice: left, right, or straight.

Evan glanced behind him.

"Going back is not an option," Ava reminded him.

Ava chose to continue forward. Evan seemed happy to merely follow Ava's lead, looking back over his shoulder every few seconds.

Layla and another vampire caught up to them and opted to go left.

While Ava was grateful they hadn't followed, she was still concerned she'd seen no sign of Duncan.

In the distance, screams filled the maze.

"Did that sound like Zoe?" Evan asked.

"No, I don't think so," Ava thought aloud. She knew full well the voice was indeed Zoe's but hoped her mind was playing tricks on her.

A flare with Zoe's name shot into the air seconds later.

Four left.

"She probably got separated from Nestor and Felix, is all," Ava reasoned. "We're fine. I doubt there's anything in here. It's most likely to see if we can conquer our fears, already having faced so much…"

"Right," Evan said. He didn't sound like he believed her anymore.

More screams resounded, and more flares shot up.

None belonged to their remaining two teammates—but whatever had caused their competitors to drop out must have been sudden and alarming.

The heavy footsteps returned. Ava and Evan turned, trying to spot the source, to find nothing but the green hedges of the maze.

All in their heads.

Ava and Evan pushed on.

Up ahead, they faced another fork: left or right.

Ava tried her best to picture the maze in her head, to picture the finish line. She turned right.

The maze opened into a large clearing, all paths leading here no matter which direction was taken. Nestor and Felix, along with Layla and her group and a handful of other competitors, stood perfectly still in different parts of the clearing.

Blocking their way forward were three massive creatures: chimeras. Each had the tawny, muscular body of a lion and three heads—a lion's with a shaggy mane, a hollow-horned goat's head, and a hissing serpent's head on top of its tail. All three chimeras stared at the competitors, preparing to pounce.

This was what had caused the footsteps. *This* was why so many had sent up flares.

As one competitor tried to approach, the creatures blew out fire from all three of their mouths, sending him running back.

Ava and Evan inched closer to Nestor and Felix, who were not far away.

"Look—around their necks," Ava whispered. "There's a ring full of keys on each one. We need to get our hands on them."

Nestor, the only captain remaining, asked, "And how do you expect to do that?"

"Sheer will and determination?" Ava offered with a shrug, then added more seriously, "One of us must be the distraction —the sacrifice."

Ava flew solo. Nestor flew next to her. Evan and Felix remained on the ground, offensively casting toward the middle creature. The creature jumped upward and shot fire out of its mouth—and Ava and Nestor narrowly missed having their brooms burnt to a crisp.

Beside them, a fairy hadn't been so lucky. His wings ignited as he fell to the ground. A flare from his teammate was sent up, and they were transported from the field.

Ava and Nestor dove toward the creature, two of its heads distracted by Evan and Felix.

The goat head locked in on Nestor, shooting flames from its mouth, scorching the boy's wooden broom. Its serpent tail snapped as Nestor got within striking distance. Nestor fell to the ground hard, and the serpent hovered over his body, prepared to strike. Nestor mouthed the words, "I'm sorry," and fired his flare.

Three remaining.

Ava was the only one left on her team in the air with a broom.

She inched closer, casting water as the chimera blew fire in her direction. The offensive attack from the creature met her defensive cast, canceling each other out.

The serpent's tail whipped toward Felix, who'd tried to get its attention away from Ava. With a snap of its head, the serpent stung Felix, sending him running back through the maze, his flare shooting up only seconds later.

Two remaining.

Evan was her lifeline. The only other person on her side in all the madness.

He struck again, distracting the creature long enough for Ava to swoop in on the lion head and grab the set of keys around its neck.

The head roared and blew fire at Ava as she turned to fly away. The flames torched the end of her broom, causing it to catch fire and burn her arm.

Ava fell to the ground with a loud thump. She rolled a few feet before she caught her bearings and turned back toward the creature, which now directed its full attention toward her.

It closed in and hovered over her. It peered down at her with its three heads, hauntingly, questioningly, as if it couldn't believe she had dared to get so close.

From behind her, Evan casted random objects to throw at the creature. It turned its heads long enough for Ava to get back up on her feet.

She glanced back at Evan, who urged her to continue, mouthing, "I'll be fine," as the creature changed its trajectory straight toward him.

She hoped he'd get his flare up in time to avoid its wrath.

One to go.

She was her team's last hope.

She had hoped they'd *all* cross the finish line together.

Ava ran forward into the far end of the maze while the other competitors still tried to get the two remaining sets of keys. She looked down at her hand, wondering what the twenty keys on the ring were for.

She rounded a corner of the maze and came face-to-face with a fourth chimera. She turned back to find a fifth — then a sixth.

They swarmed around her. She had nowhere to go.

She wished her broom hadn't been burnt to a crisp.

As they charged her, she held up her necklace. The same necklace her hands had been wrapped around when Ms. Kerpopple had found her all those years ago. The same necklace she had worn every day for the past thirteen years.

It was ridiculous. The griffins were high above the waters, back in Xarcadia. But she wouldn't surrender. She wouldn't quit with so much on the line. She had to try. She closed her eyes, content with whatever happened. As she did, her hair billowed around her head. The dirt from the ground sprayed in all directions.

A griffin—the same griffin Ava had ridden in Xarcadia—landed in front of Ava, shielding her from the chimeras. The chimeras didn't seem to know what to make of the griffin, eyeing it with curiosity and suspicion as they kept their distance.

The griffin opened its beak expectantly.

Ava had forgotten what to do until it locked eyes with her and nudged her arm. She took off her amulet and placed it in its beak. Once she did, the griffin knelt on the ground and dared the chimeras to strike, as it waited for her to climb on its back.

The griffin then rose from the ground and flew as high as the maze would allow.

Ava soared on its back, her arms outstretched, a smile on her face as it flew her up and past the chimeras and the maze.

It stopped outside the maze's exit and glanced back at Ava as if to ask if this was as far as he needed to take her. Ava nodded.

The griffin lowered to the ground in front of the towering stone wall. She hugged the griffin, then dismounted.

"Until we meet again," Ava said for the second time, but the griffin stayed close by as if to see her through to the end of the competition.

Ava stared up at the stone wall and noticed three massive locks on it. She inserted the first key into a lock, but it didn't open. She tried two more keys to no avail.

As Ava tried the fourth, then the fifth key, Layla and a few other competitors rushed up behind her.

Ava hurried as she put the sixth and seventh keys in. Each time, she waited for the wall to budge. But it didn't.

"It's a shame about Duncan," Layla yelled as she set to work on a different lock. "The chimeras circled him when I last saw him. He was in real bad shape, unable to even reach his flare. It's a shame to think what they're going to do to him."

"You're a liar!" Ava shouted.

But what if Layla wasn't lying? She hadn't seen Duncan since the start of the fourth challenge.

"Hey, don't listen to me—it'll be all over the press shortly," Layla said as she tried another key. "He's a couple of feet back if you want to see for yourself."

Ava stood, frozen, with the twelfth key in the slot, unable to move to the thirteenth.

If Duncan was in trouble, she would never be able to live with herself if she chose winning over helping him. But if she left, it meant giving up on her plans to end this when she was so close.

Ava dropped the keys and ran back to the griffin. She mounted him and directed him back toward the maze. Back to the chimeras.

Ava scanned the floor of the maze from up above for activity. Layla had told the truth.

"I can't believe she left him here," Ava said.

The griffin turned his head around and nodded at her with what seemed like sad eyes.

The chimeras circled Duncan, who lay on the ground. Parts of the skin on his arms were aflame, before it extinguished the next moment and reignited again.

Ava leaned forward, directing the griffin to swoop down, scaring away the chimeras. Ava hopped off the griffin's back.

"Duncan, are you okay?" Ava yelled, running toward him.

He'd not only been burnt, but he also appeared to have been stung multiple times. The poison from the serpent's tail left behind dark, raised welts on his skin.

Duncan writhed in pain, barely conscious. His flare gun lay several feet away on the dirt ground. Ava caught the griffin's eyes, and the animal seemed to understand. It grabbed Duncan gently with its beak and tossed him over its back. Ava jumped on, prepared to fly back and finish the challenge, hoping her keys were still there.

Before Ava could finish her thought, she heard the wall creak open. Deafening cheers from the crowd filled the air, and the maze disappeared.

THIRTY-ONE

"*Layla* won it for us?" Duncan asked incredulously. "Even after she shoved me down so the chimeras would circle me and allow her to escape? She reached into my pocket and tossed my flare gun aside. She told me *I* chose my fate."

"Not how she tells it," Ava replied. "Her speech was grandiose—she went on and on about how you sacrificed yourself, how you knew she was the one who'd be able to bring home the win."

Ava was grateful she hadn't had to listen to that speech.

In the craziness that had followed the end of the Assembly Games, she'd opted to stay with Duncan—needing her burn tended too—as the healers reversed his paralysis from the serpent's stings.

Thankfully, he'd only needed dragon's blood oil to make the poison leave his system, an antidote he'd gotten in time thanks to Ava coming to his aid.

No matter how bad it stung—and it did—that Ava hadn't won, she tried to take solace in Duncan's full recovery. She tried to remember the important things. That even though she hadn't accomplished what she sought out to do, even though she hadn't antagonized the assailant out of hiding, she'd saved her friend.

It was funny to think the reason Ava had fought so hard was to not only stop the attacks, but to also find her family—when she'd been surrounded by a family of her choosing since she'd arrived: Duncan, Tara, Colin, Mira, and Kailani.

The healers allowed them into the apothecary one at a time to visit Duncan. The school's apothecary bore many similarities to Healer Gwyn's back in Xarcadia. Warm hints of turmeric wafted throughout the room. A porcupine—one of the healer's familiar, Ava assumed—surveyed the room, monitoring all the patients closely.

The gentle aroma of turmeric relieved the tension in Ava's body with each breath she took. She was grateful for her teammates and friends. They were understanding and supportive that Ava gave up the win to save Duncan, since they would have done the same.

"I'm glad you're okay," Ava said, squeezing Duncan's hand tightly.

He shifted in his bed, a pink blush blooming on his cheeks.

"I'm okay because of you," he replied, squeezing Ava's hand back.

"Yeah, well, we seem to take turns saving each other—but by my account, I think I'm up at this point," Ava said with a laugh.

"I'll make sure to repay the favor," Duncan joked, coughing hard.

The poison still made its way out of his system, his body too weak to leave the apothecary for at least a week, the healers had said.

Thankfully, he wouldn't be alone. A roomful of other patients, Dana and Carey included, surrounded him. When Ava got there, Carey had been fast asleep. Despite their differences, Ava hoped the girl would be well enough to leave soon.

"Seriously, I know how close you were and how bad you

wanted to end this," Duncan said. "Thank you. And I have an idea. We can take everything we have to my dad and get him involved."

"That would be—"

"Duncan, my boy," a man interjected from behind them. "You came awfully close, and next year, I expect you to finish it. Don't ever let some girl like Layla Lelantos upstage you again."

A cold shiver ran down the length of Ava's spine at the deep voice. Her stomach turned at once, but she didn't understand why.

Ava turned her head.

The color drained from her face. The room threatened to spin around her. Her knees almost gave out.

The man who approached and stood in front of Ava—Duncan's dad—was the leader who'd sent all the dark ones after her in the immersive field during her History of Magic class. The man who shouldn't have been able to see her—but did.

"Ms. Jones, is it?" the man said, turning back toward Ava with a glint in his black eyes. "My apologies, I didn't see you. Thank you for your heroics today. If you will, though, I'd like to have a moment alone with my son if you could run along."

He smiled broadly at his last words. In that moment, she knew he knew. She knew it wasn't all in her head or some unwarranted fear. He knew Ava recognized him, and he was here, a foot away from her.

"Actually, Dad, we had something we wanted to talk to you about," Duncan said.

"Later ... we'll do it later," Ava said, forcing a smile. She turned on her heels, trying her best to keep her emotions in check as Duncan called to her and asked if she could visit tomorrow. She left without a reply, unable to utter a word, as she charged out of the apothecary like she was being chased by monsters, real and imagined.

That night, Ava spoke to no one. She had hardly come to terms with it herself and was not prepared to commiserate with anyone about it.

What if she was wrong? What if she had imagined it all?

Deep inside, she knew she hadn't and tossed and turned for hours as her mind waged war on her.

In the morning, she planned to somehow find a way to contact Ambrose. To inform him of her findings, that someone close to him was not only a dark one, but their leader. She didn't trust putting anything of this magnitude in the mail. Not when she didn't have Aurum shekels to pay for the protective magic to insure only Ambrose himself was able to open the letter.

Around one in the morning, Ava was about to drift off to sleep, her plan of action set, when she heard soft footsteps near her bed.

She rolled over, pulling the covers down to see Tara shuffling out of the room, appearing to be in daze or half asleep, clutching something in her hand.

"Tara, you okay?" Ava called out.

Tara continued walking. She didn't stop or turn even though Ava had spoken loudly enough for her to hear.

"Tara," she called again. But Tara stepped out of the room, leaving the door ajar.

Ava jumped out of bed and followed her.

Tara reached the base of the stairs, heading toward the game room.

"Tara, what are you doing? Seriously?"

Ava watched, incredulously, as Tara placed her palm against the wall and opened the secret passageway. She stepped through it and hurried down their normal path. She didn't even bother to seal it shut behind her.

Ava stepped through and closed it behind her so no one could follow.

She ran to catch up with Tara and placed a hand on her shoulder. Tara turned with a blank stare.

Ava stared into Tara's eyes. They were open, but there was no recognition there.

Ava took a step back, unsure of what to do other than to follow her.

At the location of Duncan and Colin's game room, Tara turned to the right and headed down the stairs, heading down to the lower levels.

Ava followed. Even though her body was sore from the day, Ava felt an overwhelming desire to protect Tara from whatever was happening to her. She'd never mentioned being a sleepwalker—but then again, she'd never mentioned she was able to create a passageway of her own, either.

Once they reached the first floor—the location of Cromwell Hall where they'd listened in on the meeting with Mr. Viscardi and Headmistress Astrae—Tara did something Ava didn't expect.

She continued down the stairs.

Ava followed Tara cautiously. The stairs opened into a large, dark area. Unlike the rest of the school, this floor appeared desolate, as if no one had ventured here in some time.

Tara roamed around, shooting fire into each of the candelabras that lined the circular room. She then made her way to its center and collapsed.

Ava ran over to her. "Tara, wake up. Are you okay?" Ava shook Tara and willed her to wake.

She didn't respond. The only movement was that of her rising chest as she took in breaths.

A heavy, ominous feeling washed over Ava.

They had to leave. They had to leave now. This was not a place she wanted to be alone, so far away from the rest of the school.

Ava looked down at Tara once more and considered her options. She could try to levitate or drag her, but the distance she'd have to do so—up several flights of stairs—would prove a challenge. She could leave and get help, but that would present a host of problems of its own. The biggest was that Ava couldn't leave Tara alone in this defenseless state.

Ava tried, futilely, to wake Tara again, so they could run out of there together.

Behind her, heavy footsteps pounded on the hard marble floor. Ava's heart skipped a beat, her eyes darted around the room as she remained protectively in front of her friend.

A man sauntered out from the shadows and into the dim light of the candelabras.

Ava let out a sigh of relief, her body relaxing.

"Ambrose, thank goodness, it's you," Ava said. "Something is wrong with Tara. She won't wake up. I thought she was sleepwalking at first, but I'm not so sure. Can you help me?"

Ava turned back toward Tara, expecting Ambrose to rush over. "I found something out about Elder Stavros—I think he may be the assailant, and it's not safe for us here so far away from everyone."

Ava turned back, but Ambrose hadn't taken one step toward them.

"Ambrose?" she asked again, unsure as to why he hadn't moved or responded to her bombshell about Duncan's father.

He met her eyes and laughed, cold and hard.

"Elder Stavros is not responsible for the attacks, at least not the ones *you* speak of," Ambrose said. He ran his fingers through his hair and shook his head.

"You made it easy," he continued. "I barely had to twist your arm to get you to trust me. You think it was a coincidence I stepped in right as Julian was about to tag you? In that most vulnerable moment? Or that a kelpie called to you, wanting to pull you under? Or that you ran out of oxygen so perfectly, you would have drowned if there'd only been one or two more minutes?

"This whole time, you've been eating out of my hand, believing that I would ever allow someone like *you*—someone who stands as a symbol to a mistake that never should have happened—to live. I've waited and waited, waiting for your parents to show their faces, waiting to wipe you all from existence, but it seems wherever they are, they don't care. Maybe they're dead, even. A real shame for me, my plans for them wasted."

Ava's stomach dropped to the floor. She tried to swallow, but her mouth dried up, leaving an acidic taste on the back of her tongue.

"I-I d-don't understand," she stammered. "You said it wasn't my fault. You told everyone it wasn't my fault and to accept me."

Ambrose sneered. "Telling the public what they want to hear about a thirteen-year-old girl was in my favor," he said. "Had that story not been leaked, you'd already be six feet under. My job is to shape the narrative, Ava, and I'm sorry, you can't be a part of that narrative anymore. I tried to let you live. I'm surprised Carey's attacks on everyone, even on herself, hasn't resulted in that stupid-excuse-of-a-headmistress locking you up." He unleashed another guttural laugh. "But, then again, she's always had a soft spot for crazy."

Something warm and wet ran down Ava's face. She raised her hands and touched it to find herself crying.

"What about her?" Ava asked, motioning toward Tara, who clutched one of the amulets Ambrose had sent Ava. "She knows nothing; I've told her nothing."

"I think we know that's not true," Ambrose said. "Even if my little gift to you brought her here tonight, there's no telling what she heard. Which is why, tonight, you'll watch her die—

before dying yourself, that is. In the morning, I'll solve the problem that's plagued the school and our security—you—as promised. I'll send search parties to investigate every inch of this place, and you know what they'll find? You and her. Murdering your best friend after she found out who you really were and then, feeling so terrible, you took your own life. I've worked too hard and come too far for anyone to get in the way of my plans."

Ava gaped at Ambrose. He was so calm for someone who talked about killing two innocent teenagers. She couldn't believe it

"Do you want to hear a little story, Ava? I mean, it would buy you a few more minutes of life, after all."

Ambrose cackled. He pulled over a dusty chair, its legs squeaking across the marble floor, and sat down with his arms folded and his legs crossed.

"You know this story—you just didn't know the main character was me," he said. "As a young man, I apprenticed to one of the oldest and most powerful witches of our time, one of the most powerful witches to ever exist, Aurora Cromwell. I tried, countless times, to reason with her, to get her to see her powers—our powers combined—could rule this world and make us unstoppable. But she decided again and again to ignore my pleadings. Talked about *doing no harm.*

"A warlock approached me shortly thereafter. He shared my views, and we plotted to steal her Book of Mystiká to do as we wished without her. Aurora cursed me, causing me to murder my whole family—something I'd wanted to do anyway—and turned me into some half-breed. She thought it was a curse, when in reality, it was the greatest gift she could ever have given me.

"She killed the warlock, took her book back, and created giant idiot dogs like Geoffrey to hunt my new kind ever since, but not before the warlock had held up his end of the deal. See, no one knows *I* was the first vampire—or that I was able to maintain all my warlock powers, unlike those that came after me. I've been superior to everyone from the start, and I have big plans for my kind and those loyal to me. Plans I intended on acting on soon before you brought a rise to The Resistance again. I want you to consider your death a sacrifice, a righteous act, like the warlock whose life was taken so *I* could continue. As was Aurora Cromwell, who met her death by my hand one hundred years later."

Ambrose stepped toward Ava with a broad smile.

"Goodbye, Ava."

He raised his casting finger and pointed in Tara's direction. He really did intend to have Ava watch her friend die.

Before Ambrose could follow through on his promise, another set of footsteps pounded the hard surface of the floor behind them.

"*Julian*, I told you to stand guard and make sure I wasn't interrupted," Ambrose snapped. "Is there *nothing* you can do right?"

For the first time, frustration broke through Ambrose's cool façade. "We wouldn't even be in this mess if you hadn't failed miserably at every opportunity you had to kill her yourself."

Unlike the first time Ava had met Ambrose, this time the tables were turned with Julian interrupting him. Whether it was planned or not, she didn't know. As far as Julian having had so many opportunities to see to her demise, she could think of at least one time he'd saved her—flying, high above the city. He could have let her fall, having good news to report back to Ambrose, but he hadn't.

Julian remained silent for a moment as he stared at Ambrose. He turned to Ava and saw Tara on the ground.

"You think I could stand outside after everything she's caused us?" Julian asked. His anger made his voice tremble as he shot daggers at Ava with his glare. "Wake her," he said darkly, pointing to Tara. "Let her watch her friend's face as she dies."

"I see," Ambrose said as he took his words in. "You think she should be awake for this? A game of cat and mouse, even?"

Ambrose considered this for a moment, then broke into a delighted laugh. "I knew you were a dark individual all these years, but I never..."

Ava had misread him. Julian had let her live for this sick, twisted moment of pleasure. A way to impress Ambrose, his master.

Tara began to wake. She got to her feet, shaky and disoriented. The amulet fell from her hand. At first, she didn't seem to understand until Ambrose began to speak.

"Would you like to do the honors?" Ambrose asked Julian. "But she," he gestured to Ava, "is mine."

"There would be nothing that would please me more," Julian said. "Your will be done, Ambrose."

Julian stepped toward the girls, his back turned to Ambrose as he approached.

Ava watched as Julian's face shifted from anger to despair. His eyes reflected sadness, regret, and love all at the same time. He mouthed the word, "Run."

At first, Ava had thought she'd misunderstood, until he did it again. Ambrose grew impatient and asked what the holdup was.

Ava and Tara exchanged a flash of understanding before they burst into a sprint.

Ambrose screamed in a strange language Ava didn't understand but knew, somehow, was evil. Right as they reached the stairs, back to the passageway, the fighting began. Bodies struck the wall, screams erupted as the men fought for their lives.

"This isn't right," Ava said, turning around and trying to go back.

Tara grabbed her arm.

"That man gave his life for ours—we will not dishonor it by going back and doing the same."

Ava and Tara raced straight to Headmistress Astrae and told her everything, not knowing who else to turn to.

While they expected her to be shocked, to be beside herself, she appeared to have had her own suspicions confirmed.

"Keep up, ladies," Headmistress Astrae said, leading the girls back to their dorms at such a brisk pace that Ava and Tara had to jog to keep up with her. Dania, the headmistress' orange fox, followed behind Ava and Tara, its head darting from side to side as if watching out for trouble.

"Mr. Viscardi and another instructor are on their way," the headmistress continued. "They'll keep watch outside your dorms this evening. No harm will come to the two of you."

Headmistress Astrae stopped in front of the entrance to Ava and Tara's dorms. She placed a heavy hand on each of their shoulders and gave a light squeeze.

"I leave you here, heads held high," she said. "You two have faced and overcome more than anyone your age ever should. So rest and know tonight we *will* determine what the outcome was between Julian and Ambrose. Carey will be restrained. You have nothing to worry about. Rest now."

Ava tried to sleep, but she could tell Tara was having just as much trouble closing her eyes for more than a minute. Neither wanted to let their defenses down until they knew, one way or another, who had survived and whether they were still in danger.

In the morning, they bided their time, waiting for Kailani and Mira to leave their room so Ava and Tara could talk. A letter appeared out of thin air and dropped at the foot of Ava's bed.

"Oooh, who can that be from?" Kailani asked, running over. "A secret admirer, maybe?"

As soon as Kailani picked up the letter from the floor, dozens of spiders crawled up her arm. She dropped it at once.

"Whoever it was, it's not worth the gossip," the girl said with a whimper.

Kailani begged Mira to help her, and two girls scurried out with anguished complaints about "spider residue."

Ava tentatively picked up the mail. Thankfully, no spiders crawled up her arms, and no snakes nipped at her fingers.

"Ava Marie Jones" was inscribed on the outside of the high-quality stock envelope in large, easy-to-read letters.

Her hands shook as she opened it. Who would send her mail, and at a time like this?

She took a deep breath and braced herself as she began to read the letter out loud. Tara scooted in close.

Ava,

This letter was to be delivered to you by a trusted confidant of mine in The Resistance upon my death.

If you're reading this, it means one of two things:

1. I fought Ambrose and defeated him, giving my life for yours and our cause.

2. I fought Ambrose and failed to defeat him, but somehow, you're still alive. Which is what matters most.

For ten years, I worked my way up through the High Court of

Magical Affairs. I'm not proud to say my methods of climbing the proverbial ladder weren't always the most ethical, but it had to be done. I want—no, need—you to know that.

After making a name for myself, I was promoted. I worked as Ambrose's right-hand man, as his trusted advisor for the last three years, all preparing for the day when you would return, the day he would learn about you. The day he would discover there was a broken chain in the bindings he has on our world. A day he would not take well to.

Your mother and I knew this had to be done, though. It was not an easy decision for her, I hope you understand.

Looking at you after giving birth, she'd thought maybe the Book of Fate must have been wrong. She'd wanted to believe that so bad, I could tell. But your mother was a powerful witch, possibly more powerful than Ambrose, having descended from Aurora Cromwell herself, a line Ambrose had thought he'd wiped out centuries ago.

Your mother knew deep within her heart, though, that it wasn't wrong. That the danger you'd be placed in was unavoidable. She only hoped, prayed, that you would be not only able to withstand what came but to survive it as well.

I know what you're thinking—I'm not your father. But your mother and I, having grown up together, were best friends.

We were Lost Ones like you. We also were covert members of The Resistance.

While the High Court wants you to believe our numbers have dwindled over the years, they haven't.

We've been waiting—waiting for you.

You are our beacon of hope in a war for our kind's survival, even more for the mortal realm's survival.

Ambrose has dark plans. Plans he's hidden from Xarcadia and Linhollow's citizens since their inception.

He's been weakening our kind. Waiting for the right moment to strike.

The attacks three hundred years ago, the Salem witch trials, everything—they were all him, his dark creatures, and his shadow souls.

Ambrose, himself, is a shadow soul.

It's impossible, I know, what with shadow souls only being able to take on physical form for mere minutes at a time usually, but it's true. I've seen it with my own eyes.

You must be careful who you share this knowledge with. There are a lot of people in the shadows, waiting for you to gleefully make one wrong turn.

The kelpie, the boat ride, the nightmares, the attacks at the school, were all him. The nightmares and attacks were a result of the obsidian amulets he'd sent you, I recently discovered. He'll never let you live in this world. He'll never let the one thing that shows he's not perfect, that his system is not perfect, live on.

Find members of The Resistance, work with them to expose him and to help us recapture our former glory, to again be a part of the mortal realm. To help The Resistance save the mortals.

This is a lot for anyone to take on, I understand that. My only hope for you is that you're still standing at the end of this. The Book of Fate didn't get that far—couldn't get that far before your mother's actions that night.

Duncan—I'm not sure if you can trust him. His father is on the Elder's Court, and I've suspected for some time he's not who he says he is. His mother works in the High Court as a cleric, and her loyalties are with her husband. Duncan's loyalties may lie with theirs.

Tara—I've been watching closely. She has a mind for the truth. She's an inquisitive being indeed. While she'll be loyal to the cause, the rest of your kind will, most certainly, side with Ambrose.

Colin—a Summer fairy with a past much like your own, I'm still unsure of. I had hoped to have more time, more time to put everything together for you—but if you're reading this, I didn't.

Use your discretion in the months to come, use your enhanced abilities to guide you, and trust Josie, at all costs. She'll reveal herself soon, if she hasn't already.

Most regrettably and with all my love,

Julian

Ava folded the letter, wanting to stuff it away before anyone else saw it. Instantly, it dissolved up into a million tiny pieces in her lap. An added security feature Julian must have put in place.

"Do we tell Duncan and Colin?" Tara asked, fidgeting nervously.

"I don't know, Tara. Who can you trust when you're about to go to war?"

Tara was at a loss for words, something Ava rarely saw. It was an impossible question and one they would have to spend much more time considering.

There were a lot of things Ava needed to consider: There had been no mention of her mother and whether she was still out there, no mention of who her father was, and no mention of what this *Book of Fate* had said—or where she could get her hands on it.

"We're kids, Ava," Tara finally managed to say, sounding smaller in that moment than Ava had ever heard her.

"I know, Tara,"Ava said. "And our enemy underestimating us because of that will be our greatest asset."

The only other thing Ava was sure about was that while many things felt impossible, she knew with a convicting faith that she'd be ready for whatever came next.

THE IMPOSSIBLE GIRL READER'S GUIDE

We hope you visit our Monarch Educational Services LLC website at www.monarcheducationalservices.com to join The Impossible Girl Fan Club and download our reader guide for TIG! It is perfect for small groups, classes, book clubs, libraries, homeschool families, and readers who love TIG and need more of Ava and Xarcadia!

ACKNOWLEDGMENTS

To my Lord and Savior, Jesus Christ, without you, my life would hold no meaning or purpose. Thank you for your unconditional love, peace, and continued faithfulness. To my husband, Justin White, this dream, this book, wouldn't exist without you. Thank you for the many months of waking up early with our daughter so I could write my first draft. Thank you for being the person who inspires me to do and dream bigger. To my daughters, Arianna and Ariel, I do this for you. To show you anything is possible with God in your heart and an idea that refuses to leave you. Dream big, my angels. To my father, Bob, you taught me no dream was too big and to always believe in the impossible. In everything I do, you are always with me. To my mother, Laurie, and mother-in-law, Jessica, thank you for being two of my biggest encouragers. To Stephanie Cotta, you're an amazing writer and you make me better too. I'm so blessed to call you family and friend. I'll never forget our first Twitter event, how tired we were, and how we kept each other going despite our exhaustion. To Jennifer Lowry, the minute I clicked on your Twitter, I knew you were the "one" for this book. Some would say that makes no sense, but we know it was God. You inspire and draw out the best in me, and I'm so happy you love Ava as much as I do. I am so honored to be a part of Monarch. Thank you. To Haley Hwang, you taught me SO much in such a short time. I'll always see you as the pot of gold at the end of the rainbow, and this book would not be what it is without you. Thank you.

To Pauline Harris, your words meant so much to me during this process. To Korin Mae, you took what was in my head and made it more beautiful than I ever could have imagined. I will treasure this cover, your art, and your work forever. To Almedia Ryan, I am so glad to have you in my corner. You are a true friend, and I'm so glad we met and are on this journey together. To every author that captivated my heart as a young girl, thank you. Because of you, I hope to be able to do the same.

About the Author

Growing up, Ashley would send her father to their local library, where he'd always be surprised to find bags of books waiting for him versus just one or two books. She's always dreamt of giving to readers what so many great authors gave to her: an escape, an adventure, and a love for thousands of well thought out words printed in the form of a book, not letting them tear away from it easily—or for very long. Ashley resides in Northern California with her husband and two adorable, feisty little girls. When she's not writing, she's reading. There are two major takeaways Ashley hopes readers have upon finishing THE IMPOSSIBLE GIRL. 1. Always believe that something magical is about to happen. 2. Remember: difficult does not mean impossible.

If you know someone is hurting or if that person is you, please reach out. Talk to school staff, family, and/or a friend. Know you are not alone. You are loved.

National Suicide Prevention Hotline: 1-800-273-8255

Crisis Text Line: Text "Hello" to 741741

National Alliance on Mental Illness (NAMI) www.nami.org